Bed 39

Hope you enjoy Bed 39! Best Wishes & Happy Reading!

Shawn Maureen McKelvie

10/6/2015

Bed 39 is available @ Amazon.com
email ShawnMcK39@aol for Book club discounts.
Please like us on Facebook!

Bed 39

Shawn Maureen McKelvie

Copyright © 2015 Shawn Maureen McKelvie
All rights reserved.

ISBN: 151529868X
ISBN 13: 9781515298687

In memory of my father, John A. Bennett, who fought a valiant battle with esophageal and gastric cancer.

Many Thanks To

THIS BOOK IS DEDICATED TO my father John A. Bennett and to my lifelong friend, Candice Ann Johnson, RN, BSN and Certified Hospice Nurse.

For years, I listened in awe to Candice's truly touching stories of the strength of those she cared for in Hospice. Those unnamed patients became real to me and I always wanted to hear more about those final moments. As a writer, I felt there was a story to be told about those months or sometimes last few days in a terminal patient's life.

In 2013, Candy and I brainstormed and thought it would be an interesting twist to tell the story as if it were being told by the spirit of a departed former hospice patient. The two of us sat at an outdoor restaurant in St. Louis's Old St. Charles Missouri river district with my brother Steve Bennett. The conversation flowed as I revealed the main character and storyteller would have his spirit attached and imprinted on the hospital bed after he died there.

For two years as I wrote this book, the title remained: *The Hospice Bed*. In these final months before publication, my husband Dr. Milt McKelvie, my sister Cheryl and Jill Lawrence, my editor, thought the title should not encourage readers to prejudge.

The story behind the first organized hospice is actually a touching love story! It is the story of Dr. Cicely Saunders and David Tasma and how he profoundly influenced her in moving forward with her dream. My dream was to integrate their fascinating story into the intriguing fictitious journey of Tomas Kaminski and others coming to the sunset of their life. I still worried that the title would only appeal to those who had a medical background or a particular interest in hospice. But I truly feel the pages of this novel will be captivating to most anyone, both male and female alike! So we worked our way through various permutations of titles and ended up with *Bed 39—* which we hope is simple, direct but also intriguing. I'm glad it captured your interest!

Working on this book gave me the opportunity to reflect on my father, John A. Bennett, and his valiant 10-year battle with esophageal and gastric cancer. Unfortunately, many of us have had family members or friends who suffered from a terminal illness. It's practically endemic. Another lifelong friend, Kathy Stephens Williams, a critical care educator, lost both parents to cancer. All three were dynamic people who left a legacy of love, learning and growth.

The last day of my father's life, my mother, siblings, nieces and nephews gathered around his bed. Moments after my daughter and son walked into the room and the entire family was present, he allowed himself to let go.

Thank you Dad for never being too tired to practice softball or help me with homework, for sharing fun stories of your childhood shenanigans, for teaching us, "honesty is always the best policy, and a little hard work, never hurt anyone."

Thanks go to my husband Dr. Milton John McKelvie for supporting my endeavor to write this second book. He was the one I'd bounce ideas off of and he's also the one who read the first, second and third revisions of the book. He is the one who made it possible to quit my day job and take off to become a full-time writer. I'm a lucky woman to have married a man with the patience of a saint.

Another continuous source of strength has been my sister Cheryl Marlin. I don't know what I would have done without her! She has been an amazing cheerleader, especially when I experienced the dreaded writer's block. My sis was there to give me that pat on the back and encouragement needed to re-start the previously elusive creative forces. I appreciate Adam Surrey for doing the preliminary edit of my book, my brother Tom Bennett for creating the first artistic draft and Debbie Borke, the graphic artist who created the awesome cover for *Bed 39*.

There is also Jill H. Lawrence, founder and CEO of Ruby Slippers, Inc., an innovative marketing, PR and communications company located in Naples, Florida. Jill was my main editor on this project. I believe we were soul sisters in a past life and I felt connected to her from the start. She is a true mentor and master of the English language. Jill is a creative force to be reckoned with and has a sense of humor to match.

A heartfelt thanks to Patti Ragan, the courageous and amazing founder of The Center for Great Apes. The center is situated on 100 sub-tropical acres in Wauchula, Florida just southwest of Orlando, and provides permanent shelter for abused, neglected, and aging orangutans and chimpanzees. Thanks to an auction to benefit the Center for Great Apes and Patti Ragan's thirty-year friendship with respected screenwriter Mark Rosenthal, I had the honor to have this incredibly wise and talented screenwriter not to mention professor of film and media arts, read my manuscript. Mark's screenwriting credits include major successes such as *The Jewel of the Nile, Superman IV, Star Trek VI, The Beverly Hillbillies, Mona Lisa Smile* and *The Sorcerer's Apprentice*.

At the time I asked Mark to read my work, I *thought* I was finished writing the manuscript and was ready to have it published. But that all changed once Mark Rosenthal was kind enough to spend over an hour providing me with the feedback that changed the whole course of my book! I went back to the proverbial drawing board and implemented every word of his advice into the newly revised and ever so much improved story. Thanks to Mark's sage advice, I allowed myself the dramatic license to creatively entwine the intriguing love story that implausibly but in fact, actually did surround the founding of the first organized hospice in London with Tomas's own love story and the events that transpired from Bed 39 over the course of four decades.

I am ever so grateful to Mark for taking the time to read my book, but also for guiding and directing me in such a propitious new direction.

I will eternally appreciate those friends and family members who read my manuscript, then shared critiques on how to make it better for the readers.

Shawn Maureen McKelvie

My sincere gratitude and thanks to all including Candice Ann Johnson, Kathy Stephens Williams, my son Chad Tenge, who is also the male model on the front cover, my daughter Lauren Corrigan, Crispin Melloh, Gay Corrigan, Kathy Chisum, Reegan Armstrong and Ella Nayor-Cull.

In my life, even when the chips were down and I barely had a coin in my pocket, the glass was always half full and I felt blessed. What makes an individual truly rich, are not the funds in the bank but those who are surrounded by family and friends who freely give their loyalty, love and support. I am one of those lucky people and thankful for those who mean the most to me.

And finally, I want to acknowledge my grandchildren, Sydney Marie, Frankie Corrigan and little Olivia Zeller, I hope Grandma makes you proud. And I thank you for the pure joy you give me! I am indeed very blessed!

Preface

As a sixteen-year-old nurse's assistant, I was uncomfortable being assigned to patients with end stage illnesses. The dying process and death itself was a frightening prospect—especially if I was expected to perform duties which would in all likelihood put me in a position to witness death itself.

Back early in the 1970s, there weren't any established hospices in the St. Louis area. As a result, many patients with terminal diseases would resort to going to various hospitals to live out their final days. The nurses and doctors would do whatever they could to minimize pain, but unfortunately back then, pain frequently went uncontrolled.

This was my first week to work the night shift and staying awake all night was a real struggle! I resorted to doing a few jumping jacks in the nurse's lounge and drinking coffee until I was almost caffeine toxic.

But on this particular night, I was wide-awake and almost uneasy about one particular patient. The air felt thick, the lighting in the hospital was dimmed due to the nighttime hours and her cries of pain echoed up the hall to the nurse's station. As a mere teenager, my thoughts were usually of cheerleading, social events at school, and homework. Now they were on death, suffering, and a feeling of helplessness. My eyes were wide as I scanned the halls to find a registered nurse to help this poor woman. My mentor was the nurse in charge that night who was at the desk and noted my concerned expression. The understanding and experienced RN stood up and placed her arm around my shoulders. She reassured me that she had done everything possible to control the woman's agony.

"Dear, go on in and try to make her comfortable," she urged.

I nodded in agreement, but was almost too frightened to walk into her room. Nonetheless, I reluctantly made my way to room 709, and as I got closer, I cupped my hands over my ears. I just wanted her pain to stop and couldn't bear the loud confirmation that it had not! My heart beat faster as I walked into her room. The only sounds were the echo of my footsteps and her screams. The room was dark, and fortunately I was able to attend to her needs without disturbing her with a bolt of bright light.

The elderly woman was grimacing when I reached her bedside, her features so contorted with pain that she was almost unrecognizable. Once I was able to shake off my fear, I slowly reached for the ailing patient's cold, frail hand. Unfortunately, the piercingly loud moans continued.

I took a cool washcloth to gently wipe her brow. The woman tightly closed her eyes as she moaned rhythmically. Strangely, her screaming stopped and now she began to make low moaning sounds, the hum of which mesmerized me.

In an almost trance-like state, I continued to run the moist cloth over her face. One by one the small beads of perspiration diminished, leaving a slight glow on her forehead. I gazed deeply at her, noting every furrow, the gray hue of her skin, the cyanotic blue tone of her thin cracked lips.

My mind wandered as my eyes continued to explore this patient's features. What had she been like as a young woman and before cancer riddled her body? My imagination roamed momentarily to another place and time, as I envisioned her as a young lady with flowing silky blonde hair and vibrant, sparkling eyes. Yes, she had kind round eyes that were almost smiling and she was so beautiful!

Subconsciously, I was smiling back at the image of youth and health I envisioned before me. Then it became clear exactly what I was looking at, something I never consciously noticed before. A small gold antique frame with an old black-and-white photo of this patient when she was in her prime stood on the bedside stand. Without realizing it, the image in the photo had registered in my mind.

Suddenly my reverie was interrupted by the reality of the suffering this patient was enduring now. Instantly I snapped back to reality. Her eyes now were wildly probing mine, as if she were desperately searching for peace. Then the screaming resumed.

Once again, my heart raced as I stifled the urge to sprint out of the hospital and back home to my family. I was just a kid who obviously had very little hospital experience under my belt. Before I worked at this facility, I'd never even been to a funeral nor witnessed death. Nonetheless, tending to others in need had been a life-long theme for me, so I knew I was in the right place at the right time regardless of how difficult it was.

I slowly took a deep breath and refocused my attention to tend to my nurse assistant duties. I knelt down to check the status of her catheter bag attached to the lower rail of the bed which was how the nurses monitored her urinary output. Suddenly I became acutely aware that the woman's sustained sounds of agony had ceased. The silence was deafening. I held my breath and wondered...why?

As I arose from my kneeling position I looked up from the side of the bed to see her face. To my surprise, her previously contorted features were now relaxed and calm. Only moments ago, her writhing face reflected how tortured she was. Now that same face had donned a sweet, gentle smile. Her blue gray eyes were open and filled with wonder, as if she had just seen something spectacular.

The sudden radical change bewildered me as I gazed curiously at the woman. Then, after a few seconds, I realized she was no longer breathing and must be dead! The incredible sight seemed like a miracle. This poor, tortured woman obviously had witnessed something beautiful, and had found comfort and peace in her final moments. Even a green-as-grass 16-year-old could clearly see that.

My rapt attention to this glorious conclusion to an earthly existence faded due to an involuntary urge to cautiously look around the room.

In an instant I felt fear creep up my spine. There was a chill in the air, and even though just the two of us were in the room and one of us was departed, I knew without a doubt, we were not alone. My imagination went wild and I wondered if her deceased loved ones were waiting in the direction of her gaze. Had she had a welcome-to-the-other-side group greeting as they all walked into the Light together? I didn't know what to think.

The woman in room 709 had not been given palliative care. Unfortunately, it did not exist at that time. Palliative care's focus is on relieving pain, stress, suffering and disturbing symptoms of those patients with serious illnesses. Today there are health care professionals who specialize in palliative care, but back in 1972, even the mere thought of it did not exist.

My two best friends and I are registered nurses who graduated back in the 70's. Over the years, I have worked in a variety of challenging arenas such as the emergency room, intensive care and healthcare marketing. My two friends have as well. These two amazing nurses are Candy Johnson, who is a certified hospice nurse and Kathy Stephens Williams, a critical care educator. The level of professionalism they exhibit is commendable and the depth of compassion in their hearts for their student nurses and patients is truly awe-inspiring. I have profoundly benefitted from their wisdom, experiences and love.

After performing more than three decades of nursing, we all experienced patients who taught us more about life than they will ever know. These patients left their permanent mark on our hearts and souls. It's unfortunate that many will go to their graves never knowing what an impact they had in our lives as healthcare professionals. Those patients taught us invaluable lessons and how to be better nurses as well as better human beings.

Many decades ago, I took care of an indigent thirty-eight year old male patient who is one of those patients who made a lasting impression on me. He was diagnosed with end-stage heart failure and systemic lupus erythematosus among other things. This auto-immune disease attacked most of his organs. For the sake of the patient's anonymity, I will call him Mr. Roberts.

I had the honor of taking care of Mr. Roberts the final two weeks of his life. Despite the critical nature of his illnesses, he shared his quick witted sense of humor with us until his last day. Mr. Roberts always greeted us nurses with a broad smile accompanied by some silly riddle he would make up on the spur of the moment. He never failed to thank us or tell us how he appreciated our help and our willingness to talk to him during our shifts.

What baffled me was the fact that there wasn't one visit from Mr. Robert's family or friends during his stay. He might have been lonely had it not been for the staff making Mr. Roberts feel as if he were part of the ICU family. The day he died, Mr. Roberts asked if I was his angel—his angel here on earth. I assured him I was until an angel with actual wings came along!

Later that evening he was surrounded by staff members who had become his friends as he took his last breath. He had an entire flock of nurse angels to whom he had endeared himself by simply being who he was at his core. Mr. Roberts did not die alone, we made certain of that!

The dying process puts an end to pretense and charades so those who minister to people making their transition back into spirit get to see the genuine essence of a person. People show up as who they really are. And we loved who Mr. Roberts really was. He was one of those special people who, I am quite certain, so many of us who cared for him remember fondly to this very day.

The premise for my book was formed due to my interest in telling a story, in fact many stories of hope, life and love. I very much want to relay that the person occupying that hospital or hospice bed is not *just* a patient, the illness does not define who they are and most certainly is not how they want to be remembered. As nurses we see the patient during the course of their illness and unfortunately for quick reference to others, they become "the man in room 30 with esophageal cancer" or "the woman in room 209 with breast cancer." We must never get so clinical that we don't remember the people in the beds are those men and women who have lived, loved, perhaps fought bravely for their country, worked hard for their education, had jobs and families who loved them.

This novel has an unusual twist in that it's narrated from the viewpoint of a departed soul named Tomas Kaminski who died in Bed 39 in the St. Louis Hospital where the novel is set. After Tomas died in 1964 at age 27, he chose to stay on earth and imprint his soul on Bed 39 rather than go into the Light and fully transition to the other side. The Light, so often described by those who have near death experiences, is the God-force portal to the other side, the spirit realm. This bright luminescence is experienced as supreme love and enlightenment.

Tomas was torn between going into the Light immediately after his death and postponing his departure in favor of staying for a time imprinted on Bed 39. He believed if he stayed with Bed 39 it would serve a higher purpose. He chose to stay in order to provide a special vessel to hold each of the many souls who occupied Bed 39 during their final days as well as to observe the evolution of the hospice movement

Once Tomas became one with Bed 39, he had powers he had not had previously. For example, he gained a keen insight and all-knowing awareness about each person who occupied Bed 39. Unfortunately, Bed 39 did not give him any special insight into his *own* personal life - in this respect he had to learn the old-fashioned way like everyone else.

But I'm getting ahead of the story. I invite you to join Tomas before he was even a gleam in his parents' eyes, so to speak and enjoy the journey that was his earthly life and his afterlife that follows. But not only is this the story of Tomas, it is also the true story of the great romantic love that literally was the catalyst for the hospice movement – the love between David Tasma and Cecily Saunders, visionary and hospice founder.

So prepare for a great read about two romances – one actual and the other fanciful. The true story of the blossoming of the hospice movement itself is part of this tale.

There are many twists and turns in these pages. You already know about one: that for now Tomas will choose to stay on the earth plane after his death and delay his trip into the Light and the other-side. You are invited to stay as well. Enjoy.

CHAPTER 1

1964
Welcome To The White Walled Ward!

―――∞―――

WHEN THE MAIN CHARACTER DIES in a novel, it's almost always at the very end. However, in my case it takes place at the beginning and my tale unfolds from there. My name is Tomas Kaminski and at the age of 27, I was coming to the sunset of my life.

Our family car was once again in the shop for the tenth time. My father had to borrow his friend's '62 Bonneville in order to drive me to the hospital. There was a softer purr of the engine as father reduced the speed of the car as we got closer to our destination. I wondered if he subconsciously thought it would prevent the inevitable, my admission to the hospital and subsequent death.

The man behind the wheel that day was foreign to me with his dull, gloomy poker face. The Bart Kaminski I knew was eternally cheerful and always smiling! I turned toward my father as he pulled out a hanky from his pocket and forcefully blew his nose. The moist yellow perspiration stains under his arms on his new white cotton shirt bore testimony to his acute stress.

There was a biting chill in the air on this late October afternoon in St. Louis. The weather was frequently unpredictable in Missouri and today was no exception. A blustery twenty miles-per-hour northerly wind whipped trees into submission. But I was well aware that although today was

55 degrees and chilly, tomorrow could be warm enough to go swimming outdoors!

I silently sat in the passenger seat as we passed several rows of small, red brick bungalows. Our car approached a group of kids who quit playing street kickball and ran onto the sidewalk until we passed by. One family was barbecuing in the front yard and gave us a friendly wave. The scent of pork ribs on a grill normally made my mouth water, however now, I was almost nauseated. Just thinking about the barbecue made me want to vomit and I covered my mouth. Thank God it was a false alarm! As I slowly withdrew my hand from my lips, I noted my frail, bony arms.

As a means of self-preservation, my mind reflected on more cheerful times. I was in a trance-like state with my forehead pressed against the door window. My father and I were two silent, melancholy bodies and I needed to drift away from this palpable sadness.

Only a mere few months ago I still had muscle mass on my sturdy frame. I was considered to be quite a catch with my good looks and keen intellectual mind that was leading me on the road to success via medical school. My strong 5'11" frame was kept lean by playing rugby in Forest Park and jogging to and from work. After a hard run, the sweat helped me slick back my thick brown hair under my silly white waiter's cap. It was a cap that looked more like an Air Force General Garrison hat! Heck, I was just a working stiff waiter trying to fund my medical school tuition. I preferred not to wear any cap in order to show off my head of shiny brown hair. My parents owned the deli though, so their rules were supreme and I abided by them by wearing the entire uniform!

I smiled to myself about the creative ways I had increased extra coins in my pocket. As a waiter and future medical student, I needed all the financial help I could get! Just between you and me, I had a tried and true method of harvesting abundant tips from our female patrons. As my hair dried, I'd strategically release a few locks of hair from under my cap. I used my finger to produce a sexy curl that hung above one brow. One day, my mother walked in and screeched,

"Tomas, what the hell ya doing fussing with your hair? Since when does my handsome son primp like a prissy lady?"

I flashed a bright smile and winked at her with my green eyes...oh, did I mention my sparkling green eyes?

I proudly revealed,

"Mother, I'm preparing my money-making game face!"

My father now caught wind of our conversation and heard my mother laugh.

"Annie, what's so funny?"

Mother unsuccessfully tried to hold her gales of laughter back as she pointed in my direction...

"It's your *pretty* son, so damn full of himself! Papa, see the cute little curl over Tomas's brow? Well, that is *his* money-maker!"

Father looked puzzled after hearing my mother's perplexing statement. He scanned me head to toe as he inquisitively analyzed me wondering what it was about his son that brought in the bucks?

My old man was hopelessly stumped, so I pointed to the lock of hair.

"Tomas, how in the hell does that little curl make you money?"

I defensively justified its existence and my excellent reason for not tucking it back under the cap.

"Father, I've been testing this for the last six months! The days I release the *money-maker*, I go home with twice as many tips! No kidding! The women love it! If you want me to help pay for college, then you better welcome my game-face!"

I was lost deep in thought as I reflected on such lighthearted times with my parents. I inadvertently roused myself from my reverie when I heard my own voice say "my game-face" out loud just as father pulled up to the front of the hospital.

My father turned off the car then slowly turned toward me. He quickly cleared his throat, wiped away a few tears, then softly asked,

"What, Tomas? What did you say?"

After a slight pause I looked at my father, sighed, then pointed to my face.

"Father, I saved up over a thousand dollars with this money-maker."

My father managed to chuckle while recalling the moment I revealed the secret of my success.

"And Tomas, you will save a thousand more when you come home." he affirmed with false bravado.

Acknowledging the reality of my situation, I slowly shook my head.

"No father, I won't be coming home this time...The money is for you and mother."

We both knew it was true, but only one of us could bear to admit it. On this gloomy late October day in 1964, my father had brought me to the hospital to die.

Eight white pillars at the hospital entrance gave the five-story red brick structure presence—at least more than it would have had without them. They made it appear to be a solid place in which to die.

The chilly morning hastened our walk up to the massive carved double doors more befitting a cathedral than a hospital, but I had gone as far as I could go on my own. Father ran inside to get a wheelchair while I waited. My unsteady gait made headway slow and precarious so cautiously I moved toward the edge of the grand stairway to be ready for my father's return with the wheelchair. No doubt about it, I mused, the exterior of this hospital was grand and impressive. Too bad I wasn't just a casual observer of architecture, but had come here to die.

The large window in front of the building caught my attention as I waited. As frail and devastatingly sick as I was, I could not help but see that the window reflected brilliant white pillow-like clouds set against the most magnificent shade of deep blue sky more evocative of Montana than Missouri. If I'd been an artist, I would have been possessed to paint it, so dramatic and stunning was the sight. I was mesmerized by the majestic scene and spectrum of colors.

My father returned to offer me a welcomed seat in the wheelchair he had rounded up. He guided the chair like an expert up the ramp bypassing the staircase. As we passed through the doors and entered the foyer of the hospital, the reflection in the window continued to mesmerize me and

I weakly attempted to turn for one last glimpse. Strangely, the grand view the window offered seemed to calm my soul. It struck me that the view was a beautiful reminder of the wonderful, blessed life I had been given, despite the shortage of years. For me, it was indeed a beautiful reflection into my final earthly home.

I had noticed in the car that my father's shoulders were slumped forward as if he were bearing the weight of the world. Now as I momentarily glanced back to look at his face I saw that he had donned an utterly blank gaze as if he were numb from head to toe. I knew he felt this all must be a bad dream, a damn nightmare and that he had to steel himself to get through it! I heard him whisper under his breath and when I listened, I heard him repeating the Lord's Prayer as he wheeled me to the elevator.

Twenty-foot ceilings soared inside this circa 1910 hospital which boasted beautiful marble pillars throughout the main entrance. It had been a grand structure in its day. Fifty-plus years later, the hospital was primarily for indigent patients.

My parents had invested every hard-earned penny they had into their deli and were struggling to break even. Not surprisingly, none of the three of us had insurance. Thus I technically qualified for the "indigent" focus of the hospital.

The architectural bones of this hospital were ornate thanks to the impressive marble pillars and carved wood molding. At first, it was a beautiful sight until you passed through the main entrance into the rather foreboding dark corridor and got into the ancient, rickety metal caged elevator.

At this point, both the scenery and smells changed drastically. This part of the hospital had not been updated or maintained in years. We encountered an orderly transporting a senile female elderly patient on a stretcher. We all entered the elevator at the same time. The plastic clamp which attached her catheter bag to the stretcher frame broke loose and was now stuck under the wheel. A thick, foul smelling urine seeped onto the elevator floor and found its way under my father's feet. He gasped and swiftly moved his feet to a small patch of dryer ground.

"Damn it, Tomas! Let's just get the hell out of this place!"

The orderly apologized as he threw a sheet over the mess. My father grumbled under his breath. He was stressed about to the breaking point, but I too sighed with his impatience, trying to placate him,

"Father, calm down, it's not the end of the world. It's just a little pee."

The clanging elevator jolted to a stop and the metal doors opened. We left one smell behind as he rolled me into an arena that assaulted our senses with a plethora of odors and sounds. The noise level must surely have been way over 80 decibels!

The nurse's station was buzzing with activity as a group of interns and medical students surrounded the resident in charge. Our arrival went unnoticed.

Father and I waited at the station for someone to look up and acknowledge our presence. We glanced around and could not help but see that this 40-bed ward was in dire need of repair. Numerous floor to ceiling cracks formed abstract designs on the white plaster walls. An overhead announcement from the hospital intercom crackled through to interrupt our ruminations. In a deep raspy southern accent, a female voice announced,

"Doctor Merkle to the I...C...U... STAT!

Apparently STAT had not been comprehended by the sought after Dr. Merkle. A couple minutes passed when a second announcement was made by a female who used a more alarmed, urgent tone.

"Doctor Merkle to the ICU STAT!"

Then a third,

"Doctor Merkle to the ICU! Right...NOW!...Ya hear?"

Every one at that nurses' station, even my father and I, laughed out loud at her last command. From the sound of it, that operator meant business! Heaven save Dr. Merkle if he didn't show up after that third announcement. I could picture the operator slamming her mic on the switchboard then rolling up her sleeves. I imagined that in a huff she slammed the door behind her and started on her vendetta to personally hunt him down to do some doctor ass-kicking!

A sign at the entrance to the ward caught my eye and I nudged my father as I pointed to it. The white sign with bold black letters sternly read: "Visiting Hours are limited to 1-7 pm. No exceptions. A maximum of two visitors per bed are permitted and no one under 15 years of age may enter the ward at any time! This policy is strictly enforced!" I shook my head and rolled my eyes. It made me sad that my best friend Seamus would not be able to bring his six kids to visit.

This ward was not a cancer unit per se, but was filled with internal medicine patients in various stages of health or lack thereof. Many patients played bedside radios which resulted in a cacophony of tunes. The result was a regular in-house "battle of the bands" with rock, blues, country and Bible preaching vying for prominence.

Oh, and a colorful group of cellmates, oh sorry, I meant ward-mates populated the beds in the large ward. One was a literal prisoner who was shackled to the bed and guarded by a nearby security officer. Long, stringy shoulder-length hair, bushy eyebrows and a twisted psychotic smile added drama to the scene. An unceasing flood of horrible vulgarities flowed from his mouth. As I watched, he pointed in my direction.

"Hey, pretty boy in the wheelchair! Tell that damn nurse I need drugs!"

A matronly looking black nurse with clipboard in hand, whisked by to reach the prisoner. I would later learn that she was the only nurse on duty to tend to all the occupants of the forty-bed ward.

A couple of elderly male patients screeched from their beds.

"Nurse Libby, please get that asshole to shut the hell up!"

Then one elderly bald man with a long pointing finger rattled on while he ate his lunch. I guess it was corn that splattered on his gown as he screeched,

"Yeah nurse, we are all sick of that bad, evil man! May God protect us all...Praise the Lord!"

The one and only nurse on this ward was obviously growing weary of her rowdy prisoner. He was wearing a devious smile as the nurse approached his metal bed.

"Roy, you are not my only patient, however, I promise if you stop cussing, I will see what the doctor ordered for your pain. No one here should have to listen to your potty mouth! We have sick people here who need rest, so you behave yourself!"

The woman wearing a white crumpled uniform turned back and swiftly walked toward my father and me. The nurse had a welcoming, friendly face. She smiled as she warmly took my hand.

"Hello, I'm Nurse Libby. I am so very sorry for the delay in your admission! There seems to be a constant shortage of nurses and today more than usual. It's just me now. But I do apologize."

The full figured nurse with a neatly cropped afro had a kind but commanding way about her where people listened and let her take control. She asked my father to take a coffee break downstairs while she got me settled into my bed.

Nurse Libby wheeled me down what could only be described as a sterile tunnel of a ward. I surmised that the ivory linoleum floors contained a sea of taupe-colored flecks to help camouflage debris and dirt.

The lack of central air-conditioning necessitated countless unsightly window units installed in various locations throughout the ward. Seemingly infinite rows of white metal-framed beds with white linens stood against the white cracked walls. A feast for the eyes it was not—with one notable exception.

Strangely, only one of the 40 beds in the ward was unoccupied the day I arrived. Unlike the other beds, this one had an ornately beautiful solid brown wooden frame—a welcome departure from the numbingly boring white "decor!"

A small gold plaque on the wooden headboard simply read: "Bed 39-donated by Dr. Cicely Saunders." I was unfamiliar with the name and didn't give it much thought. I assumed she must be a doctor on staff and was grateful for her donation as well as for my good fortune in being granted residency therein.

Nurse Libby momentarily glanced at her clipboard and quickly absorbed my numerous doctors' orders and my admitting diagnosis. As she stood in front of me, I noted some dried droplets of blood on her skirt. Nurse Libby was barely over five feet tall, however her shoes must've been a woman's size ten! I wondered if they were stretched out, hand me downs or all she could afford? I guess I'll never know.

"Nurse Libby, why in the world am I the only one who has this beautiful wooden-framed bed and headboard?"

Nurse Libby smiled,

"You are the first to christen this very special bed, Tomas! Dr. Saunders is a physician from London, who has the desire to open a cancer care facility. She gave a lecture in our auditorium to local cancer researchers and our staff physicians. I don't know all the details however, I heard Dr. Saunders trained at an indigent care hospital and felt compelled to stop by this floor. I believe she said this bed is supposed to represent a patient's home away from home. The funny thing is she was adamant about this fancy crib being labeled: Bed 39. I'm not sure why?" Thanks to Nurse Libby I was all tucked into Bed 39, but everything she just told me was merely a buzz in my ear and I didn't absorb a word of it.

I pulled the stiffly starched, scratchy white sheets up over my lap. The hospital linens didn't smell fresh like the ones at home nor were they nearly as soft. I shared a funny thought with Nurse Libby,

"These brillo pad sheets are going to be rough on my soft fanny!"

We both chortled in recognition of the truth of that statement! A hospital was definitely not the place to come for relaxation or comfort! Just as I was settled in, my father walked out of the elevator. I was heartened to see that his spirits seemed to be a bit brighter than they had been this morning. Nurse Libby noted his arrival and discreetly left to allow us time to visit with one another.

"Son, I just want to warn you," he began with a bemused expression on his face. "Your buddy Seamus is going to try to sneak his six young ones in to visit you...one at a time. He is determined that they get to see you! And yes, he is fully aware of the dreaded sign that limits each bed to a maximum of two visitors at one time and that no one under age fifteen is permitted in at all! He is quite certain those rules do not apply to his particular family!"

My "don't-fence-me-in" red-headed best friend from grade school was now an adult with six rambunctious kids of his own. My father informed me that their arrival was imminent. We both waited breathlessly for the invasion.

It wasn't long until father and I spied Seamus escorting nine-year-old Shannon into the ward. As soon as she arrived at my bedside, she ducked down to hide under the bed. He proceeded to walk each of the kids into the ward one-by-one: eight-year-old Katie, six-year-old Maureen, four-year-old Molly, two-year- old Mickey and finally the eldest, ten-year-old Patrick. Once all the space under my bed was taken, the rest of his kids huddled behind the curtain in an attempt to go undetected. Normally, the six were a noisy bundle of laughter, talking and action, but I was impressed how quiet and unobtrusive they were!

What amused me is how my ward mates wanted to help conceal the kids from the nurses. The nursing supervisor started heading in my direction when she heard laughter that sounded suspiciously childlike. That was when old Mr. Lenard in the first bed frantically called her over when he feigned a coughing spasm. He then gave a wink and motioned all clear when she went to get him medication. The collusion of patients was delicious. This unified act of kindly defiance perked every one of us up a bit! Little Katie was the first to give me a big hug!

"Uncle Tomas, you are the only one who has a pretty bed! It has a gold sign that says 'Bed 39. Donated by Dr. Cicely Saunders.' Hmmmm, she must be a very nice lady"!

I never had the chance to respond to Katie because I was so distracted by Seamus and the rest of his brood. Seamus was hard to miss thanks to his handsome face and 6'2" frame. Despite the fact that he never had much money, he always managed to look like he was going on a photo shoot whether he was wearing jeans, a suit and tie or dirty running clothes. He definitely had a way about him that attracted admiring glances.

Seamus gasped when he saw how much weight I'd lost in a matter of weeks.

"Oh my, Tomas, seeing you like this fuckin' breaks my heart!"

The "f" word brought multiple objections from his miniature tribe of red-heads. Six-year-old Maureen looked at her father and sternly reminded him,

"Dad! Mother told you no f-curse words in front of our tender ears!" She looked at her older brother for confirmation on the state of her ears.

"Patrick, are my ears still the same? Are they tough or...or different?"

Maureen immediately pushed her long red ringlets out of the way as she delicately tapped her ears as if she were in search of something awful.

Patty touched his sister's ears,

"Yep! Still tender!"

Then the two looked around to observe other pairs of ears and settled on my father. They were large with an abundance of curly gray hairs escaping from the outer canal.

Patrick gulped and reluctantly asked my father,

"Mr. Kaminski, did you hear a lot of curse words in your day?"

The old man laughed and his protuberant belly shook with each chuckle.

"Oh Lordy! Way too many to count young lad!"

All six kids gasped and covered their ears in horror! Seamus and I were smiling trying to contain our own laughter! I had to see what I could do to quell their fears.

"Kids, your ears will stay tender. Your mom doesn't want the beauty of an innocent mind to be corrupted by those bad words. Shame on you, Seamus!" I reprimanded him just before I came up with an inspired idea. "Who is up for making your dad a cuss container?"

All six kids cheered and clapped their hands, "Me, me...I want to do it!"

Maureen bolted out from behind her flock of siblings.

"I'm going to draw a picture of Dad with trash coming out of his mouth! Then I'm going to paste it on a jam jar. Dad, every time you cuss you will owe us big time!"

It maybe wasn't the best idea since the enthusiastic cheering attracted the attention of Nurse Libby. It was clear that our little hide-the-children game was over.

"Tomas, I tried to turn a blind eye and not see the little ones. But my supervisor is here and feels it's important we enforce our no-children visitation rules, so sadly I must tell you that they had better go now."

It was only an hour or so later when I was trying to be strong and not cry out for pain meds like the prisoner had done earlier. Nurse Libby had already observed the intermittent grimacing of my face and me rubbing my aching legs. She was aware of the signs of pain escalation.

"Tomas, are you OK? Are you in pain?"

I somewhat reluctantly nodded my head and told her I'd be okay. My father could also see I was uncomfortable and soon left to relieve my mom at the deli and to give me whatever level of privacy I could find in the large ward. It would be my mother's turn to visit tomorrow.

This was my first night in the hospital so naturally I was not aware of the protocol. All I knew for sure was that I was exhausted after all the activity and felt a deep, boring pain arise from every joint in my body.

"Nurse Libby, I think I'm ready for some pain medication."

My nurse responded with a look of concern on her face.

"Tomas, I need to ask you a few questions to evaluate your pain. Can you describe it for me? For example, is it burning, throbbing, stabbing and sharp, or more like heavy pressure...and is it slight, moderate or severe?"

Since I had experienced the pain many times before in the last several weeks, I was well aware of its unpleasant, typical pattern and course. The cancer had spread to my bones. The pain always started out as moderately gripping and quickly advanced to an unremitting deeply penetrating, pain in every limb.

Nurse Libby listened to my assessment, then moved closer.

"Tomas, I have been working with terminal patients for years. The doctors write orders for a silly three-tier pain scale that shouldn't apply to those with end stage cancer. It's where we give you Tylenol or aspirin for starters, then reassess your pain. If still present, then we go to step two for a stronger oral medication. Then after we have exhausted the first two steps without obtaining relief, there is step three. That's where we give a stronger pain medication like morphine or dilaudid.

"During this whole process, more time goes by where your pain may spin out of control as a result of being under treated. I can only do what's ordered, however I tell you this to reassure you. I promise not to wait long before I reassess your pain and treat it. Poor lad, I don't want you to be uncomfortable!"

She compassionately patted my shoulder then slowly walked toward the nurses' station. On her way through the ward, several patients cried out regarding a variety of needs: a bedpan, a call light that fell to the ground, water, food and to top it all off, the security guard calling for help after the prisoner bit him. Yes, the prisoner asked him for assistance sitting up and took that opportunity to take a bite out of the guard's arm while he was trying to help. Nurse Libby called for security back up while the poor guard went to the emergency room. I knew it would be a long time before she had a chance to return with my medication.

Next to my bed was a small wooden chair and beside my headboard was what would become my lifeline to the world—a window. They were rare as hen's teeth in the ward and I was already grateful it was beside my Bed 39.

I used the rail to help pull myself to my feet. I steadied myself by my new fancy bed while raising the metal blinds. Tonight I was treated to a glorious view of St. Louis from the hospital's fifth floor. There were colorful clusters of autumn-hued oak trees lining the parkway accented by a glittering city skyline in the background. The yellow, rust and orange leaves appeared momentarily brilliant thanks to a cascade of rays from the setting sun.

I watched a young mother exiting a small grocery store that was in my field of vision. She was juggling her grocery bag while pushing a stroller with an infant tucked inside as her three toddlers followed closely behind much like ducklings do when they line up to follow their momma. The mother and her children wore matching bright green sweaters. I chuckled thinking the baby probably had a green diaper to match! The green clan slowly made its way around the corner and out of my view.

Next my gaze turned to the park bench right across the street. There was a man seated smack in the center of the bench. He was wearing a dated gray suit and was maybe in his forties. He was a rather good looking man with brown hair combed straight back, very intense eyes yet a friendly face. I was five floors up when this man suddenly looked straight at me and smiled!

Needless to say I was somewhat startled and it freaked me out a bit! So much for my illusion that I was undetectable and could not be seen from ground level.

I then turned my gaze to a man wearing scrubs who was running as fast as could be to the hospital. Maybe a doctor late for surgery, I thought. He suddenly stopped in his tracks and looked directly up at me! This man's face was a twin image of the face of the man on the bench! Phew, this was beyond weird and I couldn't even blame this on my pain meds since I hadn't had any yet!

I suddenly became aware of loud snoring emanating from the once rowdy prisoner patient. My nurse must've given him a powerful tranquilizer. Peace and calm was now restored to the ward and fortuitously the nurse was focused on me.

"Tomas, time to get yourself back in bed young man!"

I looked at her and chuckled.

"Nurse Libby, I'm twenty-seven years old! Why must I go to bed at 6 p.m.?"

The woman gently took my shoulders to rotate me toward the bed. It was then I realized my legs were shaking and could barely support my own weight. Nurse Libby now had a more serious, concerned look on her face.

"That is the exact reason for my request, my dear Tomas...you were getting ready to fall."

My nurse didn't mess around with step one and gave me Tylenol with codeine. The medication didn't touch my pain and I tossed and turned for two hours before Nurse Libby pleaded with the doctor for orders to give me morphine. By midnight, the pain came back with a vengeance! My gown was half way off and tangled around my body. I was drenched from head to toe with perspiration. Nurse Libby repeated the morphine dose before she reported with the night shift nurse and then went home. I knew she had gone to bat for me and was trying her best to skirt the rules, but she could only go so far without jeopardizing her job.

By two in the morning the ward was eerily quiet and the lights were dimmed to allow patients to rest. Bed 39 was the last one on the left side in the back of this forty-bed unit. I had been looking down the row of beds toward the nurses' station to see if anyone was still up there.

Suddenly the hairs on the back of my neck stood straight up as I heard shuffling and breathing coming from the wooden chair to my left. I held my breath and slowly turned to see a man seated next to my Bed 39! I didn't even see him walk in! The light of the moon shone through my window illuminating my strange surprise visitor. He was wearing a dated gray suit with a white cotton shirt and black tie. His dark hair was slicked back and an amused expression was evident on his face as if he were enjoying himself.

"It's you! The running doctor, the man on the bench, it was you! Who in the heck are you? Is it my time and are you here to walk me into the Light?"

Tomas quickly looked around expecting to see a magnificent bright ray...

"Well, wherever the hell is that Light? I'm assuming I'm going up rather than down, right?"

The man smiled broadly which somehow made me a little less frightened. I grunted with muscular discomfort as I attempted to sit higher in my bed. I wanted to hear every word he had to say.

"Tomas, I'm David Tasma and I felt the need to visit since we have so much in common. For starters, in 1948, at the age of forty, I, too, was dying of a terminal illness..."

The stranger paused while I interjected a thought. Needless to say, I was obviously shocked at what this forty-year-old man was telling me.

"What? Mr. Tasma, it's 1964! What do you mean you were dying in 1948?"

David Tasma raised his hand as if to slow me down.

"Correction! I DIED in 1948. I too was a young waiter who was diagnosed with end-stage cancer. Additionally, you and your parents immigrated here from Poland and I, too, was raised there, however my home was the Warsaw ghetto. After the war I fled to London for a new start and a new life.

"And it was a brand new life, in a way. Who would guess that at the advanced age of forty, I would fall in love for the first—and last—time?

Would you believe that I found love from my deathbed? Yes, that happened to me, Tomas. I had two amazing months with the love of my life, before I took my last breath. I fell madly in love with an incredible woman who is helping to change the world. The woman I fell in love with donated this very Bed 39 that you are lying in right now. The love of my life was Dr. Cicely Saunders.

CHAPTER 2

Why is Bed 39 Different?

THE WELL-GROOMED MAN IN THE gray suit who had been seated next to my Bed 39, suddenly re-appeared at two in the morning. That fact alone is exceedingly odd, however, what is even more bizarre is that Mr. Tasma told me earlier he was 40-years-old when he died in 1948! My early morning visitor was not translucent nor did he look anything like I imagined a ghost might look. He had matter-of-factly introduced himself as David Tasma earlier today and appeared to be no different than any other human being during either visit.

I was suddenly possessed by an urge to touch this unique stranger. I felt like I was in Wonderland with Alice as things got "curiouser and curiouser." Mr. Tasma seemed to notice my state of being utterly perplexed as his expression turned from serious to a wide grin. He comically raised a cocked eyebrow and chuckled as he watched my finger slowly heading toward his abdomen.

"Sorry Mr. Tasma, but you told me you died in 1948. If that were true, how could you be here in the flesh, looking so dapper, so human and smiling at me, too? I need to find out if this is one of Seamus's sick jokes!"

My finger headed for the button on David's gray wool suit. When instead of coming to a stop on the button, my finger, heck my whole hand, went right through him. I'm ashamed to say I gasped out loud and almost screamed like a little girl!

David Tasma re-situated his suit as if I had messed it up with my gentle touch.

"Tomas, upon your arrival here, there was a brief moment when you wondered who Dr. Cicely Saunders was. Knowing you wanted to be a physician, I knew you would want to hear more about her. Every city has statues, buildings, murals or street signs with someone's name on many of them. Sadly, few of us think twice about what the person behind the name accomplished in order to have a monument or statue dedicated to them, or in your case, Bed 39".

Had my visitor been actual flesh and blood, I would have dubbed him "intriguing" because he fully captured my interest. But he took intriguing to a whole new level what with his fascinating conversation, baffling knowledge of me and the fact that he was as solid as vapor despite appearances to the contrary.

"Tomas, I knew you would eventually make it a point to discover who Cicely Saunders was and figure out why Bed 39 was different?" He continued.

David once again stopped talking as he became aware of the vise-like agony that was welling up inside my body.

At this moment, I wasn't able to conceal my torment and tightly shut my eyes as I put my arms across my chest and rocked back and forth. David looked at me,

"Tomas, are you in pain?"

I was intrigued with David's story about Cicely Saunders however my frenzied mind was unable to focus! I was lost in the colossal pain.

"Yes, yes David, the pain is horrible! I'm so sorry, but please, please keep telling me about her! I am extremely interested."

David looked empathetic and leaned forward. He extended his arm to gently touch my shoulder. David's touch was tender as if he thought I would crumble under his light pressure. Then he rattled off some inaudible words as his tender touch morphed into being a firm grip on my shoulder!

I suddenly felt heat migrate from my shoulders to my toes, followed by a reverse flow of relaxed cool, calm energy that went from my toes to my shoulders.

I took a deep breath and realized my pain was completely gone! Miraculously I experienced instantaneous total relief! I didn't try to make sense of it in the moment, I just luxuriated in being released from the debilitating effect of that severe pain.

What people don't realize, well maybe David Tasma does and anyone else who has experienced end-stage cancer, a constant awful aching pain gnaws away at you in those final weeks. Most of us only complain when it is to the point of being unbearable and mine had reached the breaking point. But at this very moment, after receiving the extreme benefit of David's touch, I was now totally and magnificently pain free. It was such an unbelievable relief that I started to cry. Yes, I cried like a damn baby!

Impulsively I reached forward to hug the man responsible for releasing me from my torment. When I first touched David Tasma earlier, my hand went right through him, yet now, he was warm and solid like any other man on earth and I wept on his shoulders. He took it all in stride as he continued telling me about Dr. Saunders.

Finally, I slowly relaxed the death-grip I had on him and left the shelter of his shoulder. Then I warmly clasped his hand with both of mine in an attempt to express my most sincere gratitude for the freedom from suffering he had given me.

The freedom from pain made me nothing short of euphoric. I was astonished to lean back on my Bed 39 without suffering any discomfort. Yes, I was now more than ever eager to listen to my new friend.

"Tomas, Cicely was always a compassionate soul who wanted to help the less fortunate in life. First as a nurse then as a social worker, Cicely was horrified by all the human suffering she witnessed on a daily basis. She knew there had to be a better way to minimize the misery and prepare the patient and the patient's family for their loved ones imminent death. Cicely desperately wanted terminal patients to be comfortable, pain-free and have the ability to die with dignity in the comfort of their own home or at least in a home-like environment. Your Bed 39 represents a beginning of the realization of that dream and leads the way for change for the future of cancer care."

I'm not quite sure when I drifted off into the most restful, deep sleep I had had in months, however I knew for sure that David Tasma had been at my side. When I checked my round, metal-plated bedside clock, it was almost seven o'clock in the morning! I had not awakened once during the night.

I rolled over to see if Nurse Libby was on duty. To my surprise, my mother was making her way down the long ward carrying a plate wrapped in tinfoil. As always, she was attractively dressed this time wearing brown stretch pants with an orange and brown pullover sweater and casual brown canvas tennis shoes. Mother topped it off with a long scarf draped over her head that bore a variety of autumn colors. Once she arrived at Bed 39 she leaned forward to give me a kiss made sweeter by her smile. She began to unwrap my homemade breakfast as she chattered away,

"Tomas, Nurse Libby said it would be okay if I snuck back here a little early to see you. She told me to be on the lookout for a tall, uptight looking woman with a brown beehive hairdo and an eternally mad expression. She warned me that her supervisor is a stickler for the rules and if I were to see her, I need to get myself back to the elevator STAT! That was cute of Libby to use the medical term for pronto, don't you think!"

My mother revealed a large plate of pancakes, scrambled eggs and berries she brought for my breakfast. Then she made the mistake of attempting to feed me as if I were a toddler!

"Mother! For Pete's sake! I am certainly able to feed myself breakfast. Sheesh! That is the hardest part about this whole cancer thing. It was just a couple months ago when I was playing rugby and football, tackling the opposing team and setting them on their asses. Now somehow everyone seems to think I'm helpless and not able to wipe my own rear end or feed myself!"

My mother lovingly put her hand on my cheek then apologized profusely. But then the very next thing she did was to take a comb to try to tame my wretched case of bed-head. At this point my thick hair was more than disheveled—it had gone all the way to tangled and unruly.

"Mother, how about trying to curl a long lock for my forehead to create my money-making game face? That way I might get preferential treatment from the nurses!"

That elicited a hearty laugh from my mother.

"My son, you are still the most handsome man alive and will always capture the attention of women of all ages."

She then stopped talking as she spotted a shapely, young brunette nurse on the other side of the ward. Her hair was pulled back into a neat bun just below her nurse's cap. The young nurse administered a patient's pills then turned to catch both mother and I looking at her. I could see her blush all the way from Bed 39.

"Tomas, I'm sure I know her, but for the life of me don't know from where nor do I remember her name. Hmmm...I'll think of it later. I better leave soon to open the deli. Your dad will be here this afternoon with Seamus and the kids."

Then the elevator opened and even from the far end of the ward, we could see a tall woman sporting a skyscraper of a beehive on her head. Mother quickly grabbed her purse to make a quiet and rapid get-away. That was until the prisoner woke up from his slumber, spied my mother and gave her the honor of an ear-splitting doozey of a wolf whistle. As if that weren't enough, much to my mother's dismay he yelled out,

"Nice ass, lady!"

My poor mother was both furious and mortified! I had to laugh though when she flipped him off with her middle finger held high behind her back as she walked up the ward. That's no lady, that's my mother. I'm sure if that guard and the nursing supervisor weren't around she wouldn't have left without giving him a piece of her mind!

The time was now eight in the morning and I hadn't suffered any pain since 2:30 a.m. when David Tasma's touch miraculously vanquished every iota of agony. That is until right now when it came back with a vengeance accompanied by extreme nausea! The breakfast my mother brought was now splattered all over my bed linens. I flopped back on my bed with streams of perspiration flowing down my face in too much pain to move.

The pretty nurse from across the ward came running to help me. As she ran to my bed she automatically grabbed a clean gown and pulled the curtain closed to provide privacy for me. She disappeared as quickly as she had arrived when she realized she would need a liberal supply of warm water and towels to clean me up.

"I will be right back! I just need to get a few supplies!"

Next Nurse Libby peeked from behind the curtain with an intense look of sadness on her kind face.

"Oh my dear Tomas! You poor soul! I checked my chart and noted the night nurse didn't give you any pain meds once during the entire shift! Oh my goodness, let me get you something for your nausea. Tomas, are you in pain now?"

All I could do was slowly nod my head, then whisper,

"Yes, please Libby...it's bad."

Libby quickly returned to give me one injection for nausea and one for pain. Then the pretty nurse rushed up with a tray she placed at my bedside behind the curtain.

"I'll get Tomas washed up for you, Libby."

She began organizing the bedside tray on wheels. There was a plastic bin filled with warm water, soap and other items to help clean me up, as well as a fresh change of linens. Libby uttered a quick, "Thank you, darling," to the young nurse and then patted my shoulder.

"I'll be back soon to check on you, sweet Tomas."

As humiliated as I was to have lost control like that, I noticed that my attractive young nurse didn't wear gloves when handling vomit covered sheets. Heck, none of the nurses wore them even when they drew blood! I previously asked Nurse Libby about it when I saw her draw the prisoner's blood. She told me most nurses didn't wear gloves unless the patient was known to have a contagious disease.

Nonetheless, I was surprised that the beautiful nurse changing my soiled covers didn't seem to mind getting vomit on her delicate hands. I momentarily thought that when I'm a doctor, I'll wear gloves when I have contact with a patient's body fluids. Then sorrowfully I realized I wouldn't live long enough to become a physician and wouldn't even live long enough to go to medical school.

The pain injection started to minimize my discomfort while making me a bit goofy in the process. The pretty nurse had large brown eyes which did not seek out visual contact—it seemed like she avoided eye contact. I was so weak that I failed to notice several deposits of vomit on my chin, cheek and neck. What I did notice though, was the scratchy substitute she used for my washcloth!

"Um, nurse, do you realize you are using a stiff pillow case as my wash rag?"

Once again the young woman in a crisp white uniform blushed—this time her face was as bright as the reddest apple!

"I, I, I'm sorry, however our floor ran out of towels and washcloths. Gees, it is not the first time, however I'm usually able to steal some from the floor above or below us. Not this time! I'm sorry Tomas. This is all we had and you needed to be cleansed off with something!"

I looked up trying to make eye contact and dazzle this attractive nurse by batting my sparkling green eyes and smile.

"Well, nurse, I'd rather you use your soft hands on my body than that SOS pad."

Her eyes were suddenly the size of saucers as she excused herself. It wasn't long before my new friend Nurse Libby made her grand entrance behind the old white canvas curtain that concealed my half-nude body. Nurse Libby had a hearty sense of humor and her jovial expression revealed her innate good nature.

"Tomas, Tomas, Tomas! What's the craic? And please tell me why you are embarrassing my young nurse?"

I laughed and silently wondered how she knew the Irish term "craic",

"Nurse Libby, Guilty as charged! Can you blame me for wanting to show off my 24-pack?"

This woman was so comfortable to kid around with and quite capable as a nurse, too.

"What in the world do you mean by 24-pack?"

I perked up with a confident expression as I raised my hands and pointed to my abdomen.

"I used to have a mean muscular six-pack and now that I'm a bag of bones, all I have are a pair of 12 ribs."

Nurse Libby was finishing the unpleasant job of wiping me up and taking away the rest of the vomit filled sheets. My bum was still sitting in some remains of my breakfast. Nurse Libby requested I roll over. I immediately took the wet pillow case from her hand.

"Nurse Libby, can you please put the rail down. I promise not to fall! It will be easier for you to make the bed and for me to wipe my own ass."

She soon left before I could ask her how she knew the slang word craic. Craic is a pleasant Irish term used as a greeting as well as to ask what's happening and a variety of other jovial meanings.

Suddenly another ruckus at the prisoner's bed drew my attention. My darn curtain had not been pulled back yet, but I clearly heard sounds of a struggle followed by a scream from the guard and Nurse Libby scrambling to call for security. Oh gees, never a dull moment in a place that I'm supposed to be getting a heavy dose of rest and relaxation.

The younger nurse pulled back my curtain revealing a new guard keeping watch over the prisoner now. He had been given some new jewelry with which to tightly shackle all four of his limbs. The two of us assessed the situation without commenting.

The attractive brunette nurse started to leave when I called her back.

"Oh excuse me!" I called to her. She stopped, turned and looked at me. I couldn't help but notice her brightly flushed cheeks nor could I resist attempting to make her blush a bit more. Undaunted, I continued.

"I had the pleasure of your giving me a partial bath using a pillow case as a make-shift washcloth, and I don't even know your name!"

I figured mentioning the pillow case would make her laugh and it worked!

"Tomas, my name is Mia. So very nice to meet you!"

I sat there a moment to analyze and gaze at her features. Now, like my mother, I too noticed something familiar about this woman who stood five-feet- six inches tall—plus or minus an inch or so. She had this proud, erect posture, wore only some lip gloss, but otherwise was make-up free which showcased her fresh wholesome look. There was something about her that intrigued me and made me feel healthy enough to flirt again. I then pointed to the little wooden chair next to my bedside.

"Mia, can you sit and talk awhile?"

This time Mia did not blush and instead seemed pleasantly surprised.

"Tomas, I would love to talk with you but unfortunately I only have a minute before I need to pick up dinner trays and hand out evening medications."

Our quiet conversation was suddenly interrupted by a woman's screams. Mia stood up and saw the social worker at the prisoner's bedside. Her head and neck were being forcefully twisted and cocked to one side. The prisoner whose first name was Roy, continued to yank a handful of the woman's hair! It certainly looked like he intended to snatch her baldheaded! The guard hit him with his night stick and Libby ran over to pry open Roy's hand in order to release the woman's hair from his maniacal grasp.

I couldn't help but think about the fact that there were thirty-nine patients in this ward that were a lot sicker than Roy with his uncontrolled diabetes and peripheral neuropathy. It's unfortunate that this man continued to draw help away from those patients in dire need of a nurse.

The social worker seemed shaken, but her hair was still firmly attached to her head so his attempt to de-hair her had been foiled. She left the ward shaking her head as she mumbled something about keeping out of harm's way in the future.

At 6:30 p.m. I was happy to see my father and Seamus walk out of the elevator and into the ward. Those two had become partners in crime ever since Seamus had been helping out at the family deli. Seamus wore a white T-shirt, a black leather jacket and very tight jeans. As his best friend, I was privy to knowing Seamus likes the way those jeans accentuate his *package*. The man was always on the hunt for another woman, even while visiting me at the hospital. His string of three divorces hadn't quelled his interest in launching yet another relationship.

In contrast to Seamus' breezy approach to fashion and package display and the fact that Seamus paid no homage to impending winter weather, my father was bundled up in a nice-looking, warm wool coat, with a matching wool scarf and derby that covered his bald head. They made quite a disparate pair!

Seamus grimaced as he walked down the ward toward my bed,

"Tomas, this place always smells like piss!"

I shook my head and pulled the stiff, scratchy institutional linens up over my lap. I replied flatly,

"Nice to see you, too, Seamus. Hey, where is my sweet pack of little hooligans?"

Seamus threw his head back and heaved a sigh of relief.

"Oh Jesus, all three mothers are off work this evening taking them out for pizza. Since I'm unfettered tonight, your dad and I were thinking about getting a beer after we leave. I'll drink one for you, too, Tomas! Oh, can you believe now *all three* ex-wives work in the same salon?" My father felt free to voice his opinion about the situation.

"Well Seamus, that's what happens when you dip yer stick in the same Dogtown neighborhood! These women grew up here and formed life-long friendships. Hell if I know why all three ended up marrying and divorcing the very same man. Seamus, next time you go hunting for a new woman, please leave Dogtown behind and go to the Hill or West County."

I was perplexed about my father's new vocabulary.

"Father, you've definitely been hanging around Seamus too much. Since when did you ever talk about a man's dipstick? Sheesh Father, what are we teenagers?"

When the elevator opened, a handful of big brutes from Tomas's rugby team appeared. One was carrying a frothy mug of beer down the ward. Well, that was until a stern woman with a brown beehive, the nursing supervisor, intercepted the pack and scurried them back toward the elevator. Tomas watched them be cowed by this woman and sent away without so much as a word spoken between them. Nurse Libby came to apologize,

"I'm so sorry Tomas! I tried to get the supervisor to at least let your friends come back, minus the beer, for a quick hello. But she was adamant that they leave."

At 7 p.m., the bell rang which sounded the end of visiting hours. My father had previously been upbeat, but was now filled with sadness. I'm sure it was because he wondered if each good-bye would be the last?

Mia called the night shift nurse to come in early to cover for her so she could sit and talk with me. It was like a breath of fresh air to watch her animated expressions as she shared stories about her life in St. Louis. We talked for three hours before she kissed me on the forehead and left for the evening.

It was almost midnight when Libby came back with a morphine injection for me. The attentive and thoughtful nurse would tend to give me an injection before my pain became really bad which helped diminish my suffering substantially. The other nurses would follow the standard protocol. That included administering an aspirin or a non-steroidal analgesic first, re-evaluating in an hour if the pain worsened which, of course, it always did, then the stronger oral medication came next. If all else failed, as a last resort, morphine would finally be administered.

Nurse Libby announced to me she had to finally leave the hospital—I wasn't sure how she endured the long hours and the tremendous pressure of taking care of forty patients! Her dedication was beyond impressive.

Nonetheless, she had enough energy left to give me one big hug,

"Good night Tomas. May you have sweet dreams and a peaceful, pain-free night."

I woke up around two in the morning to discover David Tasma seated in the little wooden chair at my bedside. The vise-like pain was increasing in intensity within and verged on taking control of all my senses. I knew the magnitude of discomfort would soon bring tears to my eyes. My friend from the past gently reached up to infuse a few hours peace into my world. I was his willing student and he my mentor. He was there to keep my pain at a tolerable level, but also to enlighten me about the love of his life, Cecily Saunders. He proceeded to give me a quick overview about their chance meeting in 1948.

"I was in the process of dying in a hospital in the U.K. My first social worker who had been assigned to me took another job and Cicely Saunders was the new one who had been reassigned to me. Sadly, I was alone in London with no family or friends. The only one I had had in Warsaw was my sister. When she died in 1937, a part of me died, too, and I left Poland.

That's when I found that ideal waiter's job in London. For several years I enjoyed rebuilding my life, however I then fell ill.

"Tomas, by 1948 I was in sad shape and not expected to live more than a week. The hospital specialized in cancer patients, however at the time did not have an organized or advanced treatment program for cancer patients. It really looked very similar to the ward you are in now. There was a tiered pain agenda with non- narcotic drugs given first and so on until I was finally—at the 11th hour—given drugs that could do the job. But as you know from your experience here, it is a long process to get to morphine! By that time, you're nearly insane with suffering.

"I'll never forget the first day Cicely walked up to my bed. She had an elegant stature, but at the same time was warm and welcoming thanks to her short brown pixie cut and the most warm engaging smile. It was if I was seeing an old friend. Maybe in a past life we were...well, I'm sure we were more than friends. Cicely initially had been trained as a nurse. A back injury later caused her to reevaluate her future and change professions due to the sheer physical demands a nurse must be able to handle.

"My only new friend in London seated herself in the little wooden chair next to my bed. Cicely had these funny looking cat eyeglasses, however I could see the depth of her beauty behind them."

I was eager to hear his story and I sat forward and actually crossed my legs Indian style. I hadn't been able to do that in months without experiencing loads of pain. I wondered if David could possibly realize how I loved his story about Cicely? David Tasma suddenly looked at me and smiled and I knew then he was able to read my mind!

"Yes, Tomas, I do realize you have a thirst for knowing more about her."

David straightened his vintage gray suit, which always looked perfect, and continued,

"A month before my admission, I suffered daily intractable pain. The first few days in the hospital I cried and prayed for death. That's when they sent Cicely to me and from that day forward, I prayed for more days here on earth, not less. I prayed for a long life so I could spend it with Cicely. That was not meant to be, however I had two months with her at my side each and every day."

David Tasma quit talking when we heard a voice coming from somewhere on the ward. It was strange that when David was here with me, no other patients even so much as moved in their beds, and no nurses or doctors intruded on our privacy. It was as if they all agreed to clear out so this story could be told without interruption. That's until Roy, the prisoner, shattered our peace and quiet with his foul yelling. He screamed and screamed, but strangely no one else heard him despite his strident, high decibel level—not the guard, nurses or other patients. No one except David Tasma and I gave any indication of hearing his loud outbursts. Roy looked nearly sub-human in the dimmed ward thanks to a little ray of light from the nurse's station that illuminated his greasy long hair, flared nostrils and contorted-with-evil face.

"Shut the fuck up, pretty boy! Who are you talking to back there?"

David and I ignored Roy's obscenities and when we realized no one else heard him, we simply dismissed his loud attempts to disturb us as David continued to tell his story...

"Tomas, Cicely's visits were like Christmas every day. Our connection, or reconnection if you will, was rapid and deep. As I grew weaker, Cicely asked me if I wanted to talk about dying or my last wishes here on earth. I told Cicely my wish was for her to share what was in her heart and mind with me. I wanted her to continue to make her dreams of establishing a true hospice come to fruition.

"Then this woman who had been so strong the past few weeks, truly opened up to me. Cicely came to me once she was off work and we talked the entire night. I saw the orange rays of sunset illuminate her face as she shared her deepest thoughts. Into the night, with her at my side, Cicely read by candlelight her notes she gathered since we first met. I don't know how I was able to muster the strength, however, I listened to Cicely's stories as intently as you are listening to mine. Then saw her face as she fell into a deep slumber in the wooden chair. That night was the first time we held hands through the rails of my Bed 39. I too, was in the thirty-ninth bed of a forty-bed ward.

"Cicely told me that I had had a profound effect on her life. She had always felt there should be more done to help cancer patients through the dying process. As our relationship blossomed, she realized there needed to be a whole unified approach in dealing with end-of-life issues.

"Her mind raced with the realization that care should involve multiple specialists as well as a plan to treat the spiritual, psychological, social and physical comfort level of the patient. She believed that each and every patient has the right to die with dignity with more pain control and in the comfort of their own home or a home-like environment.

"As the weeks passed, Cicely was on a mission to build that home or what she designated as her hospice. I smiled and told her day in and day out, Cicely, I will be a window to your home." There was a pause then David resumed,

"Tomas, there is another reason why I'm in your life now. In order to know the answer, you need to delve into your past. I'll lower the rail on your bed as you look out the window."

Naturally, I was puzzled and glanced out the window to see the night sky.

"David, but it's dark outside," I pointed out.

David then lowered the rail and reached over to help me up. He stood and turned the chair to face the window. I now sat in the little wooden chair and admired the star filled sky and city lights. Suddenly it was as if someone turned on a projector and I was watching an old family film. There I was as a six-year-old child back in my old St. Louis, Missouri neighborhood called Dogtown.

"This is amazing! David, can you believe it? David?..."

I turned to look but my mysterious friend was gone. It was now up to me to explore my past in order to understand my future.

CHAPTER 3

A Window to My Past...

———∞———

MY FATHER WAS A HEAVY-SET, balding man and he frequently paced back and forth as he impatiently waited his turn for the bathroom. He had developed a nervous pattern when upset: he fiddled with the long sparse hairs covering the top of his head. Today he finished fiddling with a stray hair, groaned and sighed loudly as he once again banged on the thick wooden door.

"Tomas! For Pete's sake! Please open the door now!"

As a wee lad of six-years-of-age I summoned as much volume as I could so my loud response echoed off the tiny walls of our yellow bathroom.

"Father, things like this take time. I'm not done yet!"

The elder man anxiously knocked again and I knew it was definitely time to flush the toilet. I quickly unlocked the door and sheepishly smiled at my father. He immediately grimaced as he waved in vain to diminish the foul odor that flooded from the room. He was obviously exasperated with the delay and sighed in resignation knowing now there was only time for a quick shave before work. I quickly pulled up a step stool beside my father's short, protuberant frame.

"Father, do you think rich people have more than one bathroom?" I inquired out of a genuine desire to know.

My father ignored the question, however, and continued to attempt to ineffectively wave away the malodorous scent that assaulted his nostrils. My father smiled as he paused to consider my curiosity and tousled my thick head of wavy golden brown hair. My innocent bright green eyes looked up at him inquisitively as I awaited his answer.

"Tomas, if we were rich, we'd certainly have at least two bathrooms, so I wouldn't be forced to subject myself to these smells!" Bart Kaminski then feigned a severe choking episode. "Cough...Cough...Cough!"

I covered my mouth to giggle...

"Father, you are so funny!" I told him with complete honestly.

Like most six-year-olds, I had an abundance of both energy and imagination which made it difficult for me to hold still for long. I fidgeted on the unstable step stool in the little bathroom and mimicked my father shaving. That is until several long gray strands of father's hair caught my eye. My small hand reached up and placed a few of his wiry coarse hairs that sprang untamed from the side of his head between my fingers. I curiously twirled the rogue hairs and leaned closer for a better look.

"Father, how old do you have to be for hairs to turn...turn this color?" I innocently inquired.

Big Bart Kaminski chuckled as he continued to shave. I continued to carefully scrutinize the gray hairs I had captured between my fingers. My father finished shaving, then used his palm to reclaim the hairs from between my fingers in order to plaster them back onto the top of his head. I was curious as to why my father did that. It seemed strange to me!

"Father, I can still see skin."

My father grimaced and shook his head.

To me it didn't make sense, there was an abundance of hair above his ears and even in his ears, but none at the very top of his round head! I gently grabbed one of those long, sparse hairs.

"Please, please! I want to stay here with my gray-haired friends on the side of your head! Don't take me away!"

My father chuckled, "Tomas! Please leave my hairs alone. They help cover my big barren head and make it look a little less...bald."

My father Bart spat on his hand then pressed the wispy hairs down on the top of his scalp using spittle as if it were glue. He smiled as he lingered to admire his reflection. The older man pointed to his face and confidently boasted,

"See, now I'm just one big bundle of handsome! Now out you go Tomas, I don't like an audience when I piddle."

On my quest to delve into the past, I brought up the bathroom scenario because that was always a hilarious bone of contention between my father and me. In the morning he would scratch his balls as he slowly lumbered toward the porcelain palace. I would hear my father and then race to be first in the bathroom! I'd slam the door, lock it and quickly put my little rump on the pot. It was a game to me, however, my father Bart did not enjoy it very much. No, not one teeny tiny bit! Yep, I'd usually stink it up and sometimes forget to flush and leave an unsightly calling card. A funny memory for me, however I surely won't find any profound answers to life and death by dwelling on family bathroom habits.

David Tasma's roots are from Warsaw, Poland which is also where I was born in 1937 as the only child of Bart and Anne Kaminski. My parents told me we had to flee Poland when the Soviets and Nazis invaded Warsaw in September 1939. Most of my father's relatives died during the war, however, I wonder if David and I might somehow be related?

There must be a connection to Poland or it could even be to London since that is where David Tasma met Cicely Saunders. Coincidentally, London was also my mother's hometown. Yes, it was all very confusing to me, too! My beginning started with my parents, Bart and Annie Kaminski. I will revisit what I've been told about how they first met in Warsaw, Poland.

The last half of the 1920's was a more prosperous time in Warsaw. It was during these heydays that my father Bart Kaminski met my mom Annie.

It was 1928 when my mother Annie moved to Poland from London, England. She was only 18-years-old and was fortunate to quickly find employment as a waitress in a busy Warsaw restaurant. My mother worked there for almost ten years before she met my father in 1936.

On that particularly busy day, the lunch crowd filled each and every table. As patrons flooded the establishment, the restaurant's only chef stormed out of the kitchen while hastily tearing off his hat and apron. The impetuous man yelled, "I quit," then toppled over several chairs while racing out the door. Shortly afterward, a couple of police officers walked in asking for that particular chef by name. The owner was fretting out loud, broadcasting how frantic he was to find an immediate replacement! Coincidentally, that was the exact moment when my father walked through the doors to apply for a job as a cook.

My mother thought he strutted into the deli a bit arrogantly. He waltzed past the tables decked out in red-and-white checkered tablecloths, up-righted the toppled chairs and greeted the patrons as if he owned the place. *Mr. Suave* even stooped to pick up a young woman's napkin she had dropped on the floor. The new guy then kissed her hand as if she were royalty. The table of young ladies giggled. In mere minutes, *Mr. Pseudo Stud* already had garnered deli-fans! Strangely, my mother felt giddy and couldn't take her eyes off him. He wasn't drop-dead handsome, she thought to herself, but there was something about him that set him far apart from others. Gees, what was it about him, she wondered?

The new guy straightened his necktie then cleared his throat as he asked for the owner. My mother heard the owner's gleeful and grateful response to this stranger's extremely opportune arrival.

"You're a chef? Yes? Then you're hired!"

He then quickly whisked my father back into the kitchen.

"Please put this apron on and get to work, fast!"

My father was a master at improvising anything! He efficiently and swiftly shoved orders out for my mother to pick up. He was proud that he incorporated his own little spicy twist to dishes by adding a touch of nawleka, a potent alcoholic fruit extract he took out of his pocket. That first day just happened to be one of the busiest and he triumphed despite the pressure.

"Hey Kotek! Food's getting cold!"

My mother turned to the new guy, startled by this unwelcomed nickname.

"Kotex?? What the hell!"

She scooped up the tray and sarcastically replied,

"Who the heck ya' calling Kotex? Peter-Polack? The name's Annie and don't you forget it!"

My father belted out a hearty laugh when he realized why my future mother was miffed.

"No! No, *Kotek*, is Polish for a little kitten. A cute little kitten!"

He laughed years later each time he retold the story of how they met. My father recalled,

"Yes, I called her Annie, yet she continued to call me Peter-Pole, short for Polack, for a long while. She is such a sassy Brit!"

Father was previously known for his roaming eye and never stayed with one woman too long. That was until he met my mother. The look of love never left his eyes, even after decades of marriage. She was a 5'6" full-figured, curvy woman with shoulder length ashy brown hair and light brown eyes. She had a rosy round face with a broad smile that extended from ear to ear. She was a friendly soul, however, it was not a good idea to get on her bad side!

My mother Annie was raised in Britain, however, she came to Poland shortly after her high school graduation. She had had a hard life and had helped support her family. It was certainly tough, especially as a teenager, since both parents were alcoholics. The day after graduation, she just picked up and left, just like the first chef at the restaurant.

My mother was only 18–years-old when she stowed away on a boat across the English Channel. She then spent every last coin she had to her name riding trains across Europe until she stopped in Poland. By that time she was flat broke and walked into the same restaurant searching for a job where she met my father a decade later.

One thing my mother was never accused of was talking behind one's back. That's because there just wasn't anything she wouldn't say to your face! I just sometimes wished she wouldn't force her opinions on me and everyone else she met.

My father was raised on a farm where generations of Kaminski family members built their homes on a 20-acre hillside spread. One by one most of the elder relatives passed away. But farming that hillside was not how he wanted to spend the rest of his life. Since his passion was cooking, he bid goodbye to the bucolic countryside to learn to be a chef in the big city of Warsaw.

My father Bartholomew Kaminski was known as Bart to his friends. He was short, round, balding and sported a very bad comb-over gray do. Maybe it was due to the stress of losing most of his extended family during the war. Or maybe it was because my father was really old! Hell, neither parent would ever disclose their age to me or anyone else for that matter. I was perplexed and persistent in my quest to unearth those magical numbers—the number they steadfastly refused to reveal for some unknown reason.

There were many good years in Warsaw before the war, like in 1936 when my mother and father went on their first date. That was also the day when my father first met his best friend, and one of my favorite people in the entire world, Father McCormack. Well, he wasn't a priest yet since he was only in his first year of training at a seminary in Warsaw. But he was on his way!

On that fated night, the two soon-to-be love birds, Annie and Bart, strolled down the floral lined walkway in downtown Warsaw hand-in-hand under the full moon. They were in a romantic haze since becoming quite besotted with each other since the day they met. Now on an official date, both were transported to another world as they walked together.

But their mutual reverie suddenly ended when three thugs launched an attack when they burst out from behind the bushes in front of a dark, imposing cathedral. Neither Annie nor Bart could quite grasp what was happening, so startling was the assault. One of the thugs grabbed my mother's purse and knocked her down into the bushes. She screamed loudly in protest as well as to summon help to stop the other two big hooligans from using my father as a punching bag.

My mother once again yelled at the top of her lungs for help and that was when she heard a loud creak from the ancient, ornately carved wooden cathedral doors. Out from the shadows sprinted 5' 11" Father McCormack, clergy cassock a'flyin', ready to kick some thug-ass! He grabbed the men holding down my father and gave one a left hook to the nose, then almost simultaneously flipped the other one over his shoulder. The third man knocked the priest to the ground where the robe was pulled open exposing his bare chest and boxer shorts.

Undaunted, Father McCormack quickly hopped to his feet immediately assuming a boxer stance, his right arm held inward and left extended ready to throw another punch. The three men fled with my mother's purse, however it didn't seem like she cared much.

The moon's rays shone down upon the sleek fit body of the most handsome man my mother had ever seen. It wasn't my father but Father McCormack. The half disrobed Irishman had a sleek, well-defined body and face with dark tapered brows that arched above his intense, almond-shaped green eyes. There was a bit of a raised knob in the middle of his otherwise straight nose. To my mother it was an added bonus to this near perfect, extremely handsome, masculine man.

My mother was still on the ground with her shoulder length ash brown hair flipped forward so it covered most of her face. She slowly cleared the cascading hair from her eyes. She did not want anything to obstruct her view of this warrior god! Mother was too busy taking in every detail of this half-naked man to help herself up. As the story is retold by my father, he says Annie was lying on the ground with her shoulders propped up by a bush, knees bent, skirt up and panties exposed. What made my father upset was the goo-goo eyed look on her face as she gawked at Father McCormack.

The priest rushed over to her like a dashing knight helping a damsel in distress. There was a dark, silky brown wave of hair that sensually and strategically fell onto his left brow. My father noted that his date didn't seem upset at all! Not one teeny bit. She smiled broadly and blushed while looking at his chiseled oval face and beautiful green hazel eyes that appeared to be almost luminescent thanks to the light of the moon.

As soon as he regained his bearings, Bart hurried over to assist Father McCormack. My father felt guilty being jealous of a priest or a man studying to be one. Bart was ashamed of wishing at least one of the hooligans would have bloodied Father McCormack's face...just a bit, maybe enough to take Annie's focus off every handsome, manly feature!

Father McCormack invited my father and mother into the rectory to have a cup of cocoa while they awaited the police's arrival to document the incident. The event with the hooligans had unsettled them all, but their curiosity in learning about each other trumped their upset and they quickly began sharing their life stories.

The room in the rectory looked more like an elegant library with rows and rows of books covering two of the walls. A gold framed oil painting of the Pope, an archbishop and a former priest were on the third wall and a magnificent wood burning fireplace dominated the fourth.

With this elegant room as a dramatic backdrop, all three ended up talking for hours, feeling as if they had known each other forever by the end of the night.

Father McCormack talked about his childhood growing up in an area of St. Louis, Missouri in the states. It was primarily an Irish Catholic neighborhood that had been known as Dogtown since 1850. The area was known for earth rich in coal and deposits of clay. There were numerous brick factories in the area and once railroad tracks were laid, the area's population grew rapidly. The bulk of the land in Dogtown from 1850 until the early part of the 1900's was used for coal mining.

Dogtown was a close-knit community where the neighbors looked after one another, and was an avid baseball town as well. Dogtown even hosted the World's Fair in 1904. He recounted many fond memories and talked of a brick bungalow house still there that awaited his return.

Father McCormack opened up to these two would-be strangers and explained that several years ago he had been confused about whether to become a priest or a Catholic missionary. As a missionary, he dreamed of working many long hard hours helping the disadvantaged in third world countries. He acknowledged that a chance to travel and explore the world was also very appealing.

He was an only child and once his parents passed away in an auto accident, he left St. Louis to further his education at Trinity College in Dublin.

Other than an aunt in Chicago, all his other living relatives were in Ireland. To earn extra money he boxed at a local gym in Dogtown and then continued to box for several years in Dublin. He quickly became ranked one of the top boxers on the semi-pro circuit.

From that night on, mother always had a mini-crush on Father McCormack. She told me how he sat on the opposite side of the coffee table from her and Bart. The strikingly handsome priest had the couples' full attention. My future mother noted a smudge of dirt on the priest's lower lip, however, Annie didn't dare to wipe it off for fear of revealing the butterflies and weak knees Father McCormack gave her. My father pressed his hand on top of his date's delicate hand, as if to claim her as *his* woman.

As the story is told, Bart once again leaned forward, filled with curiosity, to ask how Father McCormack had ended up in Warsaw.

The priest flashed a dazzling pearly white smile which revealed his perfectly aligned teeth before he sipped his cocoa. Each of the newly formed threesome agreed to share a bit about their backgrounds in order to catch each other up.

My parents told me many times about their first meeting with Father McCormack. He told them, "Warsaw was the first seminary program to accept me into their 1936 program." It was Father McCormack's first year when they met him. He arrived six months early in order to volunteer at the local hospital. Father McCormack's family members were frugal humble people despite their considerable wealth. The entire family felt blessed and knew it was their mission to help the less fortunate, the sick, dying, or those experiencing turmoil in their lives. Maybe it was his influence that inspired me to want to be a physician.

The first person Father McCormack met in Poland was a physician at the Warsaw hospital named Dr. Hannah. She also volunteered at the church and was the first woman who ever took his breath away. At the time, she was engaged to an army officer. The future Father McCormack was heading to seminary school, so either way, he decided he needed to not think about the beautiful doctor as anything more than a friend.

My father then shared his story about becoming the new chef at the local deli within minutes of walking through the door and how his extended family members were farmers. Then my mother shared what life had been like for her growing up in Britain with abusive alcoholic parents and how Warsaw was where she had run out of money.

At one point during the evening, the police arrived to take everyone's statements in order to make their official report of the attack and robbery. But it didn't take long until all their questions were answered and the threesome could resume sharing their life stories and bringing each other up to date. The attack shrunk to insignificant proportions compared to the powerful connection the three of them acknowledged. They agreed that the muggers were merely playing a role that would unite the three in friendship and that was all there was to it.

As usual, Annie didn't fail to mention her unremitting loyalty to the Manchester United Soccer team and that despite her difficult years in Britain, she was still a loyal fan and always would be.

It was then that the ancient clock tower chimed waking them up to the fact that it was now 1:00 a.m. They were startled at the late hour, but agreed that their meeting was seemingly destined and they remarked how comfortable they felt with each other.

Bart and Annie walked hand-in-hand as they said their good-byes to Father McCormack. Bart was secretly thankful their new friend was in the process of becoming a priest because father previously told me he surely would not have been Annie's first choice if Father McCormack were available. It was an undeniable, unsettling feeling, but he shook it off.

The couple returned outside and embraced the cool brisk air which wafted the lingering scent of wood burning. When the two were still in front of the church and beneath the light of the moon, my father gently turned my mother around to face him. She inquisitively looked into his round dark green eyes examining every feature.

His eyebrows were a little coarse and out of control thick wiry hair protruded above his ears. She noted that the wool cap concealed his balding head. Bart's nose was a bit broad with a downward slope above his curvy lips. When she added it all up, Bart was no Father McCormack, but he had a charisma about him and the most kind, gentle face. Yes, my mother liked her date and he made her happy. She smiled in response to her private musing.

That seemingly chance meeting ended up changing the lives of Bart, Annie and Father McCormack forever. The chef's and waitress's blossoming relationship became the talk of the deli. Several months later, Father McCormack married Bart and Annie Kaminski at the same church where they all met. A year later, Annie was thrilled to discover she was to become a mother. My mother loved children and was eager to have half-a-dozen or more Kaminski kids. Unfortunately, I was to be their only child.

My father initially considered moving us all back to his family farm outside of Warsaw. Unfortunately that was in September of 1939 when Poland was invaded by the Soviets and Germans. His uncle sent an urgent message to Bart, notifying him the family's crops were being confiscated to feed German soldiers, while they themselves received mere scraps. Later, when the crops failed to produce, the farm was confiscated and most of their homes were destroyed.

It became my father's quest to start fresh in a land where he would have the opportunity to make choices about his family's future and live as a free man. Nothing was more of a priority than his family's welfare and freedom was the foundation for everything he wanted to achieve, be and provide.

It was Father McCormack who provided an escape for us out of Warsaw. It wasn't the first time my parents left with just the clothes on their backs and a few coins in their pockets. This time, though, was different since they had me, their only son who was the tender age of three.

Through Father McCormack, we found what we thought was temporary refuge in Dublin. We ended up staying for several years. He would visit us whenever he had time away from the seminary. It was Father McCormack who taught me how to play Gaelic football and soccer as soon as I could walk. My father and the McCormack relatives would sit on the sidelines and cheer.

For years, Father McCormack continued to share treasured family memories of Dogtown and regale Annie and Bart about how great a place it was for a child to grow up. So it was that on one snowy Christmas in 1943, Father McCormack gave Bart and Annie their second greatest gift—I was hands-down their first, of course. The gift was the deed to his home in St. Louis—his beloved childhood home in an area called Dogtown in St. Louis, Missouri.

CHAPTER 4

Welcome to Dogtown Reflecting to 1943

THIS DOGTOWN NEIGHBORHOOD IN ST. Louis, Missouri, was so incredibly Irish that it made me feel as if I had never left Dublin. On our cab ride to our new home, I noted the flag of Ireland painted on several sidewalks. The taxi dropped us off in front of a two-story brick bungalow built in 1905. It was a cozy looking 816 square foot, two-bedroom, one-bath home in a section referred to as Clayton Tamm. A small patch of green grass was visible between the crumbled first brick step of our porch and the street—that was the full extent of our "lawn." Those crumbling bricks had not been tended to for many years since no one had been around to tend to anything. Yet after all this time had passed since any member of the McCormack family had been here, there was still an old wooden sign firmly attached to the front door that read: Welcome to the McCormack's.

There are several theories as to how Dogtown was named, however the most widely accepted is the 1876 version. The scenario goes that there were coal miners working in a huge area which is now Forest Park. But the land being mined was purchased to build a park so the coalmine was shut down and the miners had to find work elsewhere in the city. This of course forced the coal miners to work quite a distance away from their small shanty homes. While they were gone they wanted to protect their families who stayed behind with dogs for protection. When carriages would go through town, the dogs would be startled into thinking danger was imminent thus the loud chorus of dogs barking and howling were heard for miles away. The area swiftly became known as Dogtown.

After our long journey, we had finally arrived at our new residence just at sundown. To my mother's delight, our new home was just around the corner from Tamm Avenue and a street called Manchester which was a constant reminder of her hometown and her favorite soccer team, Manchester United. Nonetheless, I had a strong feeling Brits and Polish folks may be a minority in our neighborhood.

Most of the older homes were wood framed and the newer houses which were built in the late 20's and 30's, were mostly brick. Ours was the brick variety thanks to its construction date.

As far as we were concerned, heck, we wouldn't even have a home at all if it weren't for Father McCormack. It made me smile to see many of his family pictures hanging in the living room. But further exploration of our new home had to be postponed until the next day due to the late hour. So my parents tucked my six-year-old-self in bed and told me there was loads of work for me to rest up for in the morning!

That first night in our new home, I slept in the same bed Father McCormack slept in as a child. The little bedroom's plaster walls were painted yellow. They were adorned with an assortment of framed sports prints and leather boxing gloves hung on large nails. The small dark wood twin bed had a comfy feather mattress and an old green and navy plaid bedspread with white sheets.

On one side of the bed was a nightstand with a small white lamp and on the other was a dark wood rocking chair with a matching plaid pillow seat. Under the window was a cracked wooden storage chest with a bold "Keep Out" warning painted on the top. The scrawl of a child's handwriting gave away the approximate age of the person issuing the directive. Of course, seeing the warning sign made me want to open it even more! "Shall I be nosy?" I thought to myself. An emphatic "yes!" could not be stifled! I was certain Father McCormack would not mind in the least that his childhood chest was opened these many years later.

The chest easily surrendered its intriguing content. I discovered loads of books, school papers adorned with lots of A-plusses, a great assortment of cast iron cars, a box of clay marbles, a bell hop monkey, a teddy bear and some black–and-white photos of Father McCormack. It was a treasure trove of goodies just right for a six-year-old boy and I was so happy to find the photos of Father McCormack when he was about my age!

To me, Father McCormack looked way more like a movie star than he did a priest. Sometimes, I felt guilty wishing he were my father or even my older brother. I sure missed him like he actually was one. I grabbed Father McCormack's old teddy bear and we snuggled together under the covers. It wasn't long before I drifted off into a deep sleep.

I'm not sure exactly what time it was, however, in the wee hours of the morning I was awakened by a soft touch to my cheek. The glow of the full moon through my bedroom window enabled me to see a beautiful young blonde woman seated on the side of my bed. The woman extended her arm to enable her soft, gentle hand to touch my cheek. She was wearing a gray utility dress and smiled at me so sweetly with such great tenderness that I wasn't in the least bit afraid. I stared at her for a while trying to figure out who she was and why she was here when I heard her whisper,

"Hello Tomas."

My mind was going a-mile-a-minute with the appearance of this unknown visitor on the side of my bed.

"Hi lady, why are you here?"

The woman merely continued to smile while she slowly became more and more translucent. Receiving no response, I then asked,

"Do you haunt other boys in the neighborhood or just me?"

Before she totally disappeared, there was a whisper...

"I'll always be watching over you, only you, Tomas."

When I woke up the next morning I was uncertain if the blonde woman had just been a dream or if she was real. For the moment, I decided I would chalk it up as a dream, a very real and strange one! When I walked into the living room my parents were cleaning and scrubbing away at our new home. They greeted me in unison,

"Top of the Morning!" as mother continued to wash the floor and father buffed the furniture. I thought I would share my experience with my parents.

"Last night there was a pretty lady sitting on my bed. She looked like a ghost!"

My father and mother stopped dead in their tracks to listen and clearly wondered if they had heard right. They looked puzzled as they flashed a glance at one another, then probed for more information?

"Son, it was probably just a dream, however what did she look like?"

I tilted my head and dug into my short-term memory bank.

"She had a nice, kind face so I wasn't afraid. Hmmm, the lady had really long blonde hair and she kept smiling at me. She also was wearing this old looking gray dress that was the color of father's hair."

My mother's and father's mouths flew open as if they were surprised, then once again looked at each other whispering...

"Hannah?"

There was a lengthy, uncomfortable pause before they continued.

"Son, don't worry, we are sure it was a dream. Maybe she is one of your angels who is protecting you! Now we have loads of work to do here..."

When I heard my parents say that, I smiled from ear to ear.

"Yes! That's what she said! She was gonna watch over me, only me!"

My father shook his head up and down in agreement as both he and mother started cleaning again. The two suddenly started whistling at the top of their lungs! They were scrubbing so hard that perspiration dripped down their cheeks. Mother and father beamed with joy as they busted their butts scrubbing our new home. The scene struck me very funny and I started to giggle! My father looked puzzled.

"Tomas, what are you laughing at?"

I was still chuckling as I imitated big Bart with his farmer overalls cleaning while mother was whistling tunes at the top of her lungs. Both had the most goofy look of joy on their faces.

"I'm laughing at you father! You too, mother! Who smiles like that when they are working so hard?"

My parents laughed in unison.

"Son, we are so happy to have a home of our own, thanks to Father McCormack, we can't help but whistle and smile."

All three of us sat down on the dusty couch in the tiny living room. I watched as my parents silently scanned what we could see from our vantage point. The yellow walls and the array of memorabilia in my room were visible from where we sat. The oriental rug, lone red Victorian sofa and matching chair were situated on the scuffed, dark hardwood floor in the living room. And even though we had been there less than 24 hours, the three of us agreed it definitely felt like home with a capital "H"!

What I personally loved the most was the built in bookcase filled with all kinds of novels and reference manuals. Then off the kitchen was the only bathroom, where we could see part of the white claw-foot bathtub and more yellow plaster walls. All this was visible from the sofa where we sat.

We unpacked the few clothes we had arrived with yesterday. Our meager clothing was all we brought with us from Ireland and we had taken nothing away with us from Poland. But none of that was important. Here we were in the U.S.A. in a home of our own! The miracle of it all was beyond belief!

My parents took a deep breath and a moment to think of all they needed to do to settle into our new home. They were still weary from our trip. The to-do list was staggering: for starters a job for father was number one on the list, second was to register me for school, and third and fourth were to buy groceries and clean the house that had stood vacant for almost a decade.

This adult-stuff was way too much for me to think about. I was bored. Inspired by the boxing gloves on my bedroom wall, I energetically assumed a boxer stance with my fists in full motion. I was ready for a pseudo-opponent!

"Father, can we pretend fight? Like the time you met mom and the three bad guys pushed mom into the bushes, then beat you up? I can pretend I'm Father McCormack."

My father frowned immediately.

"Son, what do you mean *they* beat *me* up? No way! Now why don't you pretend to be me? You can be me, the one who rescues your mom *from* the bad guys."

My father had a pleading look on his face as I maintained silence but rolled my eyes back and forth. I was trying to figure out if my father had *his* story straight about the night he and my mother went on their first date. Heck, I was thinking really hard! I then peered out of the corner of my eye to see my mother, tightly holding her abdomen in an effort to stifle gales of laughter.

I finally sighed loudly,

"Um, father, but that's not the story I was told."

That was all my mother could take before she burst out...

"Oh my gosh, I'm laughing so damn hard, I'm crying!"

My father shook his head and held his arms high, yelling...

"Argh, I'm bad-guy-Bob and I'm coming for ya', wee lad! Arrrrrgh!"

Well, that is what Father McCormack used to say when we wrestled, not typically what a Polish man would blurt out. I do think a few years in Dublin rubbed off on my father, though.

I gallantly raced to place myself in front of my mother with fists held high as if to protect and defend her. I checked and rechecked to make sure I had a *proper* fighting fist: my thumb was *over* my fingers, not under, while covering my first two knuckles and making sure that my thumb wasn't protruding upward.

From my point of view, I skillfully acted as if I were giving the bad-guy a powerful jab to the jaw. No contact, of course, this was all play and I was only six years old. In my tiny tough guy voice I yelled,

"Didn't your mom teach you not to hit girls? Huh, tough guy? Arrrgh, your *ass* is mine!"

Once my father heard that come out of my mouth there was no more fighting. He had a surprised look as if I punched him in the gut-for real.

"Tomas, now enough of those words! Ass? Who taught you that anyway?"

I must say I looked rather sheepish and totally unaware that it was a bad word.

"Well, one of the fighters said it when Father McCormack took me to a boxing match in Dublin."

My father leaned on the coffee table as he raised himself up to tuck his white shirt back into his brown trousers. He then repositioned his red suspenders as mother helped him roll up his sleeves. Bart looked at Annie who had strands of hair falling out of her previously neatly coifed bun. Her formerly pressed, calf-length, light green floral dress with square shoulder pads was now a wrinkled mess. My parents had worn the same attire for days, however to my father, his bride Annie looked more beautiful today than when they first met many years ago. He often remarked aloud lovingly,

"We don't have much, but we always have each other. We are rich in love."

It was the first Saturday in May and we were happily and gratefully living in our new home. My mother, father and I walked to the closest grocery store yesterday to stock our empty refrigerator. The next morning I savored the mouth-watering aroma of sizzling bacon and eggs cooking in a hot frying pan. My olfactory senses were going wild and my mouth was watering like a salivating dog.

The conversation around our breakfast table flowed from subject to subject as we discussed everything that needed to be done before father hit the pavement the next day in search of a job. Suddenly our conversation was abruptly interrupted by a knock at the door. I started to get up from the table, but my father stopped me and said,

"Tomas, finish eating! I will get it."

I heard his heavy footsteps stop as he opened the squeaky door. There in front of him was a four-foot, fire-haired, green-eyed boy with a derby cocked to one side of his head. The lad spoke with a husky, gruff voice as he confidently looked up at my father,

"Hey, I heard ya' have a kid here. A kid *'bout* my age?"

Bart chuckled under his breath,

"Why yes, we do, young man! His name is Tomas. He just sat down for breakfast, would you like to join us?"

The little Irishman shook his head and declined.

"Sorry, no time, sir. I've gotta show him the ropes around Dogtown. Have him meet me on the steps, pronto."

Bart scratched his head in wonder as he headed back to the kitchen.

My father didn't know what exactly he had just experienced, but hoped fervently it was just an isolated example and not the norm of the boys in this new neighborhood.

"Tomas, there is a little mini-mobster asking for you to meet him outside. He's waiting on the front step."

In the forties, people felt safe and no one really worried about where their kids were going during the day. Once a child finished his chores, parents felt free to let them roam the neighborhood with their friends, even friends they hadn't met yet! I anxiously gulped down my morning meal as fast as I could to meet my first and only friend. As I exited the kitchen, my mother yelled,

"Tomas, be home for dinner by 5:00!"

As for my father, my mother handed him a honey-do list: fix the toilet, unclog the kitchen sink, clean out the gutters, rake the yard and that was just for starters. The list covered both sides of the sheet of paper. My mother was in work clothes with a red handkerchief tied around her hair. Her weapons to wage her war on dirt included a sponge, mop, bucket and broom. She was ready to scrub the house from top to bottom. Thanks to the arrival of the little, mini-mobster, I would now be out of their hair.

As I burst through the door and out onto the front stoop, the fire-haired boy quickly sized me up and introduced himself.

"Hi, I'm Seamus O'Leary and I live off of Tamm Avenue. I'm eight years old, how about you?"

"I'm almost seven years old. At least I will be in November! My name is Tomas Kaminski."

Seamus threw his head back and started laughing.

"What's a Polack doing in Dogtown?"

I looked at Seamus as if he had two heads. I then wanted to punch him in the nose the very moment he said Polack!

"Seamus, my family is from Poland and if you want to be my friend, you *better* call me Tomas!"

Seamus had been picking his tooth with a skinny stick and stopped long enough to say,

"Sure kid. If it makes ya' happy." And that settled that.

The two of us toured the neighborhood, discussed the St. Louis World's Fair, walked to Forest Park, then to the St. Louis Zoo which first opened in 1904. To this day it is one of the few free zoos in the country!

On their way back to Dogtown, Seamus quizzed Tomas.

"Hey, know why they call this place Dogtown?"

The red-headed freckle-faced boy pulled down his derby. It was as if he meant to discuss serious business. I recalled the cab driver discussing the origin with my parents on our arrival to St. Louis.

"Um, it has to do with all the coal miners who used to work the mines around what is now that Park...Forest Park! Years later, when the city purchased the land to build a park, there was no longer any mining to do nearby. The miners had to go elsewhere. Their families lived in shacks south of the park, so when they left to work far away, the husbands bought dogs to protect their families. The dogs barked a lot."

I smiled from ear-to-ear, confident my memory had not failed me. I was certain it had to be right. My smile faded to a frown when I saw the expression on Seamus's face.

My new friend shook his head.

"Tomas, that is all the crap the adults tell ya'! The real reason is that in 1904, a bunch of ancient tribal natives from a teeny island somewhere in the South Pacific came here for the World's Fair. On that teeny tiny far away island, these natives loved to eat dogs! Can you imagine that? The mayor or the government or whoever made the rules back then, told them they could not eat our dogs, not even stray ones! But this particular tribe didn't care, and at night, they would sneak out and it was bye-bye doggies."

I spit on the sidewalk when I heard that one!

"Seamus, now what yer telling me is a bunch of crap! No one eats dogs- absolutely no one! Not in a million years! Yuk!"

We continued walking the streets of Dogtown heading home. After a few blocks we passed an empty lot where a group of neighborhood boys were playing stickball with a broom handle and rubber ball.

Fat Freddie who was playing first base shouted out.

"Hey Seamus! We need a catcher...get your butt over here! The new kid can sit on the sidelines."

Seamus's chest puffed out knowing he was a valuable team member and needed by the older guys in the neighborhood. The opposing team was comprised of boys from Greg Avenue.

Seamus quizzed me by asking,

"So kid, who are ya' rooting for?"

Needless to say, I had a blank stare on my face and shrugged my shoulders.

Seamus's red eyebrows furrowed angrily.

"What kind of shit-bird are you anyway?"

I innocently asked Seamus,

"What do you mean?"

Seamus shook his head with disappointment and explained.

"Tomas, look around you. Do you know anyone on the Greg Avenue team?

I sheepishly replied, "No."
Seamus once again asked,
"Are we playing guys from Poland?"
I again replied, "No."
Seamus pointed to Fat Freddie.
"Now that big guy with the ugly mug on first base...is he your friend?"
Seamus waited impatiently for a reply.
I whispered, "No."
Seamus then sarcastically chimed,
"Well, ya' big goof, I *am* your friend! So ya' better be rooting for *my* team, because that's just what we do here in Dogtown. We have a friend for life and we have their backs, too. Got it?"

Seamus and I became fast friends from that day forward and we were rarely seen without each other—sort of like Mutt 'n' Jeff. Even though Seamus was more than a year older, I was moved up to the same grade. It was my passion for reading that made me excel in all the main subjects. When I was at home, it was my mission to eventually read every single dormant book that remained on the dusty McCormack shelves. There must have been a hundred of them! Father McCormack's dad was a family practice doctor and his mother a school nurse, so there was all kind of educational reading for me to look forward to tackling.

This may sound strange, but sometimes I looked more forward to reading books than eating mother's homemade chocolate custard pudding. One tempting dessert I may have given up a night of reading for was Mrs. O'Leary's famous apple raisin bread pudding!

A year passed and life carried on smoothly as if I had always lived in Dogtown. My father took a bus each day to work where he was a chef at a popular restaurant in downtown St. Louis. My mother Annie was a homemaker. That was it, at least for the time being. My father's goal was to own his own restaurant and when he does, I'm sure mother will be the manager, clean-up crew, waitress and accountant. For now, I was her entire world and she was enjoying watching her only son thrive in this new city.

Seamus and I continued to stop for a game of stickball on our way home from school each day. That is where Seamus was recruited to catch for the Tamm Team and I would sit on the sidelines doing *his* homework. Little did their team know that I was a natural athlete. Heck, after a year I was still the "new boy" to them and had to prove myself to be Dogtown worthy. Someday, maybe someday, they'd ask me to play but for now I'll continue to do Seamus's homework so we can stay in the same grade.

The school year flew by and next year I would be in fifth grade. On this particular day, I momentarily wondered if Sister Mabel caught Seamus kissing another girl in the closet. If Seamus thought about school as much as he did girls, he would be an A-student! I laughed out loud about that one.

As I meandered up Tamm Avenue, my mind wandered as I struggled to fight the sadness that swept over me when I completed another year. Strangely, it always felt as each year of my life concluded that it would be my last. I loved life, learning, reading my letters from Father McCormack, then writing him back to tell him about Seamus and my other Dogtown friends.

I think about him being here so I could share my dream of where I'll go to college someday, maybe Trinity College, like he did. Or maybe I will stay here in St. Louis and apply for medical school or go to veterinary school. My mind would race with all the exciting possibilities! I had to constantly reassure myself that the sadness over finishing the year would fade, like it always did. I'd gradually look forward to the next New Year and being a bit closer to achieving my future goals.

One rainy Sunday afternoon, my parents and I had just returned from church when there was loud banging on our door. As my father opened the front door, a river of guys poured inside like a herd of cattle. The guys from the stickball team had all been urgently pounding on the door at the same time. Seamus O'Leary, Danny McNab, Derry McDaniel and Freddie O'Toole led the charge. Freddie was carrying an injured mixed breed stray dog that had been hit by a car. No tags were evident so there was no way to tell where his home was.

"Mr. Kaminski! We need Tomas right now, sir!"

My father scratched his pate under the sparse wiry gray hairs that sprouted from the top of his head. He sarcastically yelled above the boys' frantic chatter.

"Hey Tomas, since when did you get your veterinary license?"

The commotion roused my mother as she wondered why her living room was filled with loud, sweaty boys.

"Tomas, what is going on? For Pete's sake, whose dog is that?" she asked.

I heard and came running.

"I'll explain later! Quick guys, put him on my bed!"

I put the 30-pound shepherd mix on top of one of my mother's new towels.

The pup was scared and panting rapidly. There was a small amount of blood coming from a scrape on his left shoulder and leg, maybe a result from skidding on pavement. I spoke softly to my frightened furry friend as I gently stroked his body to check for pain in various areas. The only wincing or yelping occurred when I touched his leg.

The dog's tongue was pink, which was an encouraging sign that he had good blood flow. I was no dog doctor, but I was determined to do what I could to make him comfortable and stable until we could walk him to the veterinarian's office in Forest Park.

The pup's lower left front leg above the paw looked swollen. I had read several first aid books for humans in the McCormack mix of reading material, so I attempted to reach into the depths of my recent memory bank to help the dog.

I used warm soapy water to gently rinse and clean the wounds. When my mother wasn't looking, I ran for more of her washcloths. Then I had an idea! I went into the bathroom to get the biggest band-aid I could think of, one of my mother's sanitary napkins. Unfortunately, she saw me and immediately put the kibosh on that plan of action!

When she turned her back, I snuck into the bathroom again and pilfered just one Kotex pad. It would serve brilliantly as a large bandage and splint for our patient, I surmised. Then I took some masking tape and cut it the length of his leg. I put the two sticky sides of the tape together so it would not stick to the fur any more than necessary, but left a small strip of sticky tape exposed in order to anchor the makeshift splint. It did double duty by acting as both a splint and re-enforcement to support the Kotex.

We then took our now stabilized and calmed down stray pooch to the real veterinarian's office. After a thorough examination from the professional, the diagnosis was that the dog had suffered a contusion or a seriously bruised bump and sprained leg.

The kind vet's vet charged nothing at all for his greatly appreciated services! He even gave each of us a bottle of cola for the road. Quite serendipitously, the formerly stray canine now would be taken to his new home with Freddie. Freddie had dashed home while we were tending to the dog in an effort to get his parents' approval of adding a furry new member to the family. Waves of relief washed over us all that the dog was going to be given a good home.

Somehow from that day on, the Dogtown stickball team adopted a new attitude toward me. That fact was evident the very next day when Seamus and I walked to the field so he could play stickball. This day proved to be different in more ways than one. The first difference was we usually played with rubber balls, but this day we had actual professional baseballs that one of the players brought back from a Brown's game!

The second difference was the large gathering of Seamus's female fans who were watching from the sidelines. I'm not quite sure how all the bad boys seem to always get the girls, but Seamus had a million of them!

Finally, this was officially my day of full acceptance by the Greg Avenue team. They asked me to sub in right field for *their* sick player. The Greg Avenue team was the opposing squad, the archenemy to our Tamm team. I wanted to play, but could I agree to play for *them?* I reluctantly glanced at Seamus, while nervously awaiting his approval. My red-headed, hot-natured friend grinned, then nodded "yes" as he tipped his ball cap as an unspoken sign of his new found respect for his Polish friend.

We were into the third inning and I was fortunately holding my own. I even hit a double and caught a few outfield fly balls. I heard one of the Tamm players laugh and yell,

"Oh, that was a can of corn!"

That phrase was foreign to me, however when the inning was over, one of the Greg Avenue players told me it meant the ball was easy to catch. The next time I was covering the outfield, I had to run fast and furiously, then dive to catch the ball. Fat Freddie once again yelled, "Can of corn, Tomas! That was just a can of corn!"

My cheeks were red and irritated with Freddie's banter. He was just trying to show off in front of the girls and now I was, too.

"I'm gonna take a can of corn, Freddie, and shove it up your ass!" I elegantly countered.

Instead of getting mad, the whole Tamm and Greg Avenue teams looked surprised, then laughed their butts off! Fat Freddie gave me a thumbs up and shouted,

"Good one, Tomas!"

My temporary Greg Avenue team came up for our turn at bat. The first one up to the plate was a lefty and a real power-house. The Tamm team's pitcher was 15-year-old Derry O'Malley. He was after a victory and wanted this guy out, 1-2-3! Seamus was catching and intermittently flashing broad smiles to his fawning female fans. The pitcher slowly wound up, then let the ball rip right in the middle of the strike zone. All I heard next was a loud THUD.

Seamus flew several feet backward from the force of the impact and fell motionless on the ground. The professional grade ball coupled with the powerful fast pitch hit the distracted Seamus smack on the left side of his chest with far more force than normal. I ran from the sidelines, and sprinted toward him screaming,

"Seamus! Seamus!"

The unconscious catcher was surrounded by players from both teams. I was still screaming his name as I tossed the older boys out of the way as if they were dominos. I needed a clear path to Seamus! His head was resting upon the only dense patch of clover in the vicinity as he blankly stared skyward. His eyes were no longer green, sassy, inquisitive and scheming to find another Dogtown trivia question to stump me. They were dark, open and lifeless as if God came down and took the very soul out of Seamus.

We were all standing over him when I decided to get physical. I shook my friend and cried hysterically. My first friend in Dogtown, my best friend in the world appeared to truly be dead.

All our tears were spilling onto our catcher's face and now I could hear the siren of a police car nearby. I knelt down beside the motionless player.

"Seamus! Seamus, I was rooting for you. I will always root for you because that's just what friends in Dogtown do. I'm rooting for you now to come back...please Seamus..."

The lifeless body before me didn't even look like Seamus. I felt so helpless. It was just us kids hovering around him. Many were whispering prayers and made the sign of the cross over their uniforms. The police and ambulance parked on the dirt, however I was certain they were much too late to save him.

At that moment, I stopped crying. Suddenly I was inspired by a woman's voice to take action. With all my might, I pounded Seamus on the chest just one time, but my hit was very sharp and hard. I looked down upon his face as I held my breath while hoping for a miracle, some sign of life. Suddenly his black dilated pupils which had appeared dead, instantly turned as green as the clover he laid upon in the field. Seamus' arms raised to his chest. In a weak voice, almost a whisper, he said,

"Hey shit-bird! Are ya' trying to kill me?"

The crowd cheered and started hugging one another. Derry O'Malley laughed and with tear-filled eyes he pointed to his teammates.

"See there's nothing to cry about ya' big babies! I knew he'd be okay!"

Derry O'Malley proceeded to blow his nose on his dirt covered T-shirt.

Seamus was quickly scooped off the ground by the ambulance crew and carted off to the emergency room near Forest Park. When I looked down on the ground where Seamus's head had lain, I spied a tall shamrock that rose above the rest. A four-leaf clover! I picked the clover and clutched it in my hand as I ran after the ambulance, chasing it all the way to the hospital.

My friend was admitted for a couple days while the doctor ran a series of tests to check out his heart. The good news was that Seamus would be discharged the next morning, but the doctor's orders specified that he was to remain in bed at home for at least five days following his release from the hospital. That week without my best friend was the loneliest ever and seemed like an eternity.

While Seamus was in the hospital and then home in bed, I had lots of time to read. It was a week filled with hot, humid summer afternoons. It was too hot to be indoors, where the air was still, hot and stagnant. My mother would sometimes buy a big block of ice and put it on a container in front of the blowing fan. That's how we stayed cool in the kitchen. But this hot spell included a series of days where it was almost hard to breathe! The most tolerable spot was our front porch. It was there where I read a book about how the first modern air conditioning unit was invented by Willis Carrier, in Buffalo, New York in 1902. Gees, how I wished we had a few of those units in Dogtown, or one would do just fine.

I'd read each day until the sun set, when there was no more light left to see the words imprinted on the book's pages. Then I would sit on the porch and ponder about the day Seamus died. Well, at least for several minutes.

My stomach turned when I reflected about that day. It was so surreal watching the life flow from my best friend's body and I wondered what exactly brought him back? Was it the luck of the Irish and the healing properties of the four-leaf clover? Or was it a result of the 'strike the left side of Seamus's chest with your fist one time only as sharply and forcefully as you can' guidance I clearly heard in my ear on that fateful day? My money was on the gentle woman's voice that told me exactly what I needed to do in order for Seamus to live. I was extremely grateful the blonde lady was living up to her promise of looking after me!

CHAPTER 5

Life Before Bed 39
1964

Seamus O'Leary and I graduated from high school in June of 1954. A month later he married one of his many high school sweethearts and I was best man at his wedding. A couple of months later in September, I became godfather to his first born. By 1964, Seamus had married and divorced three times. I was best man three times and godfather to all six children! There was never a dull moment with Seamus as a friend and you pretty much had to keep a scorecard to keep track.

We remained close as brothers though, especially after he nearly died several years back. I never again wanted to feel that helpless when someone I cared about or even a stranger, was dying right in front of me. I wanted to know exactly how to help them, to save them.

Seamus, the neighborhood gang and I got together for a weekly game of rugby at Forest Park. The best part was going to the local pub, where after throwing down a few beers, we'd talk about the good old days growing up in Dogtown.

I worked full-time to save money for my education and in 1957, I was accepted into Washington University's pre-med program. By 1960, my father and I both had had our dreams come true! He and my mother bought the restaurant they had dreamed of owning and would work and manage it for many years after the original owner retired. And I was accepted into medical school.

However, my father had different plans for me and asked me to place medical school on hold for a couple years. My parents desperately needed my help at the restaurant. They loved the fact the restaurant was on Manchester Road and had been a family-run business before our family took the helm. The real work started when my parents took over the restaurant. All three of us were at the restaurant 16 to 18 hours each and every day.

Unfortunately, by March 1964, I was still putting my medical school plans on hold and pretty much living at the restaurant. It was a happy place though and I looked forward to Seamus bringing all the kids in for dinner several times a week. Our discounted meals helped his struggling family out and I had the opportunity to see all my godchildren. It was hilarious to see the O'Leary clan push and shove their way through the door to see who could get to "Uncle Tomas" first. All 12 arms would be tightly wrapped around me as if it would be their last hug! Of course, I loved every minute of the hugging!

One day, four-year-old Molly O'Leary dragged this scruffy wild-haired black-and-brown stray dog into our restaurant. She asked if he could join the family for dinner...

"We can't keep him Uncle Tomas, but at least we can give him a full belly!"

I cautiously turned my head to make sure my mother didn't recognize that our furry patron had entered the premises, then nodded my agreement.

"No problem, but I'll seat you at the back corner table. I'll bring your furry friend his very own dish of stew. Just don't tell anyone, okay?"

I swear that dog knew English because he had the biggest grin on his drooling jowls and wagged his tail when he heard the word "stew." The O'Leary kids were arguing trying to figure out a name for the stray found on Manchester Road. I had a brilliant idea for a name—Harry, Harry Gregg, my favorite Manchester United player.

"Kids, how about Harry? Do you like it?"

One by one, the O'Leary kids looked at each other and smiled.

"Yes! We love the name Harry!"

Much to my mother's dismay, scruffy street-meandering Harry became our best regular patron and he showed his appreciation by bringing a few stray bitches with him every now and then. I grew very fond of him though, and tried to protect him from inclement elements by keeping him in one of the stock rooms at night when it was cold, snowy or raining. I was pretty darned sure that my mother would skin my hide if she knew! It was true that Harry was a wandering man, but he still appreciated the nicer things of life when someone offered them to him.

The next morning was a Saturday and a few of the guys from the old neighborhood and I played a game of rugby at Forest Park. After the game when I showed up for work I was hobbling like an old man. I was rubbing my sore muscles when my father walked in.

"Father, I feel like I'm almost your age with all my aches and pains! Oh and by the way, I'm not quite sure exactly how old that might be? Here I am, almost 28- years-old and you have never revealed your age to me! Father, give me a hint. How old were you and mother when I was born?"

My father rolled his eyes and almost growled repeating what I knew would certainly come next.

"Old enough to know better, son. Old enough to know better."

My mother walked into the restaurant kitchen to see if we had started preparing for the afternoon rush.

"Mother, how old were you when you married father and how long did it take to have me?"

She instantly looked disgruntled.

"Tomas, why in the world do you hope that I will suddenly relent and tell you what both your father and I have refused to tell you all of your inquisitive life? I didn't answer you before and I'm not about to answer you now or ever. That's the end of that! Please do not ask again."

My parents were perplexingly private about certain aspects of their lives, like what happened to all my aunts, uncles and cousins and, of course, their own ages. My father was clearly getting annoyed as I continued my interrogation. Nonetheless, I persevered. I gave my father a pleading look.

"Come on, father, I have a curious mind and want to know!"

"Please cease this nonsense! You are like a thick, wild, curly hair up my kolba!"

That comment of course made me roll on the floor with laughter. My father would sometimes confuse English or American slang he'd hear on the streets with Polish.

"No, father, I am the one with the hair up my butt! Not you! It is like I have a thought and won't let it drop."

My father shook his head and rolled his eyes.

"Always the 'want to know it all' *Dr.* Tomas!"

His dark green hazel eyes had an intensity that made him appear cold and calculating. Yes, he had been through much sadness, but he chose to take a positive approach to life. There was always someone who had it worse than he and he knew it... Despite losing so many family members in the war, he would always say,

"At least I have you and Annie. There are those who have no one. At least we have each other."

He was a genuinely good man with a gentle soul. One would recognize the depth of his kindness by hearing the soft tone in his voice. It was almost musical. Oh, and his laugh was contagious! His laugh sounded like a hearty roar that quickly spread across the room.

On one cooler spring afternoon when father was working at the restaurant, mother and I brought him some warm English scones from home. When we arrived, one of the patrons had just finished telling father a joke.

It must've been a doozey because from all the way at the back table you could hear father and everyone else crack up. Then one of the customers started chortling so hard he almost fell out of his seat! His wife yelled,

"Why in the heck are you laughing so hard?"

The man, almost choking on his food, replied,

"I don't know, maybe because everyone else is!"

Father loved his restaurant which quite naturally featured Polish cuisine. He was a genius when it came to making a variety of pierogi dishes and kanszanka, a traditional Polish blood sausage. If he didn't know how to cook what you wanted, then he would learn and, of course, integrate a little nawleka.

In 1964, Polish delis were not abundant in St. Louis, but word was spreading and our restaurant became busier each day. Spring was also in our favor as more locals were getting out of their houses to enjoy the warmer weather and drop by for a bite. It was clear they enjoyed seeing my mother's friendly face. She worked as a waitress and I was the waiter. I was also assistant to the cook, dishwasher and a most charming host.

I was twenty-seven-years-old when I thought I had finally met my Miss Right, Rosie. However, my mother called her Miss Wrong!

"Look at you! You're a strapping, handsome young man. You have class and that woman you call your girlfriend is trash!"

I sighed and rolled my eyes as I calmly replied,

"Mother, her name is Rosie."

The frustrated older woman now rolled her eyes and sighed,

"Rosie-Smozie! Why don't you find a nice girl? You don't think I know that she sneaks into your bed at night? Do you think we are stupid? Your father and I can tell by the smell of her cheap perfume! Rosie is not a girl you should be proud to bring home to your father and me! Does she even go to church? I don't think I've seen her there, no, no…poppa have you?" Have you poppa?"

My mother rambled on with questions erupting out of her mouth like bullets from a machine gun. Mother finally raised her voice shouting,

"Darling, poppa, I'm speaking to you!"

My father was busy slurping from a large soup spoon sampling one of his new concoctions.

"MMMMM!"

Mother repeated…

"For Pete's sake, I'm speaking to you!"

My father just shook his head and replied,

"Oh, yes."

A smile appeared on his round face knowing his response had a chance of quelling his wife's unrelenting questions. When my father was cooking, he wanted no interruptions. His focus was on what ingredients would complete the particular culinary masterpiece he was tending to at the moment.

Father opened the cabinet in search of spices to throw into his delectable new brew. Mother groaned while growing increasingly frustrated that once again, her husband was tuning her out and didn't have a clue what she was talking about.

"You! You are a hopeless old man!"

My father still deep in thought replied,

"Yes, dear. You're so right, always right. I most certainly am."

All of us quietly continued taking care of our tasks at the deli. So far as my mother was concerned, no woman was ever good enough for her son. Well, maybe a nun might have been, but that "of course" was forbidden!

One day a daughter of a friend of a friend named Pumpkin came to my parents' deli for "lunch." In reality, it was a thinly veiled attempt to blindside me with an introduction to a wealthy client's daughter.

I suddenly felt like a trapped cat cornered by a pit bull in a dark alley. Oh no! It dawned on me that my mother had set yet another would-be romantic trap for me! Suddenly I wanted to throw down my towel and ask to be excused.

My father and I were peering out from behind the kitchen door. Father gave me an empathetic pat on the shoulder as we both became painfully aware of mother's shenanigans.

Our oldest one and only female waitress became animated as she approached the table where Pumpkin was seated with her exquisitely dressed mother. My mother was proud that a woman of her stature would be a patron of our simple deli. We, as well as everyone else in the restaurant, heard her say…

"Oh, well you must meet my son!"

The hairs on the back of my neck raised and my shoulders cringed as I frantically whispered to my father,

"Help! Oh my God! Father, why does she do this to me?"

My mother proceeded to wave me toward the table. Both Pumpkin and her mother smiled as they saw me sheepishly walk toward them. As I slowly approached the table, I gave the instigator, my mother, a quick pinch on the fleshy part of her chubby back. I hope this time it hurt! I'd done "the pinch" many times before when I wasn't too happy about her impromptu set-ups. My mother just looked up and smiled broadly, then gave me a wink. Arrrgh, I thought to myself.

Now don't get me wrong, Pumpkin was not unattractive, she was just, well, plain and virginal looking. The sweet young girl had her hair pulled up in a bun with large brown eyes and flushed cheeks. Not a stitch of makeup was anywhere to be seen, despite the fact that a tad of it might have been more flattering.

In all honesty, she had a nice smile. Oh heck, who needed a Pumpkin when I already had Rosie? Rosie was voluptuous and curvy with a small waist that was almost always accentuated with a tight belt. Rosie had a swagger and a confidence knowing she could get any man. And right now, I was her man.

Pumpkin gave me a big toothy grin as she gazed up. After the introductions had been made, I heard Pumpkin loudly whisper to her mom,

"He is the most striking man I...I have ever seen! Those eyes are as green as shamrocks and sparkle like the stars above. Mom, he sure looks more Irish than Polish, don't you think so? That fair skin, rose colored cheeks and golden brown hair sure all add up to be Irish, I swear."

Pumpkin's mom laughed as she noted the twinkle in her daughter's eyes as she continued to verbally size up every detail about this particular waiter.

"I like how one long wavy curl falls onto his brow, while the rest of his mane is neatly groomed behind his ears." Pumpkin held her chest in an attempt to exert control since the mere look of him made her heart palpitate a few extra beats.

Pumpkin's mother leaned toward her daughter, then raised her hand to cover the side of her mouth,

"And, my dear, his mother told me he was accepted into medical school! He is smart, too, and going to be a doctor!"

After finishing a hearty lunch at the deli, Pumpkin Anderson and her mother waved good-bye. This was the one and only patron who had a chauffeur driven limo drop them off in front of the restaurant. Their Chauffer just happen to be on the rugby team and told me Pumpkin was big time smitten with me. Then he described how Pumpkin flashed a broad smile and waved good-bye all the way down the street. My chauffer friend witnessed how Mrs. Anderson lovingly turned to her daughter and observed her dreamy expression. Pumpkin continued to gaze out the window in total silence. Mrs. Anderson gently touched her daughter's hand as she curiously asked,

"Dear, is there anything wrong?"

Pumpkin was now somewhat speechless, and slowly turned to smile at her Mom.

"No, no mother, however, I believe I just met the man I'm going to marry!"

The deli continued to buzz with activity most of the day. By ten that evening, tables started to clear. I thought, aaah, what a relief! Customers left feeling quite content with hyper extended full bellies and smiles on their faces. The regulars waved good-bye to Annie and Bart as if they were extended relatives. Most of our customers sure felt like family to us, too!

As I was busy cleaning the table, mother walked up to further her crusade to oust Rosie and replace her with a "proper" young lady.

"Son, Pumpkin is such a sweet girl isn't she? She's perfect for you and someone you can be proud of!"

I rolled my eyes as I shook my head.

"How many times do I have to tell you? Time and time again. Please, I want to choose my own girlfriends without any help from you!"

Just then, Rosie waltzed in the door having donned one of her red low-cut dresses which displayed her ample cleavage spilling out of her dress. Rosie smacked her gum loudly as she whisked quickly toward me and said,

"There you are, darling!"

This time it was mother's turn to mutter "arrrrgh" as she turned and scurried back into the kitchen. Rosie was oblivious to my mom's non-verbal clues. As I gave Rosie a big welcome hug, Harry, the scruffy looking mixed-breed stray ran into the deli. Rosie screamed as he raised her dress with his cold nose and sniffed!

"UGH! Gawd awful creature!" Rosie sniffed with distain.

I, on the other hand, was pleased to have a visit from my furry hobo friend. Rosie seemed repulsed as I knelt by Harry and playfully rubbed his belly.

"Rosie, this is Harry, Harry this is Rosie."

Rosie sarcastically replied,

"Harry? Why Harry for Pete's sake?"

No doubt I enjoyed opportunities to explain that Harry was named after my favorite Manchester United goalie Harry Gregg. Harry Gregg was a true legend who was the Hero of Munich! Harry rescued countless teammates and even a pregnant woman after that horrible air disaster in 1958! The entire team was on a British Airways flight that crashed on take-off due to weather conditions that February day in Munich. Twenty-three passengers died, many were team members. Only twenty-one passengers survived.

Rosie put her hand over my mouth to quickly stop whatever else I was going to say.

"I'm bored...Let's get out of here!"

Much to my mother's dismay, Rosie and I continued to date the next several months. My mum ignored Rosie like the plague and Rosie returned the favor.

There was one afternoon when mum invited Mrs. Anderson and Pumpkin to join us for lunch. However, I was conveniently away watching my favorite football team, Manchester United, play Fulham. Needless to say, I had to remind my mother that I was not open to any sly match-making antics!

By June of 1964, a nagging cough kept me up many nights. Realistically my symptoms had occurred much earlier, but I had a definite knack for ignoring them. By July, Rosie frequently complained that my coughing embarrassed her—as if I had control over it.

One night while in the line to buy tickets for a movie, I could no longer stifle the over-powering urge to cough. The forceful hacking roar went on for several minutes to the point where I had to hold on to Rosie to keep steady on my feet. Out of the corner of my eye, I saw Rosie grimace and squirm as if she were irritated.

"I'm not going into the theatre if you're going to hack all through the show!"

Rosie turned to hail a cab and that was the last time I ever saw her. It was difficult to keep my mother from throwing confetti, but I missed her, of course.

In a matter of months, more than 35 pounds rolled off my six-foot frame. During that time, I was treated for bronchitis and pneumonia several times.

It never dawned on mother that I could actually get seriously sick, but by now she was extremely concerned. After all, excluding a few sniffles, I don't believe I recall any of us being ill before. Father McCormack called from some remote island to see how I was doing. Mother sent him a letter to inform him I had lost so much weight. I reassured him it was really nothing and I was on the mend.

Amazingly, the third week of September I started to feel like my old self again. All I needed was a longer course of antibiotics, according to the doctor and I happily went along with that premise. The decrease in my coughing and the improvement in my color and attitude thrilled my parents! They both seemed so happy that I was getting back to normal.

Just after dinner one evening, mum, my father and I sat around the small wooden table sipping coffee. Father excused himself to walk into the family room. He had this sly smile on his mug as he fumbled through our assortment of records. He chose one in particular, *A Lighter Shade of Pale.*

This chubby old man was trying to act like Mr. Suave, as he waltzed over to the love of his life. His outstretched arms begged for his woman to grab on, which she did, and they began to slow dance around the kitchen. They reminded me of a prom king and queen rather than a couple married for decades. My father was singing horribly off key, however, I don't think mother even noticed. Almost embarrassed, I stood up from the table.

"Umm, excuse me but I think it's time for me to leave…"

I had to chuckle at my father's embarrassingly corny moves on his woman. When I strode past the stereo, I exchanged father's tune for a fast paced Irish Jig. The looks on their faces were priceless as I did a little jig of my own. We were all cracking up now. I bent over chuckling harder at seeing the old man, trying to kick his chunky legs. My belly ached from all the laughing!

"God gave you not one but *two* big clumsy left feet!" I shot over my shoulder in a tease.

Suddenly the smile on my face abruptly changed to a grimace, as I experienced an overpowering itch in my throat. I thought surely it must've been a dry throat caused from laughing.

But then I abruptly had a strong urge to cough. Instead of the usual dry hack, an unfamiliar thunderous productive bark erupted. I coughed uncontrollably as torrents of frothy, bright red blood landed on the floor. My parents' eyes were wild with fear.

The three of us were frozen with horror as we gazed in astonishment at the splatter of crimson. The joyous merriment inside our home immediately ceased, and it became so quiet you could only hear the dripping from our kitchen faucet. That was when my mother started to cry and my father yelled, "Oh my God, Oh my God!"

My parents suddenly regained their composure and they quickly rushed me to the nearest hospital. During the next two weeks, I had a battery of x-rays, blood tests, sputum cytology, and biopsies. The specialist sat my parents and me down to reveal the bad news. The lung cancer was not only in my lungs, but had spread to several organs. I will never forget his words,

"Tomas, you have end-stage inoperable lung cancer."

I was numb and stared blankly at the surgeon. In a near trance, I sadly gazed into his eyes and remained mute. Those words…"end-stage inoperable lung cancer," played over and over inside my head. I somehow knew that medical school would not be in my future, that life as I knew it, would never be the same…if at all.

CHAPTER 6

It Sucks to be Sick

―⚬⚬⚬―

I FOUND OUT THE HARD way, there usually aren't many early warning signs with lung cancer. Once an individual like me displays pronounced symptoms, the disease is usually in advanced stages. The specialist asked me if I smoked. My reply was, "No, however everyone else in the deli does including my parents."

Oddly, after I was diagnosed with lung cancer, I came across an interesting tidbit related to smoking. For some odd reason, it stuck with me: Christopher Columbus was the first European to smoke tobacco in 1492. Instead of his fleet landing in Asia, they found Cuba instead. As Columbus and his blokes explored this new territory, they came across an Indian tribe. Columbus witnessed them drying tobacco leaves and then saw others smoking it. The Indians offered him a toke from their pipe. A couple crew members eventually brought tobacco back with them to Europe. The highly addictive and dangerous properties of tobacco for smokers and second hand smokers, would not be known for several centuries.

I read as much as possible about cancer, from the past and present. As early as 1600, Egyptian physicians were removing tumors as the only form of treatment for what was presumably lung cancer in today's parlance. In World War II, researchers discovered that soldiers who were exposed to mustard gas had suppressed bone marrow. That incidental reality lead to a treatment for lymphoma.

Unfortunately, for me, very few advances had been made in the treatment of small cell lung cancer. It continues to be one of the most challenging and difficult to treat lung cancers.

I was getting progressively weaker, and my poor aging father injured his back trying to assist me getting out of bed. No doubt my terminal diagnosis was taking its toll on the family and the business. Mother and father would take turns, one would work the deli while the other stayed home with me. Seamus was filling in as a waiter and he brought his older kids to help wash dishes and clean up. There were times now when I was too weak to even get to the bathroom on my own. I required help with just about everything. It was a horrifying downward spiral which I did not know how to reverse.

Both my father and mother had to work in order to have sufficient income. It was not the least bit optional. There was also the financial stress of not having me at work to wait tables, help cook, take care of some of the bills, and welcome customers.

Things quickly got to the point where I needed 24-hour-a-day care. I was told repeatedly that my condition was inoperable and no chemo or radiation would take this all away. So it was with the greatest sadness that I was being wheeled through the doors of this hospital in South St. Louis by my sorrowing father.

Suddenly I awoke from my sound sleep and a Technicolor replay of my recent past. Sheesh, in the past five hours by the clock, I took a journey through more than two decades of my life!

Once I opened my eyes and came back to consciousness, one of the first sounds I heard was Roy's constant flow of foul words. I couldn't wait until that man was discharged! My journey to the past offered many theories however, no definite answers about my connection to David Tasma.

To my surprise, I saw my mother racing through the ward with this excited expression on her face.

"Tomas! Tomas! I remember where I saw that young nurse! It was with her mother several months back at our deli. Her name is Pumpkin!"

The beautiful brunette nurse was at the other end of the ward when she heard my mother yell her nickname Pumpkin. Needless to say she had a look of surprise on her face. She slowly walked in my direction and once again her cheeks were bright red. "Pumpkin?"

The very same "Pumpkin" that I had avoided like the plague several months ago looked very different to me now. I guess when Rosie was around I never really looked at anyone else. I must've been crazy to not notice Pumpkin's gorgeous brown eyes and that wholesome pretty face. The young nurse had the gleam of total health thanks to her shiny brown hair and perfect porcelain complexion. Her round brown eyes seemed more intense, in contrast to her stark white professional nurse's uniform.

Pumpkin's inquisitive eyes searched for an answer trying to discover how I knew her. It wasn't until she recognized my father that her facade of disbelief was replaced with pity for the frail young man before her—me.

"Oh my goodness! Yes, yes, I apologize! You were always Nurse Libby's patient and I was on the other side of the ward. I only knew you as, Tomas. Yes! my mother and I met you at the deli! I'm sorry I didn't recognize you."

Mia paused as she took renewed interest in the patient seated before her in a wheelchair. She leaned forward to gently move aside several golden brown curls that fell forward onto my brow. She smiled as our eyes met.

"Well Pumpkin, I'm half the size since I saw you last. But, I'm not sure how you didn't recall this game face."

That was a private joke between my mother and me, of course. We both managed to have a good laugh as Pumpkin stood wondering what I was talking about. I could see Mia had some guilt of prior recognition. That realization as to who I was probably occurred to her when we sat and talked for a few hours the other day. I honestly didn't absorb Pumpkin's beauty previously and was extremely ashamed to have purposefully avoided her at the deli. Shame on me! How could I have been so blind!

My once sparkling green eyes were dull with pain and dehydration which caused them to sink deep into their orbital cavities. Now I was recalling the day at the restaurant when I met Pumpkin. Heck, I could almost see her racing heart beat through her blouse. It didn't take a rocket scientist to know she had a crush on me. That assumption was easily verified by her red blushing face every time I saw her and the multiple trips to the deli she made after we met.

But at that time, I only had eyes for Rosie, who now I realized was very wrong for me and probably for any other man for that matter. The Rosie's in life could only love one person—themself. Now I was almost embarrassed how I begged my father to wait on Pumpkin's table at the deli. My mother would beg me to give Pumpkin a chance.

"Son, she told her mother she never felt this way about anyone before. Please, go say hello, talk to her!"

Sadly, I never did.

My mother walked forward to give Mia or Pumpkin a hug.

"It's so nice to see you again! Please tell your mother hello for me!"

The two women chatted for a while before my mother left for the deli. I looked up at the beautiful woman before me and grinned.

"Ok, so what shall I call you, Nurse Mia or Pumpkin?"

Now it was Mia who was laughing,

"Oh please call me Mia, since I am no longer a roly-poly toddler." She looked up and smiled, "Tomas, you have company however, I promise to see you before I leave."

Suddenly we were interrupted by a commotion that ensued as the elevator opened.

"Why speak of the Devil!"

Seamus and his six little O'Leary's came running down between the rows of beds. Gone were the attempts to cloak their arrival. We were depending on the nursing supervisor being far, far away and everyone else turning a blind eye at the happy cloud of children.

"Uncle Tomas!" they cried, practically in unison.

All six were pushing and shoving in order to jockey to be up front, a few ended up careening into some of the other patients' beds. My sweet little hooligans didn't care. All they wanted was me, Uncle Tomas. As predicted, Seamus took one look at my pretty nurse, then tipped his hat and winked.

"Gees, Seamus, give it a rest will ya'! Some things never change," I mockingly complained.

The O'Leary kids presented themselves in a tumble of brother and sister teasing and tussling. Patrick held onto his brother Mickey's hand, then there was Shannon, Katie, Maureen and Molly. All the little O'Leary's surrounded me as if I were this interesting lab specimen. Maureen suddenly blurted out,

"Uncle Tomas, I heard Sister Agatha tell Sister Ann, that heaven may not open its pearly gates for the likes of Seamus O'Leary!" She turned to her father.

"That's you, Dad!"

Seamus almost choked on the coffee he brought in with him. When he cleared his throat, he yelled while wiping off his new green sweater at the same time.

Seamus, shook his head and threw his hands up.

"Where did this dad bashing come from anyway? We are here to see Uncle Tomas!"

Then the kids all looked at me. Have you ever seen someone laugh so hard that no sound comes out at all...only a bunch of air? Well that was me. The O'Leary kids had me laughing so hard and I loved seeing Seamus squirm in the hot seat.

"Seamus, your kids are the best medicine! Aren't you, my little munchkins? Don't worry about your dad going to heaven though, because he has truly been my angel here on earth."

Mia grinned when she heard that answer and left me wearing a big smile to tend to her other duties on the ward.

My friend Seamus was quiet now and looked around at all the ill patients in the ward and then at me. There was a look that I had not seen before on this feisty red head's face. It was probably the same look that I had on my face many years ago when I thought I would lose my best friend. The lower rims of his eyes had become red and watery. He sniffed and used his shirtsleeve to wipe his upper face.

"Oh, these damn allergies!" he feigned.

Seamus's six-year-old daughter Maureen was now on a step stool combing my hair. My golden brown locks were now shoved up into the shape of a tall cone on my head. It was certainly not my money-maker face! Seamus laughed.

"Maureen, what do ya' think this is? A beauty parlor? Come on ya' hooligans, it's time to get back to the deli!"

The O'Leary gang gave me massive hugs and kisses. They even waved good-bye to the others in the ward.

"Good-bye sick people! Get better!" they chimed in together with sincerity. To my surprise Roy smiled and those who weren't comatose, confused or writhing in pain, waved back.

I spotted Nurse Libby and Mia headed in my direction. I was sure the two were discussing how we met at the restaurant.

"Tomas, your mother told me you lived in Ireland for a couple years before you came to St. Louis! Well, Libby also spent a few years in Dublin!"

I straightened up in bed and smiled.

"Well, what's the craic, Nurse Libby?"

The nurse smiled at Tomas's use of the Irish vernacular term craic meaning, what's happening or what's new.

"The craic around the ward is you were born in Poland, then lived in Dublin before you came to Dogtown. The peculiar thing is, you are a Manchester United fan! How in the world does that happen?"

It was an exhaustive day for me, however, I managed to break a smile.

"Long story Nurse Libby and if I can have something for this wretched pain, then I will tell you all about it."

I grimaced as the pain took hold and made me double over. Mia was worried and came to my side to comfort me as Nurse Libby went for the medication.

"Please, I need to sleep, please excuse me Nurse Libby and Mia."

Blessedly, the injection of morphine I received allowed me to sleep comfortably for a few hours.

The sun had now set and the moonbeams replaced all forms of light. As I opened my eyes, I caught a wonderful, crisp, light floral scent, maybe lavender with a touch of vanilla. My head turned in order to figure out where it was coming from. The moonlight illuminated the silhouette of a woman quietly seated beside my bed. It was Mia.

When she realized I was now awake, she smiled softly. The smile exposed her beautiful straight white teeth. I didn't say a word as I gazed in wonder at this lovely woman by my side. We silently stared into each other's eyes. I caught myself wondering why I never noticed how enchanting Pumpkin was at the deli. Maybe it was just my profuse dislike of my mother arranging blind-dates and, as a result, I never gave Pumpkin, a chance. But even more likely was that I had a severe case of the "Rosie."

"Are you comfortable?" she inquired with concern.

I slightly squirmed in my bed as I took a breath to see if the deep, searing pain I felt earlier was ready to rear its ugly head again.

"Thank you, but I am fine...for now."

It was now midnight and the end of Mia and Libby's shifts. Both came to wish me a pain-free peaceful night as they walked toward the elevator. The pain injection quelled the tip of the agony-iceberg, however there was still so much more brewing beneath the surface. I was now praying for a 2:00 a.m. visit from David Tasma. I kept looking at the clock and watching the chair for my friend. My plan was to excitedly tell him about my journey to the past while I slept, however, I was much too weak to talk.

It was 3:00 a.m. when I smelled something intensely foul, like decay. I instantly raised my head to see where the odor was coming from. At that moment, I heard an electrical snapping, as if there were a short in a circuit. Then out of nowhere appeared this swirling waterspout in the middle of the floor. I frantically wondered where the nurses were. The water now seemed to heave upward with an erratic motion and I heard the slow beating of a drum. I sat forward on my bed in order to get a better look. I suddenly gasped when these pulsating serpentine fingers slowly protruded from the ever-enlarging mass on the floor! They rose higher exposing an attachment to multiple fluttering arms. As the drum beat faster, it sounded less like a drum and more like a beating heart. An evil dark mass with red eyes oscillated high above the helter-skelter fury. The sound of impending doom was upon us all!

I started to pray out loud! Roy was the only patient who heard me. He angrily raised his head from the bed and yelled,

"Shut your f-ing mouth! This isn't a damn church!"

I honestly was scared to death as the deafening beat grew faster and more frenzied. There was a dim red illumination over the frenzied storm. None of the patients awakened despite the storm of madness in the ward.

"Roy, Don't you hear it? Oh my God!"

My body was pressed firmly up against the head of my Bed 39. My knuckles were white as they gripped the metal rails.

"God in heaven, be with me now, please!" I prayed fervently out loud.

Now, it was Roy who was screaming! His body was still shackled to the bed, however the mass of appendages ripped Roy's shrieking soul into the dark pulsating mass on the floor... and into the depths of hell! I then yelled,

"David! David! Where are you?"

The fear was so piercing that my heart felt as if it would pound out of my chest! Someone must know what happened in this ward! I found myself tossing and turning while screaming for Mia, Nurse Libby...

"Please, please help me!"

I awoke to Mia looking down upon me with these sad big brown eyes. She was gently stroking my forehead with a damp washcloth while Nurse Libby had a thermometer in my bum.

"Nurse Libby, we haven't even had our first date."

The sweet matronly nurse chuckled, quickly withdrew the thermometer and patted my hip.

"And we aren't going to young man! Thank God your temp is now down to 103 degrees from 105!"

I was somewhat embarrassed and shook my head,

"Gees, can you take an oral temp next time?" I asked hopefully with my intent being more a directive than a request.

Libby sighed, "Tomas, what am I going to do with you? Dear, of course I can and will take an oral temp, unless you are in a coma or altered state, like you were this morning."

My whole bed was drenched! Thank goodness Mia found a washcloth and didn't have to use a scratchy pillow case. The sun's bright rays shining through the window were so intense that I had to squint. I contracted an instant headache. I wearily looked up—I had been through a lot!

"What time is it?

Mia reached to turn my metal bedside clock toward me.

"It's almost 4:00 p.m., Tomas, you've been out of it most of the day! I clocked out and called a nurse friend to take my shift. I wanted to be here for you."

I looked at Mia, smiled and reached to give her hand a gentle squeeze.

"I'm so grateful you are here with me."

Mia continued,

"Oh, your Dad and Seamus were here for several hours, but left for the deli and your mom went downstairs to get something to eat. She will certainly be happy to see you are finally awake! I also snuck your rugby team back here while the supervisor was at lunch. Tomas, you are a lucky man with so many people who love you."

I then had this sly inquiring expression as I glanced up at Mia,

"Um, do you happen to be one of them?"

My pretty nurse chuckled,

"Of course! How could I resist you with that cute money making game-face?"

I was amused with Mia's witty response.

"I'm going to have to get after mother for revealing the secret to my success. But lucky, lucky me, though, to have your love."

Mia stayed beside me until midnight. I heard her start to leave so I reached for her hand. When I looked up, I happened to notice the guard was no longer sitting by Roy and the bed was empty!

"Mia, what happened to Roy? Did he go back to jail?"

She raised her eyebrows as if she were surprised I didn't know.

"Tomas, Roy died last night. I'm sorry and thought you knew since you were the one to call the nurses for help. They came back to find Roy having a seizure and then he went into cardiac arrest. His heart just stopped beating."

I became silent as I thought about the horrific scene I witnessed last night— how Roy's soul was snatched out of his body and seemingly pulled to the depths of hell. Hmmm, no, there is absolutely no explaining that to anyone without sounding delusional or over medicated, I reasoned, so I stayed mute on the subject.

"Good night my sweet Mia."

She slowly packed up her purse, coat and gloves, then kissed me on the forehead before she left. I was still pretty wiped out as a result of the high fever and instantly fell back asleep.

From then on Mia was by my side on her days off and after work. We passed the time by playing silly trivia games or just holding each other's hands. It was a beautiful, heart-centered time for both of us despite the obvious severity of my physical condition. I was falling deeply in love with this beautiful angel. I berated myself for not having the eyes nor willingness to see who she was until this 11th hour of my life.

I hadn't seen my friend David Tasma for a few days, until he showed up again at 2:00 a.m. I was extremely happy to see him. David patted my hand in greeting.

"Pretty scary wasn't it?"

I instantly sat up as fast as I could which wasn't fast at all since every bone and muscle in my body was aching and the pain generated by rapid movement was extreme.

"You saw it too? It was real?"

David nodded,

"Yes, Tomas, your nightmare was real and in your mind. That is how I experienced the frightening scene. I was there with you last night, right by your side as I am now. Roy was a sick man...physically, mentally and morally. It was his time."

I coughed and held my ribs in pain.

"David, can you do that thing where you touch my shoulder and it takes my pain away? Makes me feel human for a few hours, for which I am always grateful."

David had this warm grin on his face as he reached over and gently put his hand on my shoulder.

"Yes, my dear friend."

As I started to have some relief from the pain, I was able to focus and sit still long enough to hear David Tasma's story. David would always wear his gray wool suit for his 2:00 a.m. visits with me. He had his brown hair perfectly slicked back and was quite the classy man. What I admired most though was his kind, gentle poetic soul.

"Tomas, Cicely knew there had to be a better way to treat the terminally ill. She went on to medical school in order to have greater credibility and a stronger voice in her quest to build the first organized hospice. In 1957, she graduated as a medical doctor and by 1958 she was already doing research on total pain control.

"At the time, there were scattered hospices around the world however, they were primarily run by religious orders. The patients basically went there to die with very little focus on pain control.

"Dr. Saunders wanted something more, a unified group of medical professionals to tend to the needs of the dying: an oncologist if the patient had cancer, social workers, psychologists, dieticians, a priest or chaplain and ongoing research for total pain control.

"Yes, she wanted to build the first organized hospice in the world. Those were the dreams and aspirations Cicely shared with me in her role of social worker. Once I arrived at the London hospital where I met Cicely, I was never expected to live more than a week. But the truth is, knowing Cicely gave me the will to live a bit longer, as long as possible in fact. I looked forward to hearing about her hopes and desires to bring peace and comfort to terminal patients. To find a humane way to offer better pain control was one of her cause célèbre. No one should have to tragically suffer days or months of extreme pain before their final day." David said emphatically.

"It was during this time we ended up falling in love. We shared a spiritual love and yearned for the good, old-fashioned and highly satisfying physical love. Unfortunately, that was not my reality since I was unable to leave the hospital".

I thought for a moment about the way I felt about Mia. Each day my heart skipped a beat as she walked toward my Bed 39. She always had the most beautiful smile on her face! I cleared my throat and turned to my poetic friend sitting at my bedside.

"David, it's with great sadness that I know in my current state Mia's and my love will never leave this ward. Would it be possible for you to allow me to be totally pain free with your magical touch to my shoulder? Just so I can experience some level of physical intimacy with Mia that would be uninterrupted by searing pains?"

I clasped my hands to momentarily pray before he gave me an answer. But when I looked up, David was gone and my heart sank into a deep state of sadness. I will never feel the touch of Mia's body next to mine nor the taste of her lips, I cried to myself. She will always remember me as a sick, dying man and we will never have the chance to express anything more than a spiritual love. I felt like a man cheated of not only his life, but the very essences of life that are often the zenith of human existence.

CHAPTER 7

A Spiritual Love is Better Than No Love at All

―❦―

Nurse Libby was like a bull in a china shop with all the racket she was making around my snug little corner in the ward. She pulled a tray on rollers to my bedside. It contained a small tub of warm water, soap, shampoo and a washcloth.

"Tomas, your money-making lock of hair is plastered to your forehead! Yes, your momma told me about your game face and we are going to get it back!"

I slowly rolled over and covered my bed-head.

"I'm not up to it this morning Libby."

She was always persistent and proceeded to cover me with a bath towel.

"Tomas, have you ever heard of Babe Ruth?"

I shook my head irritated and just wanted to wallow in my own sadness. Then I rolled my eyes as I attempted to resist Nurse Libby's attempt to get me out of my moody frame of mind. I just didn't feel like giving it up today. It was all mine and I wanted to harbor it for awhile, own it and be alone!

"Of course I've heard of Babe Ruth! Hasn't everyone? And what does this have to do with this impending bed bath and my money-maker?"

She looked up at me as she poured some baby shampoo on my head and scrubbed.

"Absolutely nothing, Tomas! I'm just trying to strike up some interesting conversation and do whatever it takes to get Cranky Tomas back to his old smiling self. Anyway, Babe Ruth died of nasopharyngeal cancer back in August of 1948. It was a myth that it was throat cancer. OK, I will get to the point since you look a wee bit annoyed. Would you believe..."

Libby was pouring warm water over my head to rinse my hair. I reflexively reached up to prevent suds from getting in my eyes. Libby apologized,

"Oops! Darlin', I didn't mean to get soap all over your face! OK, dab, dab dab, now back to Babe Ruth. He knew he was sick, but wasn't aware he had cancer until he pulled up to the hospital. Can you believe that? That was the era back then and sometimes now, too. Back then, doctors didn't always involve a patient with his or her care and treatment plan."

It didn't take long before my bath was finished and I had to admit I felt more human. I sat in the chair while Libby changed my bed. Libby suddenly stared at a stain on my clean pale blue hospital gown.

"Oh no! Oh no, I'm not even gonna let you wear that thing. I'll be right back."

My off white stained canvas curtain surrounding my bed was suddenly pulled back. Then a new fresh-faced nurse popped in holding a hospital gown. I looked a little closer...

"David! What a surprise! I must tell you as a man you are a good looking dude, but definitely a butt-ugly female!"

My good-natured paranormal friend grinned while he held my gown.

"You can wear this unfashionable dress that will expose your bum or...."

He reached down to open the drawer of my bedside table.

"Or you can wear your man attire."

What he did next forever changed the course of my future. David Tasma proudly reached, not for my shoulder but for my chest, my heart. This compassionately poetic man gave me the opportunity to be totally pain free and strong once again, for just awhile longer. He gave me the chance to experience Mia's love outside this white walled ward.

I heard hasty footsteps and the rustling of a bag. My curtain was pulled back and Mia stopped in her tracks and gasped as she saw me sitting on the side of my Bed 39. I had my legs casually crossed at the ankle while wearing my brown jeans, a white T-shirt under my green V-neck sweater and brown loafers. Oh and yes, the game face was back, with my clean hair slicked back and a small curl above my brow.

"Tomas! You...you look amazing!"

Mia stood looking like a deer caught in headlights. Mia had very two conflicting thoughts: "Tomas is dying, but Tomas now looks as sexy as the day we first met."

I quickly asked Mia to get a wheelchair now —fast! I didn't know how much time we had, but I wanted to leave here now so we could enjoy every minute outside the confines of this ward. This was a busy day at the deli, so my mother, father and Seamus would be working until at least 7:00 p.m.

Mia was literally jogging back to my Bed 39. She whisked past Nurse Libby, who was grumbling about needing to search several floors to find a stain or tear- free gown for Tomas. Mia opened the curtain and I flew onto the seat and used my hands to make the wheels go faster! If this one man buggy had been a car, you would have heard squealing of the wheelchair tires as we laid a long strip of rubber on the ivory linoleum floor. Mia stopped at the nurse's station to sign a release form and on our way into the elevator, yelled to Nurse Libby,

"A family emergency, Libby! We will be back later today!"

Nurse Libby was as confused as Mia when she saw my transformation. My cheeks were filled with color at the excitement of being free. The elevator door opened and Mia continued to race us through the front entrance. I put my hand up to slow her down.

"Mia, Whoa!!" Mia's laughter and smile ceased instantly when I stopped her from going out the door.

"What? Stop?"

It was then I stood up to push the wheelchair back into the hospital entrance. I stood tall, proud and was no longer frail or feeble on my feet.

" Mia, we don't need this wheelchair."

I delicately took her fingers and we ran hand–in-hand across the busy boulevard into Forest Park. Mia used her right hand to hold her sweater from blowing open and her floral blue calf length skirt swirled with the cool autumn breeze. We literally scampered across the street causing one car to screech to a stop while others honked, but we felt invincible and carelessly free to enjoy each other.

Mia and I finally stopped to catch our breath under a large oak tree with an umbrella of orange and gold leaves. Our first embrace felt so natural as if we had held each other countless times before. Mia wrapped her arms around my neck and tucked her head over my heart. Her brown hair was no longer in a bun, but flowed loosely down upon her shoulders. A few strands blew upward in the breeze, tickling my nose. We momentarily parted a few inches to look into each other's smiling eyes. Yes, our complete joy showed in every way. I could see the glimmer in Mia's eyes, the pink flush of her skin, felt the pounding of her heart against my chest, and was intoxicated by the sultry scent of her skin and hair.

I had waited so long to feel this way with a woman. We were still looking into one another's eyes when we had our first long, lingering kiss. What I thought I had with Rosie wasn't love at all. A person never actually realizes what the true emotion is until they experience it for the first time. Mia was my first love and my last.

We looked around and saw the boathouse which had been a fixture in the park since the late 1800's. Mia and I proceeded to rent a boat; our miracle continued as I had the strength to row the length of the lake. As I rowed, I closed my eyes taking in the cool scent of autumn, campfires, the vendor roasting hot dogs and of Mia. We stopped in the middle of the lake to share stories of our past and foreign lands we had visited and what we would do if we had a lifetime together. I started to row back to the shore and looked at Mia. A smile never left her face since we broke out of the white walled ward.

"Mia, as parents, I wonder who would be the disciplinarian?"

She shook her head and laughed.

"Tomas, give me a hard question, that one is easy! You are so innately playful that I would feel as if I had two children on my hands! I can visualize this so well. I'd put our child to bed, say prayers and leave thinking he was sound asleep. Then I'd hear all kinds of commotion only to find you two wrestling on the floor!"

I momentarily leaned forward to stretch my back.

"That does indeed sound like me! How could you possibly know me so well?"

Once we came to shore, Mia and I hopped on a trolley to the St. Louis Zoo. One of the things I never told her is how much I love animals, especially intelligent apes. Too bad Phil the Gorilla died in 1958. He came to the zoo as a baby weighing thirty pounds and at one time was one of the largest Lowland gorillas in captivity. Gees, I think someone said he tipped the scales at 776 pounds!

Mia and I were getting hungry and walked toward the ice cream vendor stationed under a weeping willow. We only bought one vanilla ice cream cone. It was more fun to have a reason to be close and savor the treat together.

Around the corner there was a big gumball machine with a chance to win a prize. I put in a penny and out came a blue gumball—this first one was Mia's. Then we put in another penny for mine and out came a prize. My lucky day!

When I opened the plastic container, a little gold colored plastic ring emerged. I looked up to analyze Mia's expression. She stood there grinning with her hand outstretched waiting for me to put it on her finger. Instead, I looked up hoping to find a man of the cloth who could marry us on the spot and wished Father McCormack were here right now in St. Louis.

I took Mia's outstretched hand and led her toward the edge of the lake where there was a cluster of trees. Each magnificent tree was splashed with an explosion of colorful foliage in purples, reds, oranges and golds. The wind was blowing Mia's long hair in front of her face. I stopped, turned and gently held her hair back with one hand. I desired to capture every beautiful detail of her face. Then without saying a word, I bent down on one knee and swept her left hand in mine. Mia looked amused as if she thought I was kidding and then started to giggle. My focus was on her brown eyes and I did not laugh or giggle. In my mind we would have our own ceremony right here by the edge of the lake. I would pretend this plastic ring was the magnificent 18 carat ring Mia deserved. I lightened up and smiled at the woman before me, who was acting like a teenager being asked to prom.

"My sweet Mia, please stop laughing!"

I gingerly cupped her chin in my hands in order to get Mia's attention.

"Seriously, I'm pretending we are actually getting married and in my heart, we are. Your love has had such a profound effect on me that I felt inspired to memorize a special poem for you…

"May you remember me in autumn, when the cool breeze begins to blow.
When we shared parts of our lives that no one but us knows.
May you remember me in autumn when we ran hand-in-hand.
It was then I knew our life together would be so great and grand.
May you remember me in autumn for it was then we first found love.
Without a doubt this heartfelt love was a gift from up above.
May you remember me in autumn when love, of course, is there.
T'was a cherished magic moment and I'll always keep you there.
May you remember me in autumn, winter, spring and summer, too.
For when I'm gone, my Mia, I'll spend an eternity loving you!

Mia's eyes welled with tears as she listened to my words of love. It was natural that we spontaneously shared a warm embrace which lead us into a seemingly infinite tender exchange of unbridled passion. Fireworks bursting in air would have given pale testimony to the depth and breadth of our fulfilled expression of the deepest love.

Afterward, we both fell into a deep sleep by the edge of the lake at Forest Park. When we awoke, both of us were covered with grass and fallen leaves. There was more of a chill in the air and the sun was starting to set. Panic started to set in and I felt nervous as if I were sneaking in past curfew.

There was little doubt the magic of David's touch was wearing off. I prayed I would still both appear and feel well when Mia wheeled me into the ward. I certainly would not want her to get in trouble if the magnitude of pain prevented me from even sitting up in the wheelchair!

My mother, father and Seamus were in front of the hospital frantically pacing while smoking their cigarettes. They saw us running across the street and my mother went into shock at that very moment! For more than a month, I was much too weak and frail to run. I was happy she had a chance to see me strong and on my feet, yet I didn't want to give her false hopes that I'd been cured. My mother had tears in her eyes as she ran toward me.

"Tomas! Tomas! We were worried sick! You are running and…you look so good and healthy! What happened? Where did you go?"

My mother had this built-in verbal machine gun that she fired away when the occasion seemed to warrant it and this was one of those times: her rapid-fire questions came out so fast they actually sounded like rat-tat-tat tat-tat-tat….she didn't give me a chance to respond before she fired away-again.

Seamus started to chuckle when he saw my back was covered with grass and leaves. He turned my back toward my parents and pointed to the debris on my backside. He mustered a closing argument as compelling as any Clarence Darrow could have conjured:

"Ah, my old friend Bart, please note exhibit one on your son's back. There are scattered leaves, clots of dirt, blades of grass, even a bug of some sort. Please rest assured, Mr. and Mrs. Kaminski, worry no more! It's my non-professional opinion that I don't believe any of this is from a fall and that Tomas has not sustained any life threatening injuries. Additionally, I don't believe the ducks were flying so low as to cause that little bite on your son's neck!

My father had gotten used to Seamus's sick humor and he started to laugh. My mother jabbed her husband in the side and then looked at my best friend.

"Seamus! Enough of your naughty thoughts!" But she smiled when she said it!

Needless to say, Mia was so embarrassed that she wanted to go into a witness protection program or at least hide out for a few days. Her excuse to get me a wheelchair was perfectly timed.

We were all slowly heading toward the hospital entrance. That is until Seamus stole the wheelchair with me in it and started walking the opposite direction. My mother yelled,

"Seamus! Where the hell are you going with my son?"

Seamus wore his tight jeans, his on-the-prowl black sweater and wasn't about to take his friend back before having a beer at the local sports bar—the same bar we would stop at after a rugby game.

"Annie, I mean Mrs. Kaminski, I'm not going without my beer buddy Bart, so you all better join us." Mia already had my hand as we wheeled a couple blocks to SSS-Shifty Shameless Shenanigans Bar and Grill.

The patrons inside Shifty Shameful Shenanigans were the same ones who frequented the deli so our arrival felt like "old home week." We knew and liked everybody and the feelings were mutual. When Seamus wheeled me through the doors, the place was buzzing with activity. My rugby team members and old Dogtown pals were everywhere I looked. There was a great deal of laughter, shoulder thumping and celebratory drink ordering going on that memorable night. The festive cheer would have been wonderful under any circumstance, but to be able to share all of this with the love of my life, my family and many wonderful friends was beyond belief. And I had David Tasma to thank for making this miracle possible.

Mia, my mother, my father and I returned so late the front entrance was closed and locked which meant we had to go through the emergency room. It was midnight and Nurse Libby was getting ready to leave after her shift. She stopped long enough to tuck me in and say good-bye.

"Tomas, I can't wait to hear all about it! See you tomorrow dear one!"

The last visitor of the night was someone very dear to me. He arrived as the clock struck 2:00 a.m., and I sat forward to give him a warm hug.

"David, from the bottom of my heart, thank you." I said with tears emphasizing my gratitude.

My friend once again sat in the little wooden chair next to my Bed 39.

"Tomas, the love of my life, Dr. Cicely Saunders, will be opening up the first organized hospice in the world in three more years. It'll be called St. Christopher's Hospice and will open in South London by 1967. The concept will spread like wildfire across the world and will offer not the same magic you experienced tonight, but loving, compassionate care, hope for total pain control and maybe eventually, the reality of a cure. Stay around for the ride Tomas, you'll be able to witness it all from Cicely's Bed 39."

CHAPTER 8

The Sunset of My Life November 1964

MIA REALIZED OUR TIME TOGETHER was limited so she took a leave of absence and faithfully sat by my Bed 39 and held my hand morning, noon and night. I had to smile when I saw how Mia forced that tiny plastic ring on her ring finger.

"Ok Tomas, we played trivia from the *Post Dispatch* and now I have another question for you. Ready?"

I nodded my head, "Of course, fire away."

Mia looked up at my headboard.

"OK, who is Dr. Cicely Saunders?"

I immediately warmed to the revelation and felt tremendous pride being able to share this exciting information with Mia.

"Mia, Dr. Saunders is a woman who refused to sit back and watch the inadequacies of caring for the terminally ill. She was a warrior who sought out a method, a precise plan of action to build the first organized hospice in the world. She was a nurse, a social worker, a writer who then became a physician in order to have a greater, more credible voice in the worlds of death and dying, research and terminal illnesses such as cancer and heart disease. She brought a ray of hope that those with end-stage diseases will be able to die with more total pain control, more comfort and peace. Additionally, I'm privy to know it will open in South London in 1967."

Mia sat up and raised her eyebrows.

"Tomas, how in the heck did you know all that scoop on Cicely Saunders?"

I never had a chance to answer that question since my family and friends were on their way back to visit. Mia walked up to greet them. I watched her walk away and thought how fortunate I was to have her in my life. To me, the name *Mia* meant compassionate, comforting protector of the sick. Mia, a woman who warmed my heart and made this dying man feel so, so alive.

My parents and friends who came to visit were anxious to hear any updates from Mia. It was as if they fully expected to arrive one day and hear Mia say, "You can take him home now; he's been cured!" My parents always had this look of hope, even when deep down, they knew I would never leave this hospital alive.

Mia's presence created a sense of solace for not only me, but also my family. Many evenings she would just sit and hold my hand while I slept. By the end of the third week, I truly felt we were one blended soul. I couldn't imagine a day without her.

There were several patients in this ward who were nearing death and I must say, it was both tragic and traumatic listening to them scream in uncontrolled pain. They, too, were waiting for it to be "time" for their meds. Who in their right mind would want to die like this? If I lived long enough, surely it would be my goal, my mission, to find a more humane and dignified way to treat terminal patients.

None of this was the nurses' or doctors' fault, they were doing what they were trained to do. But their training sorely needed an update! It was agonizing for professionals to watch other human beings suffer. This was especially true for professionals whose raison d'être was to lessen suffering and help the sick in any way possible.

The following morning my parents came for a visit. They both had big grins on their faces, as they waltzed through the door.

"Hello, our darling son!"

Mother was wearing this smile from ear-to-ear and father obviously had something concealed under his coat. Then to my surprise, a scruffy-headed canine poked his head out between the buttons of his coat!

"Harry! Harry Gregg, you brought him for me!"

Harry was obviously excited and squirmed to get out of my father's arms. Father worried my furry friend would be too much for me to handle.

"Easy boy! Settle down! You know it wasn't easy to catch this little roamer. Thinks he owns the damn neighborhood!"

My father eased Harry onto my bed. He proceeded to jump up and lick my face a thousand times. The touching scene of our mutual happiness filled my parents with joy. Not surprisingly, however, all the excitement caused the darn rascal to piddle on my sheets.

Father, who never owned a pet before was flabbergasted at a dog urinating on the bed! He pointed his finger while shouting at the poor pooch in Polish.

"Co to jest? Co to jest? Zly! Zly!"

The nurse assigned to my room walked in and was taken by surprise to see a canine with me. My furry friend was calm now and sat alongside me as if he belonged there. Nurse Libby came in with her white uniform perfectly pressed. She smiled and put her finger up to her lips, saying quietly,

"I'll pretend I didn't see a thing. I'll give you a bit more time to visit, however, I will be back in 30 minutes."

A half hour gave us just enough time before I felt exhausted and out of breath from all the activity. My mother's joy turned to concern as she saw my ashen face as a result of the pain medication having waned leaving me in anguish.

"Son, please, please give me Harry so I can take him home and let you rest."

I gave Harry a big hug as my father reached for my wiry friend and once again concealed him in his coat. My father leaned down to kiss my cheek. Harry simultaneously poked his head out to lick the side of my face.

"Oh father, one thing before you leave."

The older man stopped in the doorway and turned.

"Please promise me Harry will always have a home with us."

My father's smile was filled with warmth for the hobo canine. I could rest assured Harry would be a beloved part of the family.

"Of course, son. I think I'm getting fond of this feisty bugger. He makes his rounds about the block, then comes to sit in front of the deli to greet our patrons."

When the pace in the ward slowed down, Nurse Libby shared a bit of her life story. She told me her parents and extended family were originally from St. Louis. Her father was a professional jazz musician who spent several years touring Europe, mostly the United Kingdom and Ireland. Her mother finally packed up the family and moved to Dublin to reduce the distance between them. The million dollar question was, what brought them back?

Nurse Libby, paused then replied.

"The war, a grandmother's death and my eldest sister who was caring for her was dying of ovarian cancer. My husband and I were only eighteen when we came back to St. Louis and we became instant parents. When my sister died, we took on the task of raising my 10 and 12-year-old nephews.

"My husband's family immigrated to Ireland in the 1700's from Spain. They were referred to as the Black Irish referencing those who didn't have the traditionally red or light hair and green or blue eyes.

"When my sister's boys entered high school, I finally started nursing school. Yes, I was one of the older students in the class. It was caring for my sister that made me want to do more for those who were terminal," Nurse Libby concluded.

Nurse Libby's uniform was so stiff and starched that I wondered how she could move to perform her duties. This woman before me had a special confidence for a newer nurse. She had these dense, thick curly black lashes, deep, dark brown compassionate eyes and perfectly arched brows that gave her a wise and knowing appearance. Her hair was in a short natural fro. What I liked best about the woman before me was her sense of humor and broad ear-to-ear smile. She would frequently comment on the accommodations at the hospital from a patient's perspective.

"Gees, Tomas, doesn't it make more sense for the hospital decor to be more warm and inviting? For Pete's sake administrators, let's splash some color on these walls and hang some pictures! Wouldn't that make you feel a bit better being in a surrounding that looked more like home?"

I could only agree with her wholeheartedly and tell her I believed the tide was turning and that she would live to see that day come to fruition. I didn't disclose how I got my inside information and certain view of the future thanks to my direct pipeline to David Tasma.

My decline was so rapid from that point on that my dear friend Father McCormack was at risk for not making it here in time to say good-bye. He was the only priest on his Catholic mission trip in Africa. He was forced to wait for a replacement to arrive before he headed back to St. Louis to see me.

The first week of November my family, Seamus and a few friends from Dogtown held a vigil around my bed. Toward the end, Mia kept a clothing change at work and stayed round the clock at the hospital. Blessedly, someone was always here with me.

My wakeful states consisted of being more and more aware of pain and having difficulty breathing. Mia insisted that I use oxygen to make breathing easier for me. One day my eyelids were still closed when I awoke from a deep sleep. They felt too heavy to raise up to open my eyes. I attempted to open my lids half-mast in order to see what was making a loud, sonorous roar.

I attempted to moisten my dry lips with my tongue. It's a strange reality to be 27–years-old and know you have very little time left here on earth. I was half asleep and half awake. Through my drug-induced stupor, I could hear gurgling noises which were coming from my own respirations. Mia raised my head and brought a straw to my lips. I was far too weak to suck the cool liquid into my mouth. She then dipped a washcloth into the water and held it to my lips. The drops of water gradually ran down my parched throat.

Mia had quickly grown to be such a source of comfort for me. The way she gazed at me with her loving, but admittedly weary eyes warmed my heart. In my heart and in my mind, we were married. I couldn't possibly feel more in love and was so grateful I found it in the last three weeks of my life. Mia continuously wiped the perspiration from my brow. Closing my dry eyes allowed me the chance to re-moisten them. My frail fingers wandered along the white sheets to search for Mia's warm hand. Once I found it, I managed to muster up enough strength to squeeze it three times.

As I released my grip after the last squeeze, there was this compelling instinct to open my eyes. I was totally aware someone was staring at me. That was when I saw the intensity of Mia's eyes upon my face. She was now no longer able to conceal the depth of her sadness. A bright red rim lined her lower lids and much of her brown hair escaped from the now loose bun. The woman at my side though, never looked more beautiful than she did at this very moment. As I attempted to speak the dried mucous seemed to act as cement on my lips. Then finally, I was able to whisper...

"Pumpkin, I love you so much. Thank you for all you are doing for me."

Mia instantly bolted out of her chair. She hadn't heard me call her Pumpkin since the day I was admitted and was exceedingly concerned.

"Oh my! Are you feeling worse?"

She was now wide-eyed with worry! Ever so gently she grabbed both of my hands and leaned forward to hear what I had to say. What I felt for this woman was so real and genuine. In a whisper, now almost too garbled for Mia to hear, I told her what I felt deep in my heart.

"I always wanted to buy you a real ring—one that would last decades and represent our eternal love. My mother brought my grandmother's ring for me to give to you. Her eyes were wider now and a smile adorned her face for the first time in days. I put the simple silver band over the plastic one which Mia insisted on wearing, too.

"Tomas, I love you forever."

Less than an hour later I fell into a deep slumber and never woke up.

By 6:15 p.m. on November 9th, 1964, my respirations became labored, then very shallow. My condition drastically deteriorated by the second. Mia called for a priest and for an assistant to bring in my parents from the waiting area.

The priest quickly entered the room with my parents. Seamus and a few close friends came in with them. All had tear-filled faces. My mother cried and whispered to me.

"Son, why couldn't this be me. Damn it! You are too young to die."

My father brought my furry friend Harry Gregg to my bedside. Harry had keen canine intelligence and sensed my death was imminent. He lovingly nudged me with his cold nose and proceeded to whimper.

My family and friends didn't seem to notice "others" in the back of the room awaiting my last moment on earth. The priest was at my bedside reciting the Last Rites. The on-call physician arrived, took out his stethoscope and listened for a heartbeat. He proceeded to look at his watch and said,

"6:39 p.m., I'm so sorry for your loss Mr. and Mrs. Kaminski."

I felt my spirit rise from my body. Harry Gregg went from whimpering on my chest to excitedly barking. He also witnessed me gracefully floating above the bed and thought he had his friend back.

Mia, who had maintained a strong façade the last three weeks broke down and sobbed in my mum's arms. I observed what was going on around my now un-needed body. Suddenly, I became aware that I wasn't ready to leave this world and resisted the temptation to walk into the Light.

It was confusing to see those I loved crying for me when I felt more alive than ever!

No! Please Lord, not yet...please let me stay to witness a beginning of this new era in medicine. I suddenly had a vision, well more than a vision, a knowing. I could clearly see that in the future there will be a new multi-team approach to treating terminal patients.

Much research into death and dying would be conducted in order to provide the most humane, loving and gentle care for those who are dying. Hospital wings, both in and outpatient facilities will be dedicated to the care of those in their final days and these special places will be referred to as Hospices. These Hospices will have trained professionals who are well equipped to help both the patient and family. They will help resolve important issues like carrying out last wishes and helping loved ones say good-bye.

A Hospice will be a place where patients will be able to truly live until their final breath. The purpose of Hospice will not be to prolong or expedite death, but to allow a terminal patient to die more comfortably in a home-like environment or at home if he or she chooses. If the patient opts for staying in their own home in their final days, they will receive regular, frequent visits from Hospice professionals.

There are so many lessons to learn and reasons to stay, I told myself. Just for now, just temporarily, my soul will be attached to and will remain imprinted on this Bed 39 for several decades to come. In the scheme of things, since time does not exist in the spirit realm, several earth decades will go by as quickly as a blink of an eye. Then, when I have finished my mission on earth, I will enthusiastically enter the Light and proceed to the other side. The ones who come here to Bed 39 at the sunset of their lives will feel the comfort I bring, the concern I feel and know they are never alone. For most this is the end of the story, however for me, this is only the beginning

CHAPTER 9

Until We Meet Again
1974

IN THE 19TH CENTURY, PRIMARY responsibility of caring for the terminally ill fell to the family or the church. In the twentieth century up through the 70's, most terminal cancer or any end-of-life patients for that matter, spent their remaining days in a nursing home, hospital room or ward receiving no special end-of-life care mostly because none existed.

Now in 1974, a newer, vastly superior concept has emerged called Hospice where the specific needs of the dying are addressed by a team of professionals from different disciplines. The most pivotal aspects of Hospice, besides the team approach, include attention to the atmosphere in which the terminally ill patient is placed. If a person cannot die at home, although many now do thanks to mobile Hospice care, then special attention is given to making the room they *are* in more home-like, inviting and relaxing. Great attention is given to making sure the patient is comfortable and suffers as little pain as possible. This is called palliative care and goes hand-in-hand with Hospice care.

Progress of the modern Hospice movement was slow. Despite its dedication to making the dying process as easy and supportive as possible, many have misunderstood the philosophy and rationale of this movement. For some reason, human beings are not generally open to new approaches and ideas of any kind. A good case in point is that it took 20 years for the Heimlich Maneuver to be approved by the Red Cross and adopted without criticism despite the fact it was a simple, free, life-saving breakthrough that anyone could administer to prevent someone from choking to death and dying on the spot! So it is not surprising that something as complex as Hospice took a while to become widely adopted.

By 1967, word spread across the Atlantic about the first organized Hospice in the world—St. Christopher's Hospice located in South London conceptualized and created by Dame Cicely Saunders, M.D.

The concept of not fighting death, but rather making the process as comfortable as humanly possible, as espoused by Dame Saunders, intrigued the Dean of Yale School of Nursing Florence Wald, RN, who took a sabbatical in 1967 to learn as much as possible about the whole Hospice team concept for the terminally ill.

Ms. Wald is credited as being the mother of the American hospice movement. In 1974 the Connecticut Hospice in Branford, Connecticut was founded by a team headed by Professor Wald. She was supported by two pediatricians and a chaplain. This new Hospice facility with a lofty mission was the first in the United States.

By 1974, few understood that Hospice wasn't just a place to die but was a place where the patient's physical and spiritual wellbeing were paramount. Not only were the patient's needs attended to, but the patient's family's needs were as well. In addition, Hospice engaged in ongoing pain control research as well as education in order to gain greater understanding about the nature of the dying process and what would best serve those going through that process.

In 1974, terminal patients in the St. Louis area were still integrated into internal medicine floors or nursing homes along with patients who were expected to recover. There was no special expertise or support to benefit those who would not be going back home.

Mrs. Gabriella Baldini, a 79-year-old homemaker from Portofino, Italy and mother of three, had been residing in Bed 39 for two weeks. She had been diagnosed with end-stage breast cancer. By the mid-seventies, trials for using mammography and Tamoxifen for breast cancer were just in the beginning stages.

A mastectomy was the only surgical method available to treat breast cancer. Clearly, treatments were woefully limited.

Mrs. Baldini rarely went to a doctor and when physical symptoms surfaced, she continued to ignore them for many months including the oozing ulcerations on her breasts. It wasn't until her daughter Sasha observed her mother clutching her chest in pain that the older woman reluctantly revealed her open wounds. Sasha almost fainted at the sight. Thanks to Sasha's intractable insistence, that very day was the first day Mrs. Baldini had been to a doctor in over a decade, but by then it was far too late. It wouldn't be until the 80's when more wide-spread emphasis would be placed on breast self-examinations starting in high school in order to achieve early detection.

Starting in 1976, annual mammograms were available. But, for Mrs. Baldini, it was much too late and the cancer had already spread to her brain, lungs and spine. She experienced brief periods of being alert and oriented, but those episodes were fewer and more fleeting each passing day.

On this particular day, a muscular, dark haired man stormed past the nurse's station as he headed down the ward toward Bed 39. His angry, frenetic energy broadcast throughout the ward. He clearly was a man of power judging by his dominating energy coupled with his $1,000 black suit.

Mrs. Baldini's only son forcefully pushed open the heavy industrial hospital door with such power that it banged loudly against the wall. His formidable six-foot-frame bolted into the room with all the grace and consideration of a metro train barreling in at 42nd Street in Times Square. Startled by his disruptive arrival, his two siblings who had been seated peacefully beside their comatose mother instantly rose to their feet. Once they saw it was their brother, the sisters attempted to still their racing hearts.

"For Pete's sake, Angelo! Where's the fire? Can't you have a little consideration for where you are?"

Sasha's brown eyes were as wide as saucers. Her wavy long brown hair was disheveled from crying on her sister Sophie's shoulder. Fifty-year-old Sasha was the eldest with a strong, dominant personality. She and Angelo frequently butted heads in the past due to his chauvinistic attitude toward women.

Early on Sasha had focused her attention and energy to build a successful accounting firm which she accomplished with consummate skill and business acumen. Because she had been so single focused, there had never been any time for marriage or children. But much to her great surprise, she had just recently found a special someone she loved dearly and wanted to marry. It was later in the game, but better late than never at all, she told herself.

Sophie, on the other hand, was a slight, timid woman. She had chosen to give up her job as a Monsanto chemist to be a full-time housewife and mother. Both women had been holding vigil at their mother's bedside for the last 24 hours.

Angelo huffed and puffed as he quietly stood at the foot of his mother's bed. He was speechless to see his mother's current condition! Momma Baldini's once rotund frame had winnowed down to a skeletal 85 pounds.

The sight of his mother in this state triggered a flood of tears from his large brown eyes. His mind frantically searched for an explanation for the state she was in...anything other than the reality that she was at death's door. Why is she so out of it, Angelo questioned silently. Did the nurses give her that Haldol again? She had had it before and it had turned momma into a state where she simply couldn't function! That was it, he decided after his internal debate. It was Haldol!

In the midst of all this, Angelo was both perplexed and intrigued at how the hospital bed seemed to cuff his mother's now tiny body as if it were giving her a comforting embrace. But he quickly shook off that fleeting comfort in favor of venting the indignation he had brought with him to the hospital.

"Damn it, Sasha! If I weren't a gentleman I would bop you on the side of your head! What made you put momma here? She's a fighter, she wouldn't just give up and die like this! Damn you! Damn you to hell, Sasha! I can't believe you did this to momma!"

As the spirit in Bed 39, I felt I needed to break up Angelo's negative energy. There was a sudden flickering of lights every time Angelo would raise his voice.

Angelo looked up and yelled,

"What the hell is going on in this place?"

The lights began to flicker and when he screamed at the top of his lungs, I'd add a little electrical snap! Angelo instinctively ducked and then began to almost whisper.

Sasha, stretched to her emotional limit, sleep-deprived and distraught, raised her index finger to gesticulate in Angelo's face.

"Angelo, quit talking crazy! I didn't do nothing to momma but help her! This is a hospital, Angelo. It's a place where they can monitor her pain better than if she were at home. I don't know what to do for momma. I'm not a nurse, Angelo, and I work full-time! The nurses and doctors can watch her 24 hours a day here and make her more comfortable. By the way, where were you these past six months, huh? Yeah, I know, roaming around Portofino acting like some big wig! Now, please lower your voice before you wake momma."

Angelo's gaze redirected to his younger sibling in search of some answers. The smaller of the two sisters was almost cowering behind the other.

"Sophie, sweet Sophie, tell me you didn't have anything to do with putting momma here?" her brother pleaded.

There was a moment of silence as the two Italian women studied this man before them. They both recognized that he was the one their mother was always so proud of and without a doubt was her favorite. His features were chiseled to perfection. His rose-colored lips and straight athletic nose sat harmoniously in the middle of his face. To complete the unusually handsome look, his nearly black eyes were rimmed by thick curly lashes. Angelo was surely a model for Leonardo DaVinici's Vitruvian male.

Sophie ambivalently moved toward him and gently reached for her brother's hand. Her slight build and quiet demeanor gave no hint of her keen intelligence. She was the sibling who was the least willing to fight, the eternal voice of reason.

"Angelo, momma's condition quickly deteriorated after her surgery. The cancer has spread to all her major organs including her brain and her liver. It broke our hearts to see her moaning in pain. There was nothing we could do at home for her since her suffering was so extreme. Momma needed twenty-four-hour-care and for now, this is the best place for her," Sophie quietly explained.

Angelo nodded in understanding as he continued to wipe away tears. He began to reminisce to himself about that last time he saw his mother. His consciousness faded as he went back in time to a far-away place. His sister's voice was reduced to a mere buzzing in his ears.

One of the benefits of my being imprinted on Bed 39 was that I had been given an all-knowing awareness of the patients' and the family members' thoughts and lives.   As a result I knew Angelo was reflecting on happier times before he had left for Europe. He envisioned Momma Baldini making his favorite meal, home-made spaghetti noodles with meat balls. His mother, clad in a red-and-white-checkered apron, was healthy, round and jovial as she happily scurried around the kitchen looking for ways to please her favorite child's taste buds. Angelo hungrily scanned the pots, pans and oven to see what delicious morsels would be served for dinner.

"Ahh ya big lug, get outta my spaghetti sauce!" momma mockingly complained. Her Italian accent was always stronger when she yelled.

"Why can't you wait patiently like everyone else?" Momma smiled as she gave her son a big hug.

"There's no better spaghetti anywhere than in my own momma's kitchen," he declared. "Lucky me!"

His mother adjusted her dress and re-tied her apron as she watched her son sip a large spoonful of homemade sauce. It contained just the right magical proportions of fresh tomatoes, garlic, basil, oregano and onions.

"Well, maybe just for you Angelo, take another taste! Just for you! For Pete's sake, don't gulp it down like a glass of cheap wine! Wait for my noodles!"

The older woman was brimming with pride and her eyes smiled whenever she looked at her son. He truly could do no wrong. She turned a deaf ear to his profession, which was not always on the right side of the law. Momma was proud, though, and always boasted that her son was a successful businessman—which was stretching the truth almost to the breaking point. Angelo was part of an infamous criminal organization called the Mob. She bragged that he was carrying on the family name and "business" that his great, great grandfather started many years ago.

"Angelo you don't look like your poppa, but you sure do have his appetite! You inherited your Jolly Green genes from your great grandfather Victor. Your pop, as you well remember, was short, fat, bald, and sported a crooked nose on his mug that was broken more times than I can count! The man wasn't much to look at, but he was so charming. Oh, the women could hardly keep their hands off him! Can you imagine that?"

Angelo continued to sample the irresistible food he pilfered from the trays. Momma Baldini slapped Angelo's hands as he picked up a warm loaf of bread. Without missing a beat, she continued her monologue as she moved back to her command position in front of the stove. Occasionally she glanced over her shoulder at Angelo to keep him engaged in her banter as she continued to cook.

"Your poppa had a way with the women and a smile that made me melt."

Angelo rolled his eyes then grimaced as if he had eaten something rotten. He was silently imploring *"Don't go there, momma!"*

His mother, totally enraptured by her trip down memory lane and oblivious to her son's off-the-chart resistance to hearing about his parents' love life in any way, shape or form, smiled from ear–to-ear as she reflected on her deceased husband.

"Oh yes, he was so romantic. I used to call him my stud muffin!" she revealed without considering her audience.

That put Angelo over the edge. He brought the unsavory revelations to an abrupt halt with an impossible to misunderstand outburst.

"Enough! Entirely too much information!" he emphatically announced as he desperately searched for a replacement topic. When nothing came to mind, he called in reinforcements. "Sasha! Sophie! Come and help momma in the kitchen."

Sophie quietly obeyed her brother as she entered the room and began slicing bread. Sasha bellowed her resistance to her brother's entreaty from her catbird position in the easy chair in front of the television. Sunday night football was just starting and she certainly had no intention of missing a moment. Helping in the kitchen was not on her agenda let alone allowing Angelo to order her around.

"Angelo!" Sasha yelled. "Check the date on the calendar! It is no longer 1950. In case you haven't noticed, women nowadays have career options so we can do whatever the hell we want to do. Women don't have to be incarcerated in the kitchen peeling the proverbial grapes for their man. Newsflash! I'm a successful career woman. Remember me? I'm the accountant who helps keep your ass out of jail! So give me a break and help momma yourself!"

Angelo stormed into the living room where other family members and guests were gathered to watch NFL football. No one relished being around Angelo when he was angry. Everyone started to squirm except Sasha. She glared at her brother defiantly.

"Sassy Sasha, you never change! Maybe, just maybe if you spent some time in the kitchen you'd learn to cook and find a good husband!"

Sasha took a swig of beer then sarcastically laughed at her brother.

"Angelo, you're a caveman. For one thing, I don't need a man. I'm not attracted to men. Do you understand me? Sheesh! There's just no talking to you."

Angelo grimaced at the thought of his sister with another woman.

"Ugh, Somethins' the matter with your head, Sasha! It's not normal!"

Sasha had had enough of her brother badmouthing her choices in life. Just as she stood to escalate the argument to a higher decibel level, Momma Baldini shouted,

"Everyone grab your plates. It's time to eat!"

The long dinner table was set for twelve. It beckoned them all with freshly cut flowers from the garden, a profusion of wine and warm loaves of homemade bread.

Even though poppa had died 10 years ago, no one ever sat in his chair out of respect. The Baldini's had celebrated 52 wonderful years of marriage before his death.

Even though poppa was gone, the family continued the decades-long tradition of having Sunday dinners for all the local relatives each and every Sunday. Friends were often invited as well. This Sunday was no different.

The uncomfortable exchange between Angelo and Sasha was replaced by a number of free flowing conversations about sports teams, kids and politics. You could almost hear a collective sigh of relief that acrimony had turned to conviviality.

As tradition dictated, at the end of each meal momma Baldini would raise her glass of wine and say,

"Dominic my love, the love of my life, this one's for you! Wait for me darling, I won't be long." And today was no different.

Angelo sighed loudly and shook his head. "Momma, you've been saying that for the last nine years! You're never going to die, never, ya hear me! Who will make me my favorite homemade meals if you aren't around?"

Once again he repeated...now more loudly and forcefully.

"Momma, who will make me my homemade meals? Momma, our lives will never be the same without you..."

Sasha grew concerned at the nearly trance-like state her brother was in as well as the almost childlike tone of his voice.

"Angelo? Angelo!" she called to him loudly and then clapped her hands in front of his face to snap him out of it.

The sudden disruption worked as Angelo reluctantly returned to the here and now as he stood by his mother in Bed 39. They were not gathered in the comfort of momma's home as his reverie had transported him, but at her bedside in a South St. Louis Hospital ward. Despite his refusal to admit that his mother could possibly die, evidence to the contrary was so strong that even he had to admit the hard, cold fact that his mother was now at the sunset of her life. His shoulders slumped in recognition of this difficult fact as he sat down in a chair next to her. He was overcome with grief as he lovingly reached out to cradle her hand in his. He had relinquished all hope for his mother's survival when suddenly he heard the faint sound of his mother's voice.

"Angelo, you're here. Thank the Lord."

Angelo looked like a five year old who had just been given the pony he had begged his parents to buy him for his birthday.

"Momma, momma! Oh my God, we have to get you out of here!"

He bent down to wrap his arms around her shoulders to hold his mother close.

"Oh my God, I thought you were gone! Damn Sasha for bringing you here!"

Just then, a short blonde woman dressed in business attire walked through the door. The silence was so pronounced you could almost hear a pin drop. Now it was Sasha's turn to put her arm around the woman in Bed 39 and draw her in close.

"Momma, I have wanted to tell you something for so long."

Sasha choked up and wiped away her tears as she used her free hand to grab the hand of the woman who had just joined them at momma's bedside.

"I have been in love with this woman for 10 years. She is the love of my life and I felt like I had to keep it all to myself and not tell even you. But I really want you to know how happy I am and also who she is."

The blonde woman who had just arrived gave Sasha a loving look as Sasha introduced Dawn to her mother. After the introduction, the two hugged each other in greeting. Sasha suddenly pulled herself away to look at Angelo who was visibly repulsed by the embrace he just witnessed.

"Sasha! What the hell are you doing to us with this freak show? Doing to momma! You call this love?? Are you trying to kill our mother right here and now?"

The frail old woman looked angry as she reached for her son.

"Angelo! Angelo! Can't you see? Can't you see the love they have for one another? It's just as strong as the love I had for poppa. I see it in their eyes. It's true love, Angelo."

Angelo yelled his fervent objection,

"But momma! It's not..."

Momma weakly motioned the two women toward her.

"Yes, Angelo, I see the beauty and the love. I see the way Sasha and Dawn look at one another. Before I die, I need to know Sasha has your blessing."

Sasha, who had earned a reputation for her strength, uncharacteristically crumbled emotionally and burst into tears.

Revealing the deep, dark secret she had kept hidden all these years had given her such a profound sense of relief. Her secret was finally out and she at last felt free to be herself. What's more, she had gained her mother's approval!

"Momma, you know, you understood all along! I love you so very much!"

Angelo stood there staring at the ceiling as if that could remove him from this uncomfortable turn of events. But soon he brought his gaze back to his momma's face.

"Angelo, once I die, all you will have left is Sophia, her husband, Sasha and the love of her life Dawn. You all need one another. We are family and family is everything," The frail old woman said with more intensity than seemed possible considering how near death she hovered.

Sasha and Dawn celebrated momma's declaration with a kiss in front of everyone. It was as if a huge sigh of relief filled the room in recognition that the couple could now be "real" thanks to Sasha's momma's blessing.

Angelo slowly nodded his head and returned his focus to his mother.

"Momma, I'm gonna bring you home. Okay? That's where you belong. Momma? Momma?"

But much to Angelo's horror, his mother was unable to respond. Momma Baldini had fallen into what appeared to be a deep sleep. In fact, it turned out she had lapsed into a coma from which she never regained consciousness. It was almost as if her soul had been determined to rally long enough to endorse Sasha's and Dawn's relationship and to exhort Angelo to keep the family unit tightly bound. It appeared once she had made her feelings known, she was free to let go of life with a satisfying sense of completion.

The fact that she had awakened long enough to announce her unequivocal approval of Sasha's and Dawn's love for each other was a full-blown miracle. Sasha was beyond grateful for her mother's unwavering love and endorsement. She had never wanted to lie to her momma about anything, and although she had not lied to her overtly, she had not been forthcoming either. Little did Sasha know, however, that momma *always* knew and the knowledge did not change her love for Sasha one little bit. She loved all three children unconditionally. Period.

Angelo, unaware that his mother would not regain consciousness, surveyed the hospital ward with a great deal of disdain; it was no place for his beloved momma. He wanted her at home. However, he had to grudgingly admit that what he did like were the Baldini family pictures Nurse Libby had thoughtfully hung on the white walls. He surveyed the photographs of momma and poppa in their youth, at their wedding and the family at different stages in their lives. He had to grudgingly admit that the pictures added a dimension of compassion and humanity despite the stark clinical nature of the ward.

Angelo had no way of knowing how important it was to Nurse Libby that her terminal patients felt more at home during their last days. Meaningful pictures were a great way to help accomplish that, she believed. In addition, Nurse Libby would sometimes bring freshly cut flowers from her garden and place them at the patient's bedside. These touches were important to her and the fact that they seemed to make the patients more content reinforced and perpetuated these kind acts. Nurse Libby was in the forefront of nurses who sensed how important creating more home-like surroundings for terminal patients was and she would be pleased over the years to discover that her instincts were right on and that hospice would be the catalyst for making countless patients feel better in this way.

For the moment, the four of them, Sophie, Sasha, Dawn and Angelo, sat quietly at their mother's bedside. Each was cocooned in their own grief. In the midst of his despair over his impending loss, Angelo suddenly felt a firm hand give his shoulder a reassuring squeeze. Startled, he instinctively reached up and felt his father's familiar hand.

Without thinking, Angelo called out, "Poppa? But when Angelo looked up, no one was to be seen. Nonetheless, he knew without a doubt that his deceased dad had been there to give him loving reassurance.

Nurse Libby walked in to check on Mrs. Baldini. The foursome parted a little to give her access to her patient. She lightly stroked Mrs. Baldini's long gray hair that once had been wavy and black like her daughters'. The nurse then pulled her stethoscope free to listen to the dying woman's heart. In an empathetic voice, she turned to the family members to softly pronounce what none of them wanted to hear,

"I don't believe she will be with us much longer."

Angelo became flushed with irritation at what the nurse had just told the family.

"No, she's cold, so cold! Nurse, please get momma a blanket. Maybe that's all she needs."

Sasha threw her head back in frustration. She had grown extremely impatient with her brother's emotional state and impenetrable denial of what was happening with momma. It was quite clear to her that momma had said her final goodbyes.

"Angelo, did you hear and absorb anything the nurse said? What's the matter with you? We need to get ourselves together and be strong for momma."

Nurse Libby gently placed her arm over Angelo's shoulder.

"Yes, I will be happy to get her a warm blanket and will do all I can to make her comfortable."

The three siblings surrounded their mother's bed. The nurse slowly walked to the window and raised the stiff metal blinds.

"St. Louis is such a beautiful city and your momma so loved the view of the park from her window. She also loved to survey the colorful field of flowers on the property. Your mother cherished the beauty of each sunset over the foothills. She would always say, "Another day I live to see my children. Even now, your mother has peace knowing she has all of you with her now."

At that moment, a bright sunbeam came through the window and fell onto their mother's cheek as if to kiss her. For some reason, that illumination enabled them all to clearly see that death was imminent. The color of the frail woman became more ashen and blue, her respiration became slow and labored. The siblings looked down upon their mother and then at each other. Angelo gently squeezed his mother's hand. He vainly attempted to wipe back a torrent of tears as he sobbed,

"Momma, I spent so many years in Italy and now I am home. I came home to be with you and now you are, you are..."

Angelo's body was literally contorted by his heaving sobs. Surprisingly Dawn comforted him and just as surprisingly, he surrendered and cried on her shoulder as she stroked his head.

Momma Baldini's respirations changed to an audible death rattle, then suddenly ceased before the chaplain that Nurse Libby had summoned had had time to arrive. The sudden silence chilled each sibling to the core as they held each other close. Sadly they looked down upon the woman who was once the strong, indomitable matriarch of their family. There was an unusual stillness which accompanied the dead silence. Then suddenly, shockingly and totally unexpectedly, their mother bolted upright to sit tall in her bed with her hands held high! It was as if she were reaching for the heavens above!

The siblings gasped in unison and Nurse Libby ran to catch Sophie who started to faint. Momma Baldini had a twinkle in her eyes and a smile on her face as she called out.

"My Dominic!" Then she slowly fell back on the bed.

A low hum filled the room, like the soft pitch of a tuning fork. This hospital Bed 39 had been the place where momma was able to let Angelo and his sisters know without a doubt that she was fully aware they were all there in her final hour and that she had been reunited with her beloved husband Dominic.

Dominic and his adored wife embraced as they looked down upon their children. After more than a decade apart, they were finally together again, this time for eternity. The reunited twosome were testament to the truth that love never dies, that it truly lives on forever.

The following Sunday, the Baldini's gathered as usual for their traditional meal with family and friends. After eating, they stuffed a satchel with flowers, a vase and several bottles of wine made from grapes grown in their family vineyard in Italy. Twenty minutes later, the unified Baldini family walked through the hospital's elevator doors and arrived at the nurse's station.

They were in search of Nurse Libby and some of the other nurses who worked in this busy 40-bed ward so they could express their gratitude.

These loving souls had done everything they could to create the image and comforts of home for their momma in her dying days. They wanted to show their deep appreciation by placing the bouquet of flowers in the vase to adorn the nurses' station and leaving behind two bottles of wine for the nurses to enjoy after their shifts had ended.

Next the family slowly walked to Bed 39 which remained empty. The sun was starting to set sending an orange glow through the small bedside window. They opened their bottle of wine and filled several small paper cups. All three had the strong sense that both parents were with them at that moment. The Baldini children continued their family tradition however, this time they surrounded Bed 39.

"We had the honor growing up in a warm household and knew without a doubt that as parents you were always there for us."

Angelo began.

"Thank you for being the fine example of lasting true love that should exist between every married couple and the devoted unrelenting love you had for us as parents." Sophie added. "After all these years, you both are finally together," Sasha concluded. "Please, everyone raise your cups...Salute momma and poppa, this one's for you. We love you and will hold you both close in our hearts!...Until we meet again."

CHAPTER 10

For My Many Reasons Why
1985

IT'S BEEN TWENTY-ONE YEARS SINCE my death and believe it or not, after observing this hospital ward all this time, I can honestly say there were some surprising and seldom recognized communication advantages to having large, overcrowded wards in hospitals. One that comes off the top of my head is that there's not as much need to have a call light for each patient when you could simply just holler and set up a chain of hollers that rippled through the ward to alert a nurse! Oh, and some of my ward mates back in 1964 could really scream like bloody murder, too! It would practically scare the nurses to death and they'd come running back real fast. Nurse Libby would yell,

"Where is the darn fire? What no fire? Then sweet pea, don't you be screaming at me when a call light will get my attention just fine."

This buddy system worked in other ways as well. Like when the guy in the back of the ward would tell the hopefully conscious and alert patient in the next bed that he needed to pee like the dickens, but had no urinal. Urgent word of his bladder predicament would spread bed-to-bed up the row all the way to the nurses' desk.

"Hey, better hurry, the guy in back is ready to piss in his bed!" was more or less how the alarm was sounded.

Additionally, if a patient fell out of bed, then the whole floor knew about it. Despite all these "compelling" advantages of having 39 roommates, hospitals were moving toward providing the patient with more much-needed privacy.

The ward where I passed away was given a major facelift that began in 1983 and was completed two years later. The original ward no longer existed once the renovations were completed since the wing was converted to semi-private rooms. This floor was where they had primarily placed cancer patients.

In this up-dated hospital, terminal patients were no longer sprinkled among the internal medicine patients. Now end-of-life patients could even have the luxury of a private room if they could afford it.

Another change in this now progressive hospital was that it lost one of their most dedicated nurses, Mia Anderson. Each day when she would pass Bed 39, she was painfully reminded that the only man she ever loved was gone. I am, of course, proud to say that man was *me*! I once overheard Nurse Libby telling others that Mia never married nor had had children of her own, so she donated her life savings as well as her substantial inheritance to the pediatric ICU at Children's Hospital. Thank God, there was still Nurse Libby, who now was taking every course imaginable on cancer care and caring for the terminally ill.

Recently word had spread throughout St. Louis about a new scourge—a mysterious virus called HIV or Human Immunodeficiency Virus, the virus that causes Acquired Immunodeficiency Syndrome, or AIDS. This horrific disease perplexed medical professionals and was bringing wide-spread terror to gay communities all over the U.S.

By 1981, the Center for Disease Control had become aware they had an epidemic on their hands. Unexplained and unusual infections were compromising the immune systems of previously healthy young men. Massive infections and cancers were taking over and ravaging previously healthy bodies causing extremely painful deaths accompanied by protracted high levels of suffering. This epidemic was the beginning of healthcare workers routinely taking precautions by wearing gloves when in contact with body fluids and drawing blood.

Physicians were seeing more and more of what had previously been a rare lung infection called Pneumocystis Carnii Pneumonia and a no longer uncommon cancer called Kaposi Sarcoma.

The disease and its method of transmission were poorly understood for many years. The public initially believed it was transferred via hugging, kissing, and saliva. The reality was that much more intimate contact was required. It gradually became apparent that the HIV virus could be transmitted by unprotected sex, contaminated hypodermic needles or blood transfusions. Breast feeding could transfer the disease from mother to child—an unthinkable horror.

Scientists tracked the migration of the disease from primates to humans. Back in the 1930's when the bush meat trade was prevalent, it was not uncommon for humans to consume primates as a food source. The Simian Immunodeficiency Virus then mutated into a human form. The first known case occurred when a man from The Congo died of the disease in 1959. In 1969, a teenage boy from St. Louis who passed away was the first known diagnosed case in North America. He was admitted to St. Louis's Barnes Hospital in 1968 with a variety of symptoms that totally mystified physicians. His testicles and legs were swollen and covered with warts. He also had several other immune compromised diseases, one being Kaposi Sarcoma. Amazingly, an official diagnosis would not be confirmed until 1987.

Then there was the man dubbed Patient Zero by the Center for Disease Control. He was an extremely sexually promiscuous Canadian flight attendant named Gaettan Dugas. He was purported to be a carrier of AIDS and supposedly had sexual contact with more than 2,500 men in North America alone. Dugas was linked to nine of the first 19 AIDS cases in Los Angeles, 22 in New York City and nine more in eight other cities—in all, some 40 of the first 248 cases in the U.S. He later died in 1984 due to an AIDS-related illness.

By 1981, numerous cases had been reported in several larger metropolitan areas in the United States, St. Louis included. Thus here I was, face-to-face so to speak, with an AIDS patient who now occupied Bed 39. He was a 40-year-old former American rock star named Schulen McDermott.

Bed 39

He was once charming, vibrant and known for his handsome face and savvy ways. Sadly, now Schulen was in a coma dying of AIDS. Bed 39 is where he spent his final days.

Schulen was a dynamic, popular drummer in a rock band that achieved international success in the 70's. He was a gifted musician who could play piano by ear and taught himself to play drums and guitar at the age of twelve. Schulen's smooth, confident stage presence, his naturally perfect timing and uncanny ability to anticipate his band-mates' next moves were awe-inspiring. He could follow anything and go anywhere. Musical improv was his forte. Many gifts, many talents. That was Schulen—a man with remarkable musical talent and movie-star looks. Some called it a blessing and others a curse that he had such an unforgettable face. He was easily recognized everywhere he went which made it exceedingly difficult for him to lead a private life.

On top of his good looks, this rock star had abundant charisma that made him popular, not only with legions of fans but with DJ's that spanned both continents as well.

Schulen sported a thick, shoulder-length auburn mane that he wildly tossed around while engrossed playing music on stage. In healthier times, his playful green eyes would mesmerize his fans. In front of an adoring crowd, he'd bestow his flirtatious glances on the frenzied women seated in the front row. Schulen played the role of the studly macho rock star to the hilt, however, if the truth be known, he had a strong sexual appetite for both men and women.

He engaged in high-risk, unprotected sex for more than a decade. But as his health began to fail, this once highly social creature now preferred to be left alone and free from die-hard groupies.

Once diagnosed with AIDS, he constantly worried about being bombarded by paparazzi and having an overzealous reporter leak his diagnosis to a voracious media that would spread the news to every village on the planet. Schulen's desire to be alone became so profound, that a year after his diagnosis, his wish became a sad reality. He often ruefully reflected on the truth of the caveat "be careful what you wish for."

Schulen was born in a small town outside St. Louis, Missouri in 1945. He married his high school sweetheart Lilly at the age of 18 when she became pregnant. The young boy knew it was the respectable, right thing to do at the time, but was ambivalent if the institution of marriage was right for him. He adored Lilly, however, the thought of becoming a father at such a tender age frightened the hell out of him!

Even before he turned 19-years-old, Schulen had already begun to establish himself in the music industry and he had big dreams of being free to tour with his new band. He was fueled by a deep knowing that he would be world-famous someday and he was eager to get on with it! He was ashamed that at one desperate point, he tried to talk Lilly into getting an abortion even though it would be another decade before they became legalized. She would have had to take the high risk of having a back-alley abortion and breaking the law. Fortunately, she didn't consider that as an option for even a moment, which did not please Schulen one bit.

Yet it wasn't until he had his first glimpse of his newborn son Danny McDermott that he felt true joy! Schulen ended up being a model father for the first six years of Danny's life.

Danny idolized his daddy and was by his side as much as humanly possible like a mini-Schulen shadow. Despite Schulen's great initial reservations, fatherhood fit him sublimely! He was so proud of his red-headed clone that he took him to his local gigs to show him off and even brought him up on stage to sing a short father-son duet.

Schulen used to laugh when Danny would say, "Dad, I like that song 'Don't Slap Me When I Cheat.' But, does it mean *cheat* like on a test? Phew, I wouldn't blame the teacher for being mad!"

So great was the child's adoration of his father, he would regularly report that he had practiced singing while Schulen was at work. Danny had an ear-to-ear smile on his face in anticipation of his dad's bear hug and effusive praise that would follow this revelation.

"Let me show you, Dad. I know all the words to 'Don't Slap Me When I Cheat.' Now watch me dad, I sing just like you!"

Danny began to slowly wiggle his little hips as he strategically placed the pseudo hair-brush microphone to his lips with one hand, then wave the other in the air as he belted out the precise lyrics to his father's song.

> *I can't help being that kind of guy*
> *Who has that hopeless roaming eye.*
> *"One" is not in my DNA*
> *So don't blame me if I want to play!*
> *I know I'm bad and I'll take some heat.*
> *So woman please-don't slap me when I cheat!*
> *I can't help being that kind of guy*
> *Who has that hopeless roaming eye.*
> *For now you are my only dame…*
> *Until I capture another flame.*
> *Ouch! I know I'm bad and I'll take some heat*
> *So woman please-don't slap me when I cheat*
> *I can't help being that kind of guy*
> *Who has that hopeless roaming eye.*
> *Until I came home one sunny day*
> *And saw a note YOU went to play,*
> *it said,*
> *Honey, I know I'm bad and I'll take some heat*
> *But man, don't slap me when I cheat!*
> *Don't slap me when I cheat.*

Schulen roared his admiration and appreciation for this remarkable performance. He was impressed that his son had memorized the entire song. Now little Danny was truly guaranteed one song on stage at his dad's gigs.

Audiences loved watching the precocious five-year-old sing on stage. His performance always drew wide-spread laughter and wild applause from the crowd.

Lilly, on the other hand, scolded Schulen for teaching Danny a song that was disrespectful to women and monogamous relationships.

"Schulen, I hate that song! I want Danny to learn to be a gentleman. Please don't teach him that damn garbage!" Lilly said with the full courage of her conviction. Schulen chuckled retorting, "But Lilly, he thinks it's a song about cheating on a test!" and that would conclude the debate.

By the time Danny turned six, Schulen's fame started to escalate. Now he was singing at larger venues like Kiel Auditorium in St. Louis, and various major event venues in both Chicago and Los Angeles.

Inevitably Schulen's career caused the demise of his marriage to Lilly. After the divorce, he left the United States to spend more than a decade in non-stop global tour-mode, only to finally return to St. Louis a couple months prior to his death.

When Danny McDermott walked to Bed 39 it was the first time he had seen his father in 17 years. Danny was now a grown man with a son of his own.

The butterflies in his stomach would not be still as he thought of all he wanted to say to his father. He wondered what his dad would think when he saw him walk through the door after all these years. Would he even remember him or be able to recognize him? Danny could not deny the anger he felt at being abandoned by his father for a life on the road. His head and heart were filled to overflowing with conflicting thoughts and emotions.

Nurse Libby escorted Danny to his father's bedside. Much to Danny's dismay, he quickly discovered that his father had fallen into a coma earlier that morning. All plans for a soul-searching dialogue between father and son became moot.

The room was darkened since the sun had set an hour or so ago and few lights had been turned on to compensate. Only a dim light on the bedside table illuminated his father's face. The face Danny stared at was not at all consistent with the face he remembered from childhood. If the nurse hadn't purposefully brought him to this particular bedside herself, he would have thought this man couldn't possibly be his father.

Ever the keen observer, Libby noted the dismay and confusion on this young man's face, then patted his shoulder.

These loving souls had done everything they could to create the image and comforts of home for their momma in her dying days. They wanted to show their deep appreciation by placing the bouquet of flowers in the vase to adorn the nurses' station and leaving behind two bottles of wine for the nurses to enjoy after their shifts had ended.

Next the family slowly walked to Bed 39 which remained empty. The sun was starting to set sending an orange glow through the small bedside window. They opened their bottle of wine and filled several small paper cups. All three had the strong sense that both parents were with them at that moment. The Baldini children continued their family tradition however, this time they surrounded Bed 39.

"We had the honor growing up in a warm household and knew without a doubt that as parents you were always there for us."

Angelo began.

"Thank you for being the fine example of lasting true love that should exist between every married couple and the devoted unrelenting love you had for us as parents." Sophie added. "After all these years, you both are finally together," Sasha concluded. "Please, everyone raise your cups...Salute momma and poppa, this one's for you. We love you and will hold you both close in our hearts!...Until we meet again."

CHAPTER 10

For My Many Reasons Why 1985

IT'S BEEN TWENTY-ONE YEARS SINCE my death and believe it or not, after observing this hospital ward all this time, I can honestly say there were some surprising and seldom recognized communication advantages to having large, overcrowded wards in hospitals. One that comes off the top of my head is that there's not as much need to have a call light for each patient when you could simply just holler and set up a chain of hollers that rippled through the ward to alert a nurse! Oh, and some of my ward mates back in 1964 could really scream like bloody murder, too! It would practically scare the nurses to death and they'd come running back real fast. Nurse Libby would yell,

"Where is the darn fire? What no fire? Then sweet pea, don't you be screaming at me when a call light will get my attention just fine."

This buddy system worked in other ways as well. Like when the guy in the back of the ward would tell the hopefully conscious and alert patient in the next bed that he needed to pee like the dickens, but had no urinal. Urgent word of his bladder predicament would spread bed-to-bed up the row all the way to the nurses' desk.

"Hey, better hurry, the guy in back is ready to piss in his bed!" was more or less how the alarm was sounded.

Additionally, if a patient fell out of bed, then the whole floor knew about it. Despite all these "compelling" advantages of having 39 roommates,

"Mr. McDermott, the medical social worker has been trying for weeks to get in touch with Schulen's closest family members. I'm so glad you responded to our call. How long has it been since you last saw your father?"

Danny stood there in stony silence for a moment before he answered. Then he entombed glumly,

"Seventeen years."

Libby felt his sadness and spoke in a gentle tone.

"Please, let me take your coat and encourage you to make yourself at home and take as much time as you need. Do you want me to stay with you both for a while?"

The young man slowly shook his head no.

"After all these years, I want time alone with my father, but thank you for your kind offer."

Nurse Libby warmly patted his shoulder as she replied,

"I will be in again to check on you and your father. If there is anything I can do, just press this call button. Before I leave, I just wanted you to know, your father had been alert until a few days ago. The staff just adores him. He always makes us laugh. Oh, the man is full of personality! Sorry, I didn't mean to rattle on. I'll hush for now and let you visit with your father."

Danny sighed despondently as he looked down at his father. The only marker that triggered a scintilla of recognition was his long thick eyelashes. Schulen was only 40 years of age, however he looked like a tiny, frail old man. Sparse strands of long auburn hair studded his balding head. Schulen emitted a musty medicinal smell rather than the Old Spice scent Danny recalled from long ago.

Danny sat on the chair next to his father's bed, much too afraid to touch the "patient." He stared intensely at Schulen's boney hands folded across his chest. As thoughts crowded his head about his childhood and what he had hoped to say to his father, Danny suddenly became aware that each breath his father took was becoming slower and farther apart. The only sounds besides the slowed breaths were the ticking of the clock on the wall and the distant buzz of activity at the nurses' station.

Surreal disbelief made the young man dizzy. After flying more than 10 hours and rushing to the hospital only to discover that his father was no longer alert or even aware he was at his bedside was devastating. Silence dominated until Danny could no longer stifle his tears and surrendered to sobbing into the palms of his hands. After several minutes he briefly regained his composure as he listened to the tick…tick…tick of the clock. Young Danny McDermott then stood up, gathered his composure and spoke to his father.

"Dad, I'm not sure if you can hear me, but I have flown a thousand miles to speak my mind. I have been planning to visit you for years, never realizing the time I had would be cut short."

Danny blew his nose vigorously, then wiped away more tears.

"I loved you so much, Dad. When you left Mom and me that day, you never said you wouldn't be back! How in the hell could you leave me? I was your only son and you were my world. You know, for months I'd sit on the porch step after school knowing that you would be pulling up any minute. But you never, ever did."

Danny leaned closer as if he were waiting for his father to open his eyes or speak. It was almost impossible to comprehend that this frail shell of a man was once so vibrant and strong. Schulen had been a multi-talented maestro who performed grueling 30-minute drum solos seemingly effortlessly, and alternately would sing or rock out on stage with an acoustic guitar. But those glory days were long gone.

Now his father's pale blue hospital gown covered numerous unsightly purple lesions that populated his skeletal body. His complexion was dusky and jaundiced.

The slender, well-groomed young man had his thick auburn hair neatly pulled back in a ponytail. His tear-filled emerald green eyes gazed at his father mournfully. The young son looked collegiate wearing his navy sport coat with a crisp white polo shirt and khaki pants. He briefly looked upward the ceiling as if searching for some sort of assistance and answers then started to slowly pace about the room as if he were a professor preparing to speak in front of his class.

"Dad, I thought you'd want to know that I'm a professional musician and I taught myself to play many instruments, just like you. What I've found I enjoy most though, is singing. Unlike you, the world does not know my name. Nor do I play in large auditoriums or have a need to run from the paparazzi. The only people I perform for are those who attend my church.

Danny continued his discourse all the while wiping tears from his eyes.

"I know you'd be proud to know that I've been told my singing is so beautiful that I've made a few church members cry. The good kind of tears that make you smile through them."

Danny sat down again, this time moving his chair closer to the bed.

"Strange, how I always imagined myself yelling at you if I were ever to get a chance to talk with you. I was sure I would be screaming at the top of my lungs! Lord knows how angry I have been about how you abandoned me and how deeply you broke my heart.

"I've read in the papers how you traveled the seven continents, so I just don't understand how you couldn't stop once to see me, not in 17 years? What did I do to deserve that? I just never thought I could ever forgive you."

The young man resumed his pacing around the room while emotionally moving his arms to punctuate his heart-felt monologue.

"For years I prayed for God to lessen my pain. The way I loathed you, well, it just wasn't healthy. I often wondered how I could call myself a Christian while harboring such incredible hatred. But, today when I walked in and saw you lying there so helplessly frail and so close to death's door, I knew you were already battling enough just to stay alive and you didn't need to contend with me as well. I felt that my fight was finally over and all I wanted to do was hold you in my arms."

The young man, tears still streaming down his face, cupped the palm of his hand over his father's hand. Kindly Nurse Libby once again returned.

"Do you have any other siblings?" she inquired. Danny wiped away the moisture from around his swollen eyes.

"Not that I'm aware of. I believe I'm his only son."

Nurse Libby was aware of rare visits from a few former lovers, both male and female, however, she never knew he had a son. No one who visited ever claimed progeny.

"Looks like you've spent the day traveling. Can I get you anything, tea or some coffee?"

Danny straightened himself up in the chair.

"No thank you, but could you tell me how long my father's been here and what it is that's killing him? He's so young!"

The nurse gave a big uncomfortable sigh. She felt quite uneasy answering this very innocent and justifiable question. Nurse Libby pulled up a chair next to Danny as she gave him another empathetic pat on his shoulder as if to apologize in advance.

"Your father has been with us for the last five weeks. He is a delightful man who was kind enough to sing a few of his old songs for us nurses when he first arrived.

"That was before your dad became too weak," Nurse Libby continued.

"He told me he started to lead a hermit-type existence the last two years when his health started to fail. He still had his engaging wit though, and a sense of humor up until a couple days ago."

Danny politely interrupted.

"But, what type of disease does he have?"

The gray haired nurse leaned closer to Danny.

"My dear, Mr. McDermott is dying of AIDS."

At that moment another nurse poked her head in the room and asked for Nurse Libby's assistance in another room. She pardoned herself,

"I will be back, my dear, please call if you need me sooner!"

Danny's head was spinning while trying to comprehend how his father had contracted AIDS. Knowing he didn't have much time to spend with him, he realized it just didn't matter, not how, not why, not when. The fact was he was now finally at his father's side after years of separation.

"Dad, I wish we had more time, even an hour of your knowing I am here. Do you remember how I made you laugh when I would sing that quirky song on stage, 'Don't Slap Me When You Cheat?' You were so proud you'd yell, "That's MY son!" After a long night we'd go home and tell mom all about it.

"Phew, she would get so mad. I think she hated your song, Dad, but that was when I felt the closest to you, when we would sing together."

Danny smiled at the memory. Then he sighed and shook his head in disbelief. The somber young man started to rock in the chair holding his head while grabbing fistfuls of his own hair as if to rip it out.

"Damn, I thought our meeting would be so different, and I thought we would have more time, that we would work through our problems and have decades to grow close and rekindle our relationship as father and son. I had planned to see you years ago, but it somehow never happened. Only this week I found out you were dying. Mom finally told me where you were."

Danny tried to compose himself as he stood up and walked to his Dad's guitar that stood in the corner of the room. It was the one Schulen played earlier this month when he performed some of his songs for the nurses.

"Dad, when I was fifteen years old, I wrote a song for you. I hope you don't mind if I play your guitar and sing it for you. It's called

For Your Many Reasons Why.
I'd sit up on the porch and look into the sky.
Then counted all the stars for your many reasons why...
you left me.
How could it be so easy to walk right out that door
Was my mere existence such a laborious chore.
How could it be so bad when all I did was love?
So I'd sit upon the porch and look into the sky
Then count all the stars for your many reasons why...
you left, me.
Did you ever stop to think as days turned into years
That our lives could be so different without the lies or fears.
How I needed you to be there or just to give me one more chance...
I'd do anything to make you see.
I'll do anything for a father's love to be.

So I'd sit up on the porch and look into the sky
Then count all the stars for your many reasons why...
you...left...me.

Danny finished the song and gently placed the guitar by the bedside. His father's features seem to soften, as if he heard his son's song. Then, one lone tear trickled down Schulen's cheek. Danny felt this overpowering swell from within his chest and swallowed hard in an attempt not to cry. He reached out and squeezed his Dad's hand. With an urgency in his tone because he felt like there was still so much to say, yet not much time, Danny continued.

"Dad, I, too, have a son who has a head of thick auburn hair like you and I. Knowing the depth of love I have for my own son makes me wonder how you could possibly have left me so easily. What could make a father just pick up and walk out that door forever is totally beyond my comprehension.

"But I never lost interest in you over the years. I collected every newspaper article and one time I even drove to one of your concerts at Radio City Music Hall. Unfortunately, I was mugged on the way and both my ticket and wallet were stolen. When I finally made it to Radio City, I told security I was your son in the hopes they would let me in, but the guy just laughed and ushered me out the theatre door like you see in a bad movie."

Danny paused as he wiped his own tears.

"It was with pride, however, that I listened to your concert from outside and yelled to passers-by, "Now that's my father! Do you hear me world, that's my father!"

Danny abruptly ceased talking as his father coughed and became more cyanotic.

The young man became anxious recognizing that his father's death was imminent. Danny rushed to the door and yelled,

"Nurse! I need a nurse in here, please!"

He quickly returned to his father's side leaning his face close to his ear.

"Dad, I hope you can hear me now. My dear father, I harbor no ill feelings toward you. I do love and forgive you."

With that uttered from the deepest part of his soul, Danny felt a distinct inner shift and tremendous relief. So great was the shift that a serendipitous event was triggered. A fairly forceful cool breeze blew through the opened window which dislodged a piece of paper that had been tucked under a book on the bedside table. Danny watched the note swirl round and round until it finally landed in his lap as though being delivered by an attentive butler.

Danny was astonished to discover that the paper was actually a small envelope addressed to him. On the front of the envelope his father had written, **To My Son...My Many Reasons Why. Love, Dad.**

Only Nurse Libby, Sister Mary Patrick and Danny McDermott witnessed Schulen's final mortal breath that autumn of 1985. Afterward, Danny quickly glanced at the note his father had handwritten in order to glean the gist of its content. A brief scan revealed that this note was his father's heartfelt attempt to explain why he had left and was a most sincere expression of regret, as well as the pain and suffering Schulen himself had experienced over the years due to the self-imposed separation from his son.

The young man carefully tucked the envelope into his pocket—he was eager to read the note it contained word for word, but wanted to do so in the privacy of his hotel room. Danny knew that a careful read of the content was going to trigger more tears shed, but would also help heal his heart. He was most grateful that his father had taken the time and gone to the effort of putting pen to paper in an attempt to explain, but most importantly, to apologize and ask for his son's forgiveness.

As Danny stood at his father's bedside he became aware of the pronounced scent of Old Spice aftershave lotion which suddenly filled the room. Danny, entranced by the meaningful, familiar aroma, became even more amazed when he clearly felt a warm embrace from an unseen source.

Danny knew without a doubt that his father had heard every word he had spoken including intuiting those that were unspoken, and that he was there with him now and always would be. Once again tears streamed down his cheeks, however, this time it was different. They were tears of bittersweet happiness, the kind that make you smile.

CHAPTER 11

What's the Craic?
1990

By 1990, A HOSPICE-DRIVEN MOVEMENT was sweeping across the country which triggered the creation of hospital environments that were more aesthetically pleasing and comfortable for the patient and the patient's family. A full-blown hospice facility would follow. Things were definitely changing for the better.

The cancer wing at the hospital in St. Louis that housed Bed 39 was still semi-private, but at least patients were now given the option of paying for a private room. This was not a full-fledged hospice yet, however strides were being made to attract more clientele thanks to the more inviting, home-like hospital rooms in the cancer wing. Walls were no longer institutional stark white, but were painted a softer light caramel or beige hue. Patients were still surrounded by the stereo-typical furnishings, however, bedspreads often were pastel sage or blue in lieu of stark white.

Studies that had been conducted decades ago showed that small doses of narcotics administered around the clock seemed to help keep pain under control better than the formerly prevailing approach of waiting to administer pain meds every four to six hours when such long pain lapses would allow pain to become severe and out of control. Once on the loose like that, pain was almost impossible to rein in. The trick was to keep it fairly under control with small, frequent doses.

The medical community was becoming more aware of hospices popping up all over the country and would refer terminal patients to them in increasing numbers. It was likely that this hospital would transition into one in the next several years.

Over the last decade, I'd seen quite a few terminal patients occupy Bed 39 who died from colorectal cancer. The incidence and mortality of colorectal cancer is highest in both men and women of the black race. Like many cancers, early detection is key in order to treat it before it has a chance to spread to other organs. Which brings me to the current occupant of Bed 39, Mrs. Edith Bailey.

Mrs. Bailey fervently believed in her home remedies learned while living in the deep south, but not in doctors nor preventative screenings. The seventy-year- old was born and raised in Selma, Alabama.

At the age of 17 she met a traveling laborer named Frederick Bailey from The British West Indies. The two eventually married and moved to St. Louis where Edith had her first child. In twelve years, Edith gave birth to seven children. Today in 1990, the youngest is forty-year-old Tyrone who has Down's syndrome.

The older woman worked two jobs most of her life in an attempt to give her children a better life and good educations so they would never have to depend on anyone to take care of them. She was especially sensitive to the need to be self-sufficient and self-sustaining since she herself could not depend on her husband Frederick. He ended up falling in love with a woman at work and moved out when Tyrone was only a baby. Mrs. Bailey struggled with taking Tyrone to his numerous doctor appointments as well as paying for them. In addition to Down's, he had epilepsy which necessitated many hospital stays to get his seizures under control.

Somehow or other Edith managed to work to earn money for her seven children. But the decades since her husband left only brought on stronger and stronger feelings of anger and resentment within Edith. At first her negativity was just aimed at men, but eventually it branched out to include women as well. The entire human population in general made Edith's blood boil.

Edith was still working two jobs when she was given her diagnosis. A few months later, Edith's condition deteriorated to the point where Tyrone had to move in with his sister Violet and her family, and Mrs. Bailey was admitted to the hospital.

Edith had many of the risk factors for colorectal cancer such as heavy smoking, obesity and high blood pressure. A risk factor she had less control over was the genetic reality that her mother and grandmother also died of colorectal cancer.

The older black woman had simply ignored the fact that she had lost 50 pounds from her 300 pound frame in less than a month. She also failed to be alarmed by changes in her bowel habits, was chronically fatigued and continuously had a feeling of fullness in her lower abdomen. Still she pushed it to the back of her mind and did nothing.

What prompted her to finally seek medical attention was blood in her stool. Unfortunately, by then the cancer had spread to her liver and lungs. Now here she was, a terminal resident of Bed 39.

Today, Edith was fumbling and grumbling with her tangled, uncooperative robe. At that moment her daughter Violet and son Tyrone walked in to visit with her in Bed 39.

Edith greeted them harshly with an accusatory,

"You're late...again!"

Fifty-two-year-old Violet was an elegant black woman dressed in a stunning hot pink wool coat and matching hat. Her hair was perfectly coifed and hung just above her shoulders. Dutifully she extended her arms to hug her unwelcoming mother, however, Mrs. Bailey only stiffened and frowned.

Forty-year-old Tyrone smiled broadly with pure delight when he saw his mother. The last week had seemed like an eternity without her! Childlike Tyrone had a teeny afro, a short, chubby frame and a delightfully playful personality.

Even though Tyrone had Down's syndrome he had attended regular high school classes. He loved school so much that once he graduated, he continued to work as the school janitor so he would not have to leave. Everyone absolutely loved being around Tyrone with his cheerful, happy disposition and willingness to help everyone.

Mrs. Bailey, ever the whirling vortex of unmitigated rage, erupted once again at her two adult children,

"Don't just stand there; help me get this dang robe off! Not everyone is cold and stiff yet! Violet, can you ask the nurse to turn down the heat? They are probably all too busy playing cards at the desk to tend to the needs of an old, sick woman!"

At that point, Libby was the only nurse who dared to joke around with Mrs. Bailey. The rest were cowed by the woman's round-the-clock ill temperament, but not Libby. She could see past that. The older nurse, wearing her signature wire-rimmed glasses, walked confidently through the door at that moment in time to hear the crack about card-playing nurses.

"Yes, my darling Mrs. Bailey, I was playing cards and can you believe I lost the last hand on the river?"

Violet frowned at her mom's sarcastic and uncalled for comment,

"Mother, please be nice! Libby, I'm sorry you had to hear my mom's last unjustified comment about nurses."

Violet took note that strangely enough, her mother didn't stiffen up when Libby walked over to give her a hug.

"Oh, my sweet Edith knows she's my special patient. How can I help you, dear?"

Mrs. Bailey started to relax with Ms. Libby present,

"For one, you can help Violet get this robe off me, I'm burning up!"

Nurse Libby and Violet were trying to gingerly assist Edith in untangling her robe. To their amazement, they discovered that Mrs. Bailey was wearing one of the old T-shirts her son Derrick bought her two years ago from one of those funky T-shirt shops in Florida. It read:

"I CRAPPED TODAY...DID YOU?"

Before anyone was aware of Mrs. Bailey's diagnosis, it was a standing joke in their household that momma's mood was dependent on if she had had a BM that morning. Violet had not seen the shirt in over a year and raised her hand to stifle a giggle. Her brother Tyrone turned and looked to the corner of the room, then back at his mother. He tittered as he told his mother,

"Mom, Nana Jackson is laughing! She said your T-shirt is funny!"

Edith Bailey shook her head as if she were confused.

"Boy, what in tar nation are you talking about? Nana Jackson's been dead for twenty years!"

Her son innocently leaned toward his mother and proceeded to point to the corner of the room.

"There she is now! You have all kinds of folks in your room! Plain as day. All here to see you momma."

Her son's eyes were round as saucers as he pointed his chubby index finger to count the invisible visitors.

Edith Bailey scratched her head.

"Tyrone, I'm gonna tell the doctor that your new seizure medicine is making you hallucinate!"

Tyrone continued…

"…three, four, five, six people in that corner!" he declared, undaunted.

Tyrone's skin was deep black like his father's, however his eyes were light honey brown like his mother's own Poppa Jackson. His innately sunny, happy disposition masked the fact that he had any problems whatsoever, but in reality, in addition to Down's syndrome, Tyrone had a congenital heart problem and had suffered some vision loss. Regardless, he never uttered a single complaint.

Mrs. Bailey pampered Little-T, her nickname for her five-foot-tall son Tyrone, so much when he was growing up that he didn't learn to walk until he was four years of age. Of course, he saw no need to make the effort since his mother carried him everywhere they went until she simply could not physically do it anymore.

There were precious few things or people that triggered a smile from Mrs. Bailey, but Little-T was one of them. Mrs. Bailey looked at the youngest of her seven children with pride and smiled broadly. Only three were still living in St. Louis while the others were scattered in various places around the world.

Tyrone returned the favor of a smile to his momma and informed her of his immediate intention.

"Little T is gonna give his momma a *big* hug! I missed you so much!" Tyrone's hug was like a strong vise grip on his mother as he accentuated the sincerity of his words with action. His childlike face displayed a wide, toothy grin which betrayed his strength. The scene warmed Violet's heart.

As much as Edith loved her son with every fiber in her, she could only take so much affection. Without giving it any conscious thought, she struggled to set herself free of his embrace.

"Don't get all mushy on me, boy! Please, you're gonna break a few ribs!"

Tyrone momentarily felt sad when his momma struggled out of his embrace.

"Momma, doesn't everyone love hugs? I save the big monster one's for you!"

His mother would normally resist anyone invading her personal space, even her own children. But not Tyrone. He was special. Still, an internal mechanism deep inside Mrs. Bailey limited the amount of loving attention she was willing to receive even from her beloved Tyrone.

"But momma, I miss you so much! When are ya coming home? Remember, you told me you'd read me the encyclopedia. I brought one for you. It says...'A.' I want to learn more like the kids at school and maybe go to college someday like Violet!"

Tyrone proceeded to pull out the encyclopedia from his backpack. He may work as a janitor, however, he enjoyed looking studious like seniors preparing for college.

Nurse Libby walked into the room and noted Tyrone holding the encyclopedia.

"My, my Little-T! What do you have there in your hand?"

Nurse Libby had talked with Mrs. Bailey each day since her admission and knew the woman's pet name for her youngest son. The boy excitedly walked up to the kind nurse and showed her the "A" book.

"My momma said we would learn something out of our encyclopedia books. We don't have the whole alphabet, 'cause my momma didn't have enough money. She just bought four at a garage sale before she came to the hospital. I have cataracts, so I don't see so good anymore so I can't read it myself."

Nurse Libby couldn't resist smiling at sweet Tyrone.

"Young man, I need to give a few patients their medications. Could I come back in 15 minutes? It would be my pleasure to read you one story!"

Even Mrs. Bailey's heart warmed with Nurse Libby's willingness to be a part of their family. Violet was seated quietly enjoying her brother's banter with Nurse Libby and her mother. The nurse promised to return then exited the room. Mrs. Bailey then turned to her daughter.

"So, where's that so-called husband of yours?"

Violet rolled her eyes in frustration. She was growing tired of repeatedly hearing her mother's paranoid warnings about her husband leaving her someday for a younger woman.

"Mother! Anthony and I have been married for 22 wonderful years. He is my best friend! For the life of me, I do not know why you treat him that *way*? You've got to stop hating on *all* men! I'm sorry Dad left you, but not every man is going to break his wife's heart. Not every relationship is a bad one, nor is every man."

The older women shook her head,

"Darlin', just don't come crying to me when he does..."

Nurse Libby returned unaware of the tension between Mrs. Bailey and her daughter as she pulled up an extra chair next to Tyrone. Libby situated her substantial bottom on the chair in an attempt to get comfortable. She then ceremoniously repositioned her wire-framed glasses on her nose as if in preparation for a reading of great import and meaning.

"So Tyrone, what story do you want to hear from the 'A' book?"

Tyrone straightened his spine and sat tall in the chair. He took a moment to glance at the pages, flipping them to the right and then to the left, in order to see what pictures or words especially interested him.

"Nurse Libby, my great Nana Jackson was from Africa. Can you read me something about it?"

The nurse turned a few pages to find information about the second largest of the seven continents.

Nurse Libby so admired Tyrone's enthusiasm to learn and once again smiled.

"Little-T, did you know that Africa is so large that you could fit all of Europe, the whole United States of America, China, India and maybe a few others into the continent! Can you believe it? It also has the largest desert in the world called, The Sahara." She read on for a few minutes and then closed the book.

Tyrone hated hearing the end of the story of Africa. He wanted Nurse Libby to go on and on. Nonetheless, when the time came Tyrone reluctantly stood to leave with his sister Violet. She helped her brother put on his coat and lovingly tied his scarf around his neck to keep him warm.

Nurse Libby flagged Tyrone over and said,

"Little-T, may I have one of your monster hugs before you leave?"

Tyrone's face brightened up and he rushed over.

"Sure can, Nurse Libby! Sure can!"

Tyrone gave the older nurse a monster squeeze and then looked at his mother.

"Momma, your turn!"

Mrs. Bailey defensively raised her arm and yelled,

"Young man, you just head on out that door or you'll make Violet late for the kids."

Little-T formed a circle with his arms in front of his chest as if he were flexing his muscles.

"Sending you an air hug instead...comin' attcha momma!"

Mrs. Bailey playfully raised her voice while motioning her daughter and son out the door.

"Go on, walk that way and out the door, you two!"

The last thing Violet said as she left was,

"Tomorrow I'm bringing you a respectable night gown instead of that T-shirt!"

As she walked out of the hospital, Violet reflected on how blessed she felt to have a team of nurses, social workers and the rest of the amazing staff at the hospital who gave with all their hearts to take care of her mother. They truly cared about their patients, treating them like family—especially Nurse Libby. Violet felt she was in a class by herself!

Early the next morning, Nurse Libby poked her head in the door
"How's the craic, Mrs. Bailey?"
Old Mrs. Bailey moaned then slowly rolled over while struggling to open her heavy lids and decipher if Libby was asking about her bum rather than using the friendly Irish greeting meaning news.
"Wha? What? How's my *crack*? Ugh! It's tired and sore! Don't you ever go home Nurse Libby? What the hell time is it anyway?"
Nurse Libby opened the curtains allowing the bright morning rays to shine into the room. The colors of the fresh flowers sitting in a vase on the window sill seemed more vibrant. The soft blue paint on the walls was lined with comforting wood framed pictures of the green English countryside. There were two cozy warm chairs like one would have at home. The room was not the typical sterile environment you'd see in a regular, run-of the-mill hospital. This place was different; the hospital rooms were intentionally decorated to look less institutional and more inviting to patients.
Nurse Libby's uniform was a bit wrinkled after her 12-hour shift. She was in her sixties now, no longer a young woman and the long shifts took their toll on her. The stubborn nurse, though, felt it was the patients who kept her alive, the patients who gave her the will to move on since her beloved husband had died last year.
"Mrs. Bailey, I worked a 12-hour shift, I'm tired but not *too* tired to take you for a stroll on this beautiful spring morning. Now let me help you get dressed *and* woman, I know that T-shirt of yours is a bold-faced lie! You did *not* take a crap this morning, or I would have known! Here, let's get you washed up so I can put something pretty on you."

Nurse Libby wheeled Edith around the grounds of the hospital while the two welcomed the sun's warm rays and the pleasant breeze on their faces. Edith enjoyed this grand little escape from Bed 39. Libby also took her on a short tour to see the magnificent, awe-inspiring oil paintings that hung along the north stairwell, then to the chapel and pastoral care to visit with the staff.

Edith hated to admit it, but she had not felt this relaxed all week. During this respite with Nurse Libby, her attention was diverted from dwelling on the fact she was dying much sooner than she wanted to.

Nurse Libby looked down at her friend and giggled,

"Edith, you better wipe that smile off your face or someone might think that you're enjoying yourself!"

Mrs. Bailey chuckled along with Nurse Libby,

"I am, you old coot! *And* you better stop working so hard or I won't have anyone to give a rough time, well, other than my family. Now take me back, I need to sleep."

The wheelchair must've been as old as the woman upon it. It loudly creaked and squeaked with every roll down the hall. But despite the noisy chair, by the time Nurse Libby reached Bed 39, her patient was sound asleep. For the first time since she arrived, there was no longer a grimace or furrowed brows on her face and her lips were upturned. Yes, Nurse Libby noted with great pleasure, she was definitely smiling in her sleep! At least for a moment, that exact moment, Edith found contentment and peace in her earth-bound world.

The old woman slept soundly for several hours, even through lunch. Sister Mary Patrick, who had volunteered at the hospital for the past twenty years, was seated next to Edith when she opened her eyes. The nun was rocking in the chair quietly praying her rosary.

"Sister Mary Patrick, you *do* know I'm Baptist, right? Have you got any ministers in the house?"

The slender nun ceased rocking then stood to reach for Mrs. Bailey's hand.

"Mrs. Bailey, you do tickle me with your dry wit and I happen to like your feisty personality. You remind me of my sister, God rest her soul!

Oh, she had this kind heart underneath a very rough exterior. Much like you, I know you have a good soul."

Mrs. Bailey semi-snorted, and then cleared her throat.

"Well, if you like me so much then will you be a dear and hand me my T-shirt? That one on the other chair," Mrs. Bailey motioned with her hand in that direction.

Sister Mary Patrick picked up the T-shirt, took a moment to read it silently to herself, then reread out loud what was printed on the front.

"I CRAPPED TODAY...DID YOU?"

Sister Mary Patrick emitted an appreciative, hearty belly laugh.

"Oh my! Why in the world would you want to wear this shirt each day?"

Edith looked down then sighed, as she gingerly grabbed the T-shirt and held it to her heart.

"It's special. That's all."

The nun knew when to listen as she continued to hold Edith's hand. The room was quiet at this precise instant, but the silence was finally broken by Edith as she cleared her throat in order to make a declaration.

"This T-shirt was the last gift my eldest son Derrick gave me before he left St. Louis two years ago. I haven't seen nor heard from him since. Won't even return my phone calls. It's a silly gift I know, but it's special because of who gave it to me."

The nun saw a different person emerge for a moment—a woman who was vulnerable and deeply sad who used anger, bitterness and an unpleasant temperament to conceal her pain and suffering.

"Then my dear Mrs. Bailey, what are we waiting for? I think it's time to display your precious gift. I don't know about you, but it personally makes me smile."

The T-shirt was back on Mrs. Bailey by the time lunch arrived. The continual feeling of fullness was growing stronger and it suppressed her appetite more each day. Pain gnawed at her back, hips and legs. The doctors were certain tumors had spread to the bone. After an injection of morphine, Mrs. Bailey fell into a deep, yet troubled sleep evidenced by great tossing and turning.

Before long the old woman realized someone was calling her name. She tried to pull herself to consciousness and out of the cocoon of sleep. "Mrs. Bailey, Mrs. Bailey?"

She recognized her oncologist standing at her bedside trying to rouse her. Edith grumbled and rolled the other direction as she threw the blanket over her head.

"Lordy, Lordy! What is this? Grand Central Station?? How's a gal supposed to get some sleep with y'all coming into my room every two seconds? Can't I die in peace?"

The husky physician had a short, gray, no-nonsense crew cut. By now, he was well aware of Mrs. Bailey's cantankerous ways. He gave her time to vent and then cautiously proceeded to evaluate his patient regarding her pain level, overall comfort, emotional and physical states and of course, assessed if there had been any further deterioration caused by the disease.

The older woman fidgeted in her bed while watching the clock. Then suddenly Edith heard clumsy footsteps racing down the hall. She also heard Violet's high pitched voice send forth a warning to her brother,

"Walk, Tyrone! Don't run down the hall!"

Tyrone burst through the door holding an encyclopedia high in the air. He was so excited that his rapid speech was slurred.

"Momma, I have the 'K' book! I already started reading while waiting for Violet. In the ' K' book, I chose to read about a really great man! Martin Luther King was an American…ah…Civil Rights…er…activist," he reported measuring his words. "He wanted people to be judged by who they are on the inside rather than the color of their skin. He gave a famous speech, too, called 'I Have A Dream.' I don't know all of it, but something like all men are created equal, oh and I know he meant women, too, momma!"

Mrs. Bailey smiled yet seemed distracted by who was walking in with Violet. It was Violet's husband, Anthony. The woman couldn't help smirking, then sighing quite loudly. In a flat tone Mrs. Bailey grumbled,

"You're late…again! Were you *delayed* at work *again*, Anthony?"

Violet and her husband glanced at each other, confused by Edith's question.

"Don't go there, Mother!" Violet implored. "Please, let's make this a nice visit. Oh, and I am expecting Pastor Virgil to stop by. He's bringing a few ladies from the choir to see you."

"Goodness!" she remarked with surprise as she saw them pour through the door. "Here they are! Come on in, Pastor Virgil, ladies. Momma say hello!"

Momma, overheated and nervous with a roomful of company, frantically fanned herself, then quickly shed her robe in response to her rising internal body temperature.

Pastor Virgil and the ladies from the church choir stood at the foot of Edith's bed with eyes as big as baseballs. It was Tyrone who started to roar. He laughed so hard he held his left side and wiped tears from his eyes.

"Momma, you're wearing that funny shirt in front of Pastor Virgil!"

Violet, embarrassed by her mother's insistence on wearing that darn thing, slowly pulled the bed covers up to conceal the words. It was time to change the subject and redirect the focus to the company who had just arrived.

"Mother, I told Pastor Virgil about your favorite song and they wanted to come to sing it to you."

The pastor held up his arms to direct the choir singing *Amazing Grace*. The three harmonized beautifully until Mrs. Bailey started to grumble yet again! The old woman began to repeatedly point to her chest. Thump, thump, thump, she drummed on her sternum with an emphatic finger.

"Pastor Virgil! Can you look here real close, *real* close. Do you see what this is? It is called a res-per-AAAAA-tion. That's right, a respiration. That means I'm still breathing, so don't you and those church ladies come here and start singing me funeral songs!"

Violet, Anthony, Pastor Virgil and the women from the choir were flabbergasted at Edith's rude response to their kind gesture. Poor Pastor Virgil tried to explain the meaning of *Amazing Grace* and how it wasn't just a song sung at funerals. Edith didn't want to hear another word.

"Why don't you just put a tombstone at the head of my bed? For Pete's sake! I think I'm ready for some peace and quiet now." she said dismissively.

Violet was growing concerned about her mother's increasing anger and disagreeable outbursts. And she was mortified that such a nice gesture by the three choir members and the pastor was cause for her mother to act in such an offensive manner.

"Mother, we just wanted to make you happy. You always loved that song. No, you did, it used to bring sweet tears to your eyes. We didn't intend to upset you. Please tell me how I can melt that cold, icy exterior of yours? Please, let me in, I'm your daughter."

Tyrone gently tugged at his momma's T-shirt.

"Momma, is Nurse Libby here tonight? I wanted to show her the 'K' book and tell her how much I learned about Dr. Martin Luther King, Jr.! Did I tell you he won the Nobel Peace prize?"

Edith waved her hand in a downward motion as if to slow Lil' T down.

"No baby, Nurse Libby isn't here tonight. You can tell her about it tomorrow.

"Now I think it's getting late so y'all better head on home and let momma sleep."

Tyrone cautiously moved forward and asked,

"Can I give you a monster hug, momma, or an air hug?"

Edith rolled her eyes and replied,

"Little-T, you better send me an air hug. I'm kind of sore tonight."

Tyrone, who was quite the actor, flexed and growled as his arms formed the familiar C-shape in front of his chest mockingly assuming the position of a strong man.

"Monster air hug coming your way! Bye momma, I love you."

Violet's husband Anthony could hardly wait to get out of this uncomfortable situation. He dreaded every moment with his mother-in-law. He practically pulled Violet off her feet when they exited the room and then breathed an audible sigh of relief.

The next morning seemed more like midnight as a mass of dark gray leaden clouds filled the sky. Sheets of rain pelted the window while the clatter of thunder made Mrs. Bailey shudder.

She had never liked storms, even as a child. Edith, who seemed so fearless and strong at an early age, used to hide in the closet every time it stormed. A sudden bolt of lightning cracked, flashing a brilliant white glow across the room. It startled Mrs. Bailey, but she didn't allow any outward indication that it did. "Show no fear," was one of her mantras!

Despite the gloomy weather, it turned out to be a busy day for Mrs. Bailey. The hospice aid came in to help her get washed up, the medical social worker sat down to chat, then Sister Mary Patrick and even Pastor Virgil, who clearly did not hold a grudge, visited! Thank God he was a forgiving man.

By the end of that rainy day, Mrs. Bailey doubted she had the energy to visit with her own family members and decided to call Violet to tell her tomorrow would be a much better day. But just as she picked up the phone, Violet walked in, tears streaming down her face. Her daughter was so distraught she couldn't speak.

Before Violet found her voice, Mrs. Bailey welled up in anger, yelling.

"I told you that no good cheating son of a bitch was gonna..."

Mrs. Bailey's face was flushed with rage and she had both fists balled up from a burning desire to punch Anthony in the nose!

"Where is that bastard anyway? Did you catch him in the act with his secretary? I don't know why you married him in the first place! I knew he was trouble from the very beginning!"

Mrs. Bailey was fired up and continued to ramble on while Violet violently shook her head back and forth repeatedly,

"No, No, No!"

"Mother...just hold on..."

"Please..."

Violet quickly raised her hand to stop Mrs. Bailey from saying another word.

"Mother, mother please stop...it's Tyrone...he's, he's dead."

Those words hit Mrs. Bailey like the last lightning bolt that had severed the sky earlier. The woman sat there with her mouth gaping open, every muscle paralyzed. Such an unthinkable turn of events was not even a remote thought in Edith's mind as she had mentally projected the future for her children. No, no, no! Little-T had many years ahead of him, she had been certain! And today Little-T was going to bring her the 'K' book and talk about Dr. Martin Luther King, Jr. He was going to laugh at her funny shirt or tell her about what he did at work or remind her of his dream to go to college someday.

Violet interrupted Edith's thoughts and began to fill in the blanks. "Earlier that morning, one of the history teachers at school asked Tyrone if he wanted to discuss his hero, Dr. Martin Luther King, Jr. in class today," Violet started. " You know, momma, how the students all adore sweet Tyrone who was eternally excited to share what he had learned from his four encyclopedia books A, K, F and Z.

"Momma, the teacher told me no one would have ever guessed that Tyrone only had an IQ of 70! She said this morning he gave the most eloquent speech to her class. Little-T explained what he had read in his favorite 'K' book. He even used gestures to make his point and 'scanned' the room with his index finger as he began his monologue to get the students' full attention," Violet reported.

"All of us, yes, all of us in this room and in this world, should be able to walk with our heads held high, knowing we are free from prejudice and free of racial discrimination," the teacher said Little-T announced. According to the teacher, he held his arms out in wonder as he asked, "Please, tell me how, how people could possibly choose to like or dislike anyone because of their sex or the color of their skin, when instead judgment should be based on their goodness within. That's what counts! It should be so *easy* to choose respect, acceptance and love; it should be easy for all of mankind to do what's right to make our world a better place. But why is it so hard for so many?"

Violet explained that the students clapped for Tyrone and then, one by one, they all stood and cheered. After that, Tyrone left the classroom and went back to his duties as a janitor, a janitor who somehow with the pure goodness in his heart, managed to change the lives of everyone who met him.

Tyrone was so happy because he had done so well and gotten such a positive response. Violet recounted that he mopped the floors wearing an ear-to-ear smile. Apparently just thinking about how he finally memorized that long speech made him giggle.

Tyrone excitedly left work on a mission. Instead of going home, he decided to run to the hospital and share the good news with momma. He was on his way when he ran straight into the path of an oncoming car and was killed instantly.

After telling her terrible tale, Violet sank to a chair and sobbed uncontrollably. But Edith was frozen in place and remained like a statue in her bed that neither moved nor spoke.

Sister Mary Patrick, Nurse Libby and Pastor Virgil ran to Mrs. Bailey's bedside the minute they heard the tragic news. They gathered around Mrs. Bailey's bed and prayed. Violet stroked her mother's back and cried with the others. Edith sat for hours in a catatonic state, never shedding a tear, never averting her glazed stare from the wall.

Nurse Libby gingerly rolled down the head of Bed 39 in the hope that her patient might be able to sleep. But Mrs. Bailey was literally in a state of shock, and remained emotionless as she stared into space. It wasn't until around 3:00 a.m. when tears finally and blessedly erupted from the grief-stricken woman. Nurse Libby, angel that she was, was by her side when the flood gates opened. Pastor Virgil hadn't abandoned her either, but was taking a quick chair nap when he was roused by the woman's wailing.

"Little-T was supposed to be at *my* funeral," the bereaved mother cried in protest. "Libby, he wasn't supposed to die before me, it's just *wrong*! Yesterday before Little-T left, he asked me for a hug and I made up some damn lame excuse to avoid it! For years I have shunned any display of affection from my own children! Pastor Virgil, what kind of mother am I? I am a sinner and I pray that I can live long enough to make it up to my children, and that somehow both Little-T and the Lord above will forgive me."

Pastor Virgil responded by starting to sing Mrs. Bailey's favorite song. He knew this time it would somehow comfort her.

Amazing Grace, how sweet the sound.
That saved a wretch like me.
I once was lost but now am found;
Was blind but now I see.

There were over 500 students, friends and family members at Tyrone's funeral. Pastor Virgil presided over the funeral giving a touching speech about Tyrone and his life.

Sister Mary Patrick, Nurse Libby and other staff from the hospital were also present to show their support and pay their last respects. Mrs. Bailey, rocked to the depth of her soul with Little-T's death, experienced a number of epiphanies. She suddenly realized she had spent too many years choosing to be angry, choosing to hold onto resentments, when all along she had a choice to love, and a choice to be happy. Her children had poured out so much love to her, but sadly she had often rebuffed such displays.

Later back in the hospital, Mrs. Bailey was finally surrounded by six of her children, including the son she had not spoken with in two years who had given her the infamous T-shirt. Little did she know that Tyrone and Nana Jackson were there, too, joining the crowd. They watched with pride as this woman who was once so very lost had now managed to finally find the true beauty of love within her family.

That day her children witnessed something in their mother's eyes which they had not seen in decades. They all agreed it was peace and blessed freedom from festering anger and resentment. It should have been so very easy to choose love, they reflected, but finally she did and that fact was apparent to each and every one of them.

Mrs. Edith Bailey died the next morning. Moments before drawing her last breath she raised her arms as she laid in Bed 39 and whispered softly,

"Lil'-T, momma is ready for one of your monster hugs."

CHAPTER 12

1995
Cowboy Jack and the Western Sky

IT'S HARD TO BELIEVE I'VE been dead since November of 1964, keeping vigil here at Bed 39. It was only three years after my death when Dr. Cicely Saunders established the first organized hospice in the world—St. Christopher's Hospice in South London, which opened in 1967. Then in 1974, The Connecticut Hospice became the first organized hospice in America thanks to the efforts of Florence Wald, M.D.

Now of special interest to me, the first hospice in Poland was opened in the mid 1970's. One by one, organized hospices were being established worldwide. It was a heartening trend.

My imprinted spirit has watched this hospital come a long way from consigning terminally ill patients to an overcrowded 40-bed hospital ward. Later it morphed into several smaller wards, then to a semi-private cancer floor and now finally, in 1995, to a one-of-a-kind free standing hospice facility in St. Louis, Missouri. It was an evolution I have been privileged to observe.

Thank God Bed 39 was always quite special thanks to the donation made by Dr. Cicely Saunders herself. I was in the good company of sheer royalty, or at least the energy of royalty, thanks to imprinting my soul on the bed she donated. From the beginning, the elegantly framed wooden bed has been appointed with a fancy gold plaque with Dr. Saunders' name on it. The bed's timeless beauty kept it in continual use without thought of replacing it and appropriately and thankfully now in 1995, it's been moved into one of the rooms in our first hospice unit! I am so joyful over this evolution, especially since I stayed behind to watch it happen. Coincidentally, and for now, Bed 39 is in room 39, no longer the 39th bed in a very long ward.

For admission to hospice the prerequisite for admission doesn't have to be cancer. Any terminal illness where the patient is in the end-stage of life, like dementia, pulmonary disease or like Cowboy Jack, end-stage heart failure qualifies for hospice.

Jack Walker was a 65-year-old farmer diagnosed with terminal heart failure. The older man, though, "corrected" the diagnosis to a *broken heart*, since his wife of 45 years had passed away six months ago. It wasn't long after his dear Josefina's funeral that Jack suffered a massive myocardial infarction. Unfortunately, while the stubborn fool was in the hospital, he signed himself out against medical advice, only to suffer yet *another* heart attack!

The depressed economy hit the farming industry hard, real hard, and the man felt like his ranch couldn't do without him pretty much 24/7. In reality, the bigger concern was that Jack felt the urgency to be home, where he felt closest to Josefina.

Long ago, Josefina and Jack started a lovely tradition for the two of them. It happened by accident when mission-driven Josefina angrily rode her horse to where Jack was mending a split rail fence and demanded that he get on his horse and follow her. Josefina had had enough of Jack distancing himself from her by immersing himself 110% in work. His routine seven days a week, 365 days a year was: Jack would wake up at the crack of dawn, swiftly chug down his coffee, shovel in breakfast and then race out for a day's work on the farm. Often the sun would set and Jack would keep working. More often than not, they would pass like ships in the night with little if any interaction between them.

For 13 of those hours each day, Jack would feed and groom the animals, cut, roll and load hay, administer routine vaccines, trouble shoot any mechanical problems, mend fences, gates...the list was never ending. But no matter where Jack was, his hound dog Ernie was always close behind. Sad thing was, Josefina wasn't.

Josefina, if truth be told, was feeling like Ernie spent more quality time with her husband than she did. Sadly, during the last four months the two barely had said good morning and good night before the punishing cycle started all over again on a relentless daily basis. Jack was a quiet man by nature who felt idle chatter was a waste of time because it supposedly siphoned him away from taking care of necessary chores. So Cowboy Jack remained mute most of the time, not because he was being purposefully mean, but because he had merely gotten his priorities woefully mixed up. He believed the farm to be more important than his relationship with his wife. Being male, he adopted a single focus so predominant among men, and was oblivious to everything except the needs of the farm.

One day his wife's bottled-up feelings of being alone finally erupted until she just couldn't take it anymore. Josefina was in the barn shoveling muck when she suddenly threw down the shovel, possessed with a take-no-prisoners mission. She quickly mounted her horse to have a little *talk* with her husband.

Jack stopped tightening the fence wire when he heard the sound of hoofs and saw Josefina riding toward him. Sensing Armageddon, Jack whispered to himself,

"*Oh, Nellie.*" Jack had no idea what had precipitated Josefina's arrival that interrupted his work, but he was pretty darned sure he was about to experience the end of the world as he knew it!

Jack could see by the look on her face he was in some kind of trouble, he just couldn't fathom what nor why! Josefina pulled the reins on her Palomino, straightened her back and raised her head high. In a no-nonsense, don't-even-think-of-messing-with-me voice she yelled,

"Jack Mitchell Walker, I want you to STOP what you're doing right now, ya hear me? We need to talk!"

The 6'6" tall man with his sturdy, muscular frame and signature cowboy hat, was the spitting image of John Wayne. *Nobody* ever gave him lip, absolutely *nobody*, well, except for Josefina. When his feisty Hispanic wife was angry, it wasn't "*purdy*."

Jack raised his cowboy hat to smooth the wavy strands of brown hair that were soaked with sweat. He sighed and momentarily seemed to cower away from this woman possessed. Josefina's brown eyes were intense, almost piercing and when they flashed like they were flashing now, he knew she fiercely meant business. Their dog Ernie put his tail between his legs and whined as he sought refuge behind his master.

"Damn it, Jack Mitchell. Get on your horse and follow me. Now!" she commanded.

The cowboy's dark, thick eyebrows furrowed at this annoying and unexpected interruption. Jack kicked the dirt and pouted like a spoiled child.

"I'm already a month behind on this work, woman!"

Josefina quickly turned back one more time giving him a withering "if you want to live, follow me" look; Jack knew she meant business. He grumbled to himself, but remained silent while he mounted his beautiful black 16-hand thoroughbred. Josefina slowly galloped ahead, mute.

Off and on throughout their decades of marriage, Jack would have cyclical periods where he became so immersed in work that he forgot how to love, how to enjoy life and family. Each cycle became longer than the last, making her wonder if someday the distance he put between them would become their permanent way of life.

Josefina was deep in thought about how to turn their relationship around. The two rode quietly on the dirt trail before coming to a magnificent valley filled with wild flowers. She stopped to admire the remarkable beauty of the valley's verdant, grassy meadow and appreciate the floral scent that wafted in the crisp air.

Josefina dismounted and tied her horse to a tree. Her husband audibly exhaled, then shook his head in preparation for *the talk* he knew was imminent.

The two sat side-by-side, looking straight ahead for several minutes. Jack slowly turned to gaze at his wife. The gentle breeze was blowing Josefina's long silky black hair away from her face and shoulders, exposing a beautiful, yet utterly defeated face. Her silhouette riveted Jack as she continued to drink in the beauty of the vast valley below.

All they heard were birds chirping, leaves blowing and Ernie loudly chewing sandspurs off his brown and black paws, next to Jack. Yep, Ernie had followed his master and the horses all the way to this remote corner of the ranch.

Jack continued to admire his wife's youthful elegance, which took him way back to memories of long ago and how they first met. A release in tension between the two of them had occurred without so much as a word being spoken. Jack scooted over, narrowing the gap between him and Josefina. The hound-dog in turn rolled on his back closer to Jack, occasionally slapping a big paw on his lap in an attempt to gain Jack's attention.

For once, Jack didn't notice the proffered paw for he was too focused on his wife. He had to grudgingly admit that the distance he had put between them these many months made her seem more like a stranger than his wife. However, he was now acutely aware of the comforting warmth of her body next to his and the lavender scent of her skin. Ahh, the wonderfully familiar, he remembered.

Jack lightly draped his arm over his wife's narrow shoulders. A random memory made him smile as he looked at Josefina. He chuckled out loud.

"Do you remember our first dinner together?"

The question seemed to immediately strike a humorous chord with his spouse. Josefina couldn't help but laugh,

"Of course! How could I forget? You ate as if it would be your last meal. You dribbled steak sauce all over your white button-down shirt! Thought it would be my first and last dinner date with you, Jack Mitchell!" The diminutive woman smiled as she turned to look at her husband.

Jack raised his hands in defense,

"Hey, I was only a 17-year-old-kid who was so nervous about our first date that I didn't eat all day before I picked you up. When I saw that big hunk of juicy steak on my plate, my taste buds went into overdrive, which made me drool like old Ernie here. You've gotta admit I have me some manners now, woman!"

Josefina shook her head, "Is that so? Well, just last week I walked in the kitchen and you had my fresh blueberry pie all over your cheeks and pie crust crumbs had been dropped all over my kitchen floor!"

Jack rolled his eyes toward his furry canine kid.

"Ok, I guess it's time to fess up. Ernie jumped up and knocked your pie off the stove. You warned me about what would happen to *MY dog* next time he got into your baked goods. So there was only one thing for me to do—let him out, smear blueberry pie on my face and take the rap."

Ernie was snoring with his pink belly up, totally unaware his sweet sleepy face festooned with upturned floppy jowls was creating a soft spot in Josefina's heart.

"Ok, my dear husband, your old pup gets another pass due to your honesty."

Their laughter sounded musical as they reminisced about all they had shared over the years. For the first time in ages, there was a torrent of communication between Jack and Josefina.

After a couple hours had passed, the brilliant glow in the Western sky illuminated the true beauty of their love. Their joint journey to the setting sun created something magical that day, a momentous resurrection of their love. No matter how busy, troubled or stressed the two from that landmark day on were, they always made it a point to take the time to mark the passing of another day watching the sunset together at that very spot overlooking the verdant valley.

When Josefina passed away on a cold winter day in December, Jack and Ernie carried on the ritual. He found sunset was the perfect time for him to be able to communicate with Josefina after her passing. Jack clearly felt her presence and knew she was there with him and Ernie. It gave him great peace to know she was present and her spirit was very much alive.

Jack Walker's multiple heart attacks since his wife's death caused his heart to become so weak that his organs were failing from lack of oxygenation and blood-flow. He had benefitted from hospice home care for a while, but the physical and medical demands had become too extreme for his family to handle, thus he reluctantly consented to spending his remaining days in Bed 39 at the new hospice facility.

The diminutive Sister Mary Patrick wheeled Jack up to his room when he arrived at hospice. The distraught man took one glimpse then started yelling! Nurse Libby couldn't help but hear the commotion and came running.

"Hello, Mr. Walker. I'm Nurse Libby. Please, tell me why you're so upset."

The man squirmed and started to roll his wheelchair out the door.

" Dagnabbit nurse, it's just *wrong* putting me in this north-facing room! I need a view of the Western Sky. I must be in a room where I can watch the setting sun and talk to my dear Josefina! Can't do that in this room."

Mr. Walker wheeled himself down the hall with Nurse Libby in rapid pursuit.

"Just hold your horses, cowboy Jack!" she ordered as they careened around a corner. I have news for you! Good news!

It just so happened that Nurse Libby was aware of an available room with a perfect view of the park's rolling green hills and the western sky. The elderly nurse smiled, and then waved at Sister Mary Patrick to accompany her and Mr. Walker to Bed 39. Mr. Walker looked up to see the elderly nurse push his wheelchair in a different direction. "Nurse Libby, dang, I should be pushing you in this wheelchair! How old are you anyway?"

The broad-shouldered, gray-haired nurse shook with laughter.

"Cowboy Jack, I may not be a spring chicken anymore and some folks may call me ancient, but I can still beat *you* in a foot race! So let's head on to your brand new room with a western view!"

Mr. Walker enjoyed having a nurse with a sense of humor, and someone who was feisty like Josefina.

"Nurse Libby, get this cardiac carriage a movin'! Yee haw! Giddy up now, ya hear!"

When Nurse Libby, Jack and Sister Mary Patrick entered the room, the curtains were wide open. This western view showcased green meandering hills and a nature trail. The sun was shining down upon beautiful, strategically planted rose gardens surrounding an angel statue. Dotted upon the hillside were scattered wild daisies. All three were quiet as Jack absorbed the lovely landscape. Jack cleared his throat then spoke in almost a whisper.

"Ladies, this room will be just fine." The smile that accompanied the statement really said it all.

When a patient was first admitted to hospice, the flurry of activity usually lasted for the first hour or two. Initially the patient was greeted by the nurses, including the aides and pastoral care staff or volunteers. Later throughout the week, a number of hospice team members such as the physician, counselors, social services staff, a dietician, and someone from physical therapy introduced themselves to get to know the patient for many reasons including identifying his or her needs, special requests and preferences.

One of Cowboy Jack's most fervent requests was to have his dog Ernie visit him in hospice. His aging 15-year old canine-child was now considered a senior citizen by his veterinarian. It was hard enough to be without Josefina, so he dreaded being away from his constant canine companion as well.

Mr. Walker's son, Henry, was currently taking care of Ernie while his Dad was in hospice. Another concern for the family was that Ernie had been diagnosed with lymphoma almost a year ago. The trip to the vet was triggered when Jack noticed Ernie's lymph nodes were enlarged and he had lost weight. Jack was horrified to learn that Ernie had canine lymphoma which is similar to Non-Hodgkin's Lymphoma in humans. Lymphoma is a cancer with two specific types of white blood cells, T and B cells, which are lymphocytes. Lymphocytes are a part of the immune system that help the body protect itself from illness and disease. Lymphoma is the most common cancer in canines and without treatment, the life expectancy is only two months following diagnosis.

A local non-profit organization had assisted Jack by paying for Ernie's chemotherapy. The veterinarian told him that with a combination of chemotherapy and drugs, Ernie had an 80 - 90% chance of going into remission.

Remission would be formally declared when Ernie had a complete resolution of all the signs and symptoms of the disease.

Unfortunately, since there was no cure for lymphoma, even with state-of-the-art chemotherapy and radiation, the prognosis was only a life span of 14-16 months. Canines in general do respond favorably to chemotherapy and suffer minimal side effects. Sadly though, less than 5% live to or beyond 24 months.

Nurse Libby walked in and noted all the pictures of Ernie and Josefina in Cowboy Jack's room.

"You know what, Cowboy Jack?"

He replied in his low-pitched voice...

"What my lovely, Libby?"

Nurse Libby scooted a chair closer to Cowboy Jack. "It took years for this hospice to be established right here in St. Louis," the kindly nurse explained. "A one of a kind facility! Well, I bet you may think I'm crazy, but I have a feeling there will be hospice veterinarians someday, doctors who will see the patient through to the end of their life. Hey, maybe even animal hospice facilities, too! No one wants to see animals or humans suffer, right? Maybe some veterinarian offices will eventually have grieving rooms large enough for the whole family to be with their pet until the final moment. Yes, then maybe grief counseling, too, for the owners."

Cowboy Jack looked out the window and kept watch for his son, well, for *both* of them. The human and the furry one were scheduled to visit today. Jack Walker's son, Henry, had lived out of the country until his mother Josefina passed away. After his mother passed, Henry made the difficult decision to uproot his family in order for them to move in with his father.

Unfortunately, Henry and his wife both worked full-time and were not always available to tend to Ernie or his father Jack's physical needs. A home-care hospice nurse had been coming to the home throughout the day for several months, however, Jack's condition had deteriorated to the point where both father and son felt an in-patient hospice was needed. The hospice staff worked cohesively as a team in order to assess Jack's needs and address his and his family's concerns. Shortly after Jack arrived and got settled in, Henry walked in to visit his father. His son was a tall man like his father, however much more slender in build than Jack with darker features like his mother. On the leash next to him was old Ernie.

"Hey Dad, look who I brought?"

Jack sat up in bed and smiled from ear-to-ear when he saw both sons, one human, the other canine. Once the furry son saw Jack in the bed, the weak, cancer-riddled black–and-tan coonhound jumped up on the bed to be as near as possible to his beloved master. Ernie was about two feet tall and used to weigh close to 80 pounds. He was now emaciated after losing 25 pounds due to the ravages of cancer. But this coonhound wasn't calling it quits just yet!

Coonhounds are also referred to as scent-hounds because of their amazing specialized olfactory ability. If there were a raccoon anywhere within a mile radius, Ernie would be on the critter's heels. Amazingly, it was Ernie who smelled the scent of cancer on Josefina. And now it was clear he knew Jack's heart was an issue. While Ernie had hopped up on Bed 39 to be closer to Jack, he suddenly raised his head, sniffed multiple times, then turned his head downward in order to poke his nose between the buttons on Jack's flannel pajamas. Jack thought it was hilarious!

"Dagnabbit! This dog doesn't miss a *thing* does he? Ernie knows I have an ailing heart. Don't ya boy? Who needs a doctor when we have good old Dr. Ernie, right here! Son, remember how Josefina complained about Ernie licking her left ear? Dang, that dog was like a duck on a June bug about it! Sometimes your mother would get mad as a wet hen because he just would not stop!" Jack paused to cough and clear his throat.

"Yep, I told her that everything about that is just wrong, 'cuz Ernie doesn't sniff like that when everything is okay! Gees, your mom would get testy and say,

'You trying to tell me he's sniffin' my head because I'm crazy? Well, that's not funny at all!'" Jack recalled with a bittersweet laugh.

Henry was smiling while his Dad told his story. Both men were petting the sleeping coonhound. Every time Ernie heard his name mentioned, the dog would open one sleepy eye, then slowly close it again. Henry scratched his head,

"Dad, how long was it before mom saw a doctor?"

Jack shook his head, rolled his eyes and sighed.

"Dang stubborn woman, she just refused to think my furry son here could actually *smell* a medical problem. Hmmm, maybe it was two months later, when she complained about having difficulty seeing. That very next day while lunging the horses, she fell down. Told me she had the worst headache ever and couldn't get her feet to work."

Henry looking sad, nodded his head.

"Yes, I will never forget your call. I took the first flight out and tried to tell myself the whole way that it wasn't anything bad. Deep inside, though, I knew that as strong as mother was, it had to be very serious in order for you to call an ambulance."

There was a tear in his father's eyes as he recalled that dreadful day.

"It was in the emergency room when she had a seizure and then another which threw her into a coma. That's when I learned that my Josefina had an aggressive form of brain cancer. As I'm sure you recall, she never woke up after that day, never had a chance to watch even one more sunset."

Henry became uncomfortable recalling such horrifying memories. He started fidgeting in his chair and then stood up to stretch.

"Dad, I better head on out now. Nurse Libby said Ernie could stay overnight with you. Would you like that? I brought him some food I got from the veterinarian's office. The food is specifically for his cancer diet—high-protein low-carbohydrate. That is what they feed dogs with cancer nowadays!

"Funny, I didn't know they had such a thing. Here is a big overstuffed pillow-bed for Ernie, since I know the staff doesn't want him sleeping directly on your bedspread or sheets."

The two men hugged, Jack whispered his thanks to his son and his great pleasure to have Ernie stay behind with him. Then his son grabbed his coat and left for the evening.

Jack was thrilled with the news that Ernie could stay, but sad his son was leaving. He marveled that the overnight dog visitation was so heartily approved by hospice. He felt overwhelming gratitude for this surprising endorsement.

A little later one of the nurse's aides took Ernie out after she fed him. The dog then retired to his new pad on the floor next to Jack's bed. The two slept comfortably the entire night like old times again.

In the morning, the hospice aide fed Ernie, made sure Jack had his breakfast tray and then took Ernie outside for a brief stroll.

Shortly after, Nurse Libby walked into the room and couldn't resist grinning at the patient and his dog. Ernie had crumbles of food mixed with slobber on his snout and Jack's gown and chin were decorated with dribbles of ketchup. The older nurse chuckled,

"My, my, Mr. Messy, let me get you a little napkin!"

Jack was surprised that *he* was who Nurse Libby was calling Mr. Messy.

"Dagnabbit! You're just like Josefina! That wife of mine was more like a proper city-slicker when it came to manners.

"Jack, you're using the wrong fork,

"Jack, you dripped hamburger grease on your new shirt,

"Jack, you don't have to eat the whole chicken in one bite!"

The man paused then went on as he gently tapped his heart.

"But I loved that woman. Funny how I used to make excuses for spilling on myself,

"Josefina, did you feel that earthquake? Shook the food right off my fork!

"Josefina, the spoon's too small! My pudding fell right off it!

"Josefina, you are the vision of pulchritude which makes me shiver with passion!

"I normally don't know big words like pulchritude, but I looked *beauty* up in the dictionary. I wanted as many words as possible to describe my wife. Know what Josefina said to that one, Nurse Libby?"

The kindly gray haired nurse sat in the chair next to Jack's bed, interested in what he had to say next,

"No, please tell me, Mr. Walker!"

The thin, fragile patient straightened up in bed, then cocked an exaggerated eye as if he were making his wife's facial expression. "My Josefina had a real attitude and said,

'Puke-ritude? I make you sick, Jack Mitchell? Now that 's not nice is it? Not proper at all! Next time you and Ernie dribble all over my floor, I'm going to buy you both bibs!'"

Jack, tickled at his own words, slapped his leg while laughing. Ernie got excited and thought he was signaling him to come up and join him on the bed.

"Nurse Libby, my Josefina was always prepared for everything, strangely, even her own death. Two weeks before her hospitalization, Josefina called our son and asked if he could visit soon. She also insisted we see her aunts, uncles and cousins in her old hometown. I didn't understand it, however, she had this particular look in her eyes that I didn't question. She bought each of them a stained glass sun-catcher with a cross. I thought that was strange since it wasn't Christmas or a birthday or anything like that. But, Josefina had a kind heart.

"I just thought it made her feel good to leave a present for each of them."

Nurse Libby empathetically patted Jack's knee.

"The Lord works in strange ways, Mr. Walker. He allowed Josefina more time to say good-bye to those she loved. They say that whenever a bright ray reflects light through a sun-catcher, your departed loved one is near. Those who were dear to Josefina have something beautiful to remember her by and will know she is there with them."

Cowboy Jack looked down at Ernie and then at Nurse Libby.

"I told Ernie that I'll be damned if he dies before me! Better be strong for me Ernie, my heart couldn't take another loss. When Josefina passed away, I took her urn and rode my horse to the same spot on our property that we've been going to together for the past 14 years—that gorgeous, verdant valley. Those moments we had under that old oak tree, watching the sunset each night, saved our marriage. I nearly destroyed our union thanks to my danged single-minded focus on work. Once we met at that spot at the end of each day, I suddenly remembered how much I truly loved her. So it was only fitting I sent her ashes aloft on that spot. It felt so right for me to open the urn, and release my precious Josefina's ashes into the wind. They blew upward and then into the western sky, toward the setting sun..."

That afternoon, a social worker arranged to have a veterinary staff member take Ernie for his chemotherapy session. Mr. Walker's color was more ashen that evening and he was much too weak to even feed himself. Nurse Libby gave Jack some oxygen to make him comfortable.

It was after lunch when he developed intense mid-chest pressure and became diaphoretic. Nurse Libby was with Jack most of the day. She was growing steadily uneasy about his condition and felt it necessary to call Jack's son and suggest he come to hospice to see his dad.

The chest pain reoccurred again for 10 minutes, and then subsided after another dose of morphine. Despite Jack's weakness, he insisted on being put into his wheelchair, and rolled to the window.

"Please Nurse Libby, it's almost 'that' time," he implored. She couldn't refuse him, of course.

What gave Jack comfort was gazing out the window so he could talk to Josefina. As the orange glow of the sun slowly crept behind the rolling hills, he began his discourse.

"Dang, woman, I know it wasn't easy to put up with me all those years. I'd get my head so wrapped up with work, so worried we'd lose the farm, that I put my total focus and energy into the ranch. I knew I had a bad heart, but I still wanted you to have a home when I died. Never did I think you would go first! Thank God you finally got pissed off enough to talk some sense into me!

"Josefina, you made me realize that even if we lost the farm, we still had each other, but if I continued shutting you out, if I lost your love, I would have nothing.

"The last fourteen years out of our 45 together were the happiest. You weren't just a wife, but my best friend, too, and only God knows just how much I miss you now."

The man seated at the window stared up into the sky, as if he were searching for something or someone. Little did he know that Josefina was gazing back. She saw her man, who so strongly resembled the Duke with his handsome good looks, imposing tall frame and broad shoulders. Yes, in her eyes, he was still that man. She did not see a frail dying patient in a wheelchair; she saw her Jack, who was a vision of pulchritude, a true beauty in all phases of his life including now.

Ernie was responding well for six months on chemotherapy. It was not the cancer that caused his death. It was a broken heart. Both Jack and his beloved coonhound, Ernie, died the same day. So Jack did not have to feel the pain of another loss but the joy of a reunion with those he loved, including his canine son.

When the coroner came to take Jack Walker out of Bed 39, Nurse Libby and Sister Mary Patrick both remained and sat by the window. Neither woman said a word as they gazed at the brilliant reddish orange ball on the horizon.

Strangely, the blazing glow seemed to light up the entire celestial sphere, and even the room. As the sun gradually lowered behind the rolling foothills it fittingly reminded them of the slow closure of curtains on a Broadway stage following the finale. Of course, this *was* the end of a memorable play, a love story about Jack and Josefina. This *theatre of life* will only play this story once, because there will only be one Cowboy Jack and one Josefina. But now for the encore...

Jack Mitchell Walker's memorial service was held later that week in unincorporated West St. Louis County, at the very spot where he and his wife rekindled their love fourteen years ago. Friends, family and relatives rode horses to the clearing where the valley was vibrantly green treating them to a dazzling display of colors offered by the wild field flowers in the meadow below. Nurse Libby and Sister Mary Patrick traveled by horse drawn wagon carrying the urns.

Bed 39

As the sun began to set, Jack's and Ernie's ashes were released into the orange glow of the Western Sky—the very same farewell Josefina's ashes had been given by Jack.

Nurse Libby thought she saw movement out of the corner of her eye down in the valley and quickly turned to check it out. In awe-inspired amazement, the nurse suddenly and clearly saw Jack and Josefina riding their horses into the Light with Ernie running close behind. Before he rode completely out of sight, he turned one last time, then waved. Nurse Libby nodded her head while slowly raising her hand in acknowledgement.

"Good-bye my dear, Cowboy Jack, good-bye to you and your western Sky."

CHAPTER 13

2000
Lunch with An Angel

DURING MY TIME HERE IN Bed 39, I've witnessed incredibly kind acts by countless devoted health care professionals who truly inspired me. There are two nurses in particular who have warmed my heart and made me smile more than any other persons. Those nurses are, of course, my Mia and Nurse Libby. Libby was only thirteen years old when she first met her future husband, Clarence. He was a shy, intellectual young lad who paid another student to deliver a box of chocolates to Libby on Valentine's Day. Clarence worked for one solid week at his dad's hardware store in order to earn money for Libby's candy. He spent another week composing a special poem he hoped would touch her heart and get her attention. He was totally smitten with her, but doubted she was even aware he existed. This poem would do the trick, he was sure, if only he could find the right words. He'd write, then erase, write a little more, then erase, write *again* until he finished, then erase the whole darn thing and start over. In the end, 13-year-old Clarence came up with these words for Libby:

> *Don't know if you ever realized...*
> *How your friendship would be my Nobel Prize.*
> *You're everything I'm not, but want to be.*
> *Looks, charm and wit, like a real celebrity.*
> *I have the brains and I work hard, too.*

> *But what I don't have yet...is you.*
> *Your chocolate brown eyes make me melt.*
> *A feeling I've certainly never felt.*
> *My Valentine I hope you'll be...Please Dear Libby, consider me.*
> Love, Clarence.

Clarence hid behind an old oak tree as his friend gave Libby the box of chocolates. Once he heard her voice, he peeked out ever so slightly in order to see her response. His heart went from literally palpitating out of his chest one minute, to almost coming to a dead stop, when he heard her say,

"*Clarence? Who in the heck is Clarence?*"

Libby liked the delectable chocolates as well as the friend who delivered them. And she wasn't kidding when she asked who Clarence was. She had no clue, but his friend was another matter.

The two dated for the rest of the school year. Poor Clarence was always too embarrassed to force the issue or to even admit he was the one who sent them to her. It wasn't until they were in the same Algebra class that Libby became impressed with the "smart boy." She eventually asked Clarence to tutor her after class.

Fortunately, within a few weeks both she and Clarence were both making A's. Their study sessions led to a good friendship but nothing more until their junior year. Heck, Libby never connected Clarence as being the same one who gave her the chocolates and the poem in the 8th grade.

During the summer of their junior year, Clarence worked six days a week at his father's store. By the time school started, he now had money for more fashionable attire as well as a bicycle built for two. In addition, all the heavy lifting at the hardware store packed some muscles on his previously scrawny frame.

The young man had such high intelligence that he didn't need to invest hours of his time studying like most kids. Instead, he spent time volunteering with a local accounting firm. His vision of the future was clear. He wanted to be an accountant someday and have Libby as his wife. That first semester of their junior year, Clarence and Libby had geometry together.

He marveled that this beguiling young woman had the most gorgeous brown eyes that seemed to see into the very core of his shy soul.

Clarence thought he might finally be getting into the groove of learning about women. He sure had enough flirt with him that summer at his Daddy's hardware store. Heck, one older woman even pinched his bum as he packed her order into the back of the car. Yep, there were others, too. Truth be told, many females flirted with the now tall, dark and handsome lad at the hardware store.

There was something different about Clarence. He was the eternal gentleman who never flirted back even when the most popular girl in school came to see him at the store. One day she walked into the store as if she owned the place, then slowly waved a card containing her phone number in front of his face. The seductive sorority girl rubbed the card up and down his brawny chest before she stuffed it into his pocket and left.

Clarence's dad witnessed what had just brazenly transpired in front of his eyes. He hooted and hollered at how women were going to great lengths to win his son's affection. The older man grabbed the note that was none-too-subtlety decorated with a red kiss emblazoned on it.

"Son, you have certainly been good for my business this summer!"

Clarence sadly shook his head and replied,

"Dad, there's only one woman my heart has room for and unfortunately, geometry is her only interest in me.

That next Saturday both Libby and Clarence were scheduled to study for geometry. Clarence pulled up in his bicycle built for two. He slowly walked to the door, fearful that Libby would be mortified at the thought of a date, but determined to find out if his fantasy had any chance of becoming reality. He doubted so, but was resolved to discover whatever the answer may be.

Clarence knocked on the thick wooden front door. His knees were weak and his respiration was rapid. He thought he might faint, but mustered his determination regardless.

Libby answered the door wearing a sky blue sweater and a tan skirt. Clarence, dazzled by her appearance, sheepishly asked her if she would like to go eat instead of study. His world stopped still as he held his breath waiting for her response. Truth be told, Clarence surprised her and she was sincerely puzzled by his suggestion to do something fun as opposed to cracking the books. But there on the back of his bicycle built for two she spotted a picnic basket.

"Libby, I packed us a lunch in hopes you'd say yes."

The young woman turned, then looked deeply into his pleading, almost black eyes,

"Gees Clarence, do you know how long I've waited for this moment? I thought you would never ask! Oh, and by the way, I've *always* been good in math!"

Libby gave him a wink as she ran to climb on the bike. Relief flooded Clarence and joy made his heart pound uncontrollably. He knew he was the happiest man alive!

The two scampered playfully as if they were children. Libby waved her arms up in the air as Clarence peddled downhill. Her skirt blew in the wind somehow reflecting how free and relieved both felt about entering a new dimension in their relationship.

"Look, no hands, Clarence!" Libby giggled.

Together they cycled several miles through the scenic rolling green hills of Ireland then later through Phoenix Park in Dublin. An inviting spot caught her eye as they were about to pass it by. Libby frantically pointed to a small area under a large alder tree. Clarence was quick to respond and brought them to the perfect spot for their picnic. Libby wasn't used to riding bikes for so long and it showed. She walked to the tree as if she were still on a saddle. Clarence looked at Libby and laughed. Everything she did and everything she said amused this young man. After what seemed like an eternity of pining away for Libby, he could not believe she was showing interest in him. Thrilled doesn't begin to describe his euphoria.

The two sat across from one another and talked endlessly for hours under the shade of the alder tree. Time truly did seem to stand still as their magical day faded into evening. A chill filled the air after the sun went down and Clarence noticed Libby was shivering so badly that goose-bumps were forming on her arms. He summoned all his courage as he moved close to her and took her in his arms partially to warm her up and also to kiss her. He gave her a long, lingering passionate kiss—one that he had imagined for so many years. Now, finally, it was reality. He met no resistance from Libby. The two embraced as they watched the setting sun. So intent were their hours of conversation that the lunch went un-touched that day—without a doubt, their time together had indeed finally come.

Libby and Clarence married shortly after graduation the following year. They had more than fifty amazing years together before Libby's dear husband Clarence passed away. Clarence always called Libby his angel, his gift from God. He never once changed his mind!

There was another person who felt Libby was her hero and the closest thing to an angel earth side. A young woman walked up to the nurses' station at 12 noon and called to Libby who was at the desk. The fair blonde-haired woman dressed in a forest green sweater and plaid skirt fidgeted at the desk.

"Nurse Libby, do you remember me? I'm Cheryl Edwards. You took care of my mum, Madeline, when she was in Bed 39."

The older woman approached her with a broad smile on her face.

"Of course I do, darlin'! You are a nursing student right?"

The young woman gave a sigh of relief knowing she was recognized.

"Yes! Yes, Nurse Libby. You remember! I want you to know what a blessing it was to have you as my mum's nurse. Don't know what she and my family would have done without you! I'm sorry for just walking in today, but I was wondering if I could buy you lunch in the cafeteria. You see, I'm a junior in nursing school and would like to ask you a few questions about hospice."

Nurse Libby was flattered that she was being pursued in order to share her hospice experience. Nothing was dearer to her heart other than Clarence.

"Yes, I haven't eaten yet, so I would be pleased to join you!" the RN responded.

Cheryl Edwards brought two bowls of piping hot pea soup, two raisin scones and a pot of tea to the table for their lunch. Once seated across from one another, the young woman pulled out her notepad and pencil ready to record Libby's insights and knowledge.

"My mum was only 45 years old when she died. It was heartbreakingly premature," Cheryl told Libby as tears welled up in her eyes. "She died only four weeks from the date she was diagnosed with cancer."

"My mum, father, brothers, sisters and I were in a state of denial about the terminal nature of her ovarian cancer," she remembered. "I guess that was pretty obvious to the staff here. The entire hospice team helped us cope with and eventually accept her prognosis, but you especially made the greatest impact on us and helped us the most.

"In fact, you were such an inspiration to me that I am considering becoming a hospice nurse. I have so many questions like how does someone know when to come to hospice and what is the difference between hospice and palliative care? I hear about both and am confused about how they differ.

"I know we just have lunch to discuss this, however anything you can share will be appreciated. Just jump in and tell me what comes to mind about any aspect of it. I am all ears."

The older nurse tilted her head as if she were going through a mental rolodex of people and events over the last four decades, took a deep breath and began. She momentarily reached for the scone, but put it back down as she began to talk.

"Alright, there's a load of information to put in a nutshell over lunch. I'll share with you what I can, but there's so much more you'll need to know. This hospice movement is still in its infancy, but will begin to explode in popularity by the 21st century, mark my words.

"There are already free-standing hospice facilities popping up all over the world. The public is becoming increasingly aware of the options available for themselves and their loved ones who are diagnosed with a devastating disease or end-stage illness. "

As Libby spoke, a couple of nurses walked by while excitedly waving their greeting when they spied the older, highly respected nurse.

"Hi Nurse Libby!" they chimed in unison.

The older nurse flashed them a warm smile,

"Hello my darlins'! Have a great day!"

She then turned to the inquisitive young woman across the table from her.

"Sorry my dear, now where was I? Oh, oh yes, palliative care and hospice are related, but as you know, they are not the same, but do go hand-in-hand. Hospice is appropriate when the referring physician believes that all medical treatments have been exhausted for the patient and death is likely to occur within six months of the referral.

"This means medical professionals officially acknowledge that the condition is terminal and, in spite of having explored the absolute best quality care and advanced treatments, there is nothing more the doctor can do to heal or treat the disease. Of course, sometimes the patient may not have a desire nor the will to seek further treatment or participate in experimental studies. It's a difficult process of letting go because everyone involved recognizes a cure at this point is unlikely short of Divine intervention. The patient just wants to be as pain free and comfortable as possible for whatever time they have left.

"As I mentioned, usually hospice care begins when the patient has around six months or less to live. That's not set in stone, though. The patient may opt for at-home hospice care or choose to move into a hospice facility."

The older woman looked up and paused in case Cheryl had questions, but hearing none, she resumed.

"In the case of palliative care, it's a specialty that focuses on relieving the pain, symptoms and stress of a disease or chronic illness. It doesn't have to be cancer necessarily or even an end-of-life situation and there typically isn't a time frame for treatment. The point is to reduce pain as much as possible and make the patient comfortable for as long as possible.

"There are, unfortunately, many patients who have to deal with chronic illnesses for a number of years, not just six months or less. In the case of palliative care, more aggressive forms of medical treatment may be instituted in order to obtain greater relief of symptoms. Oh, in some of these cases, the patient may even be awaiting a cure or participation in research trials when the opportunity arises."

The younger woman nodded her head and smiled back at Nurse Libby. "This is all starting to make sense to me!"

Libby took a sip of tea and continued. Once again she reached for the scone, but thought better of the idea so she could continue with a single focus.

"Now there are many times when a hospice patient may be given palliative care such as when a tumor is growing so rapidly that it's causing pain or the person is short of breath due to an ever-enlarging tumor. Their physician may even order the hospice patient a dose of chemotherapy or radiation to shrink a tumor to minimize discomfort. Because after all, no one wants the patient to suffer and anything we can do to make each day easier is a big benefit. So there may be a period of time where the hospice patient needs palliative care.

"The wonderful aspect of hospice and palliative care is that it engages a whole team of healthcare professionals who all work together. They share information about the patient with each other in order to develop a comprehensive care plan for the patient. When an individual finds out his or her condition is terminal or chronic, that is the time to call on palliative or hospice professionals— often both.

"As you found with your own mum, sometimes time is short for professionals to assist the family or for the patient to cope with the prognosis. When diagnosis to death is rapid, then it's imperative to quickly put together advanced directives so the family will know what their loved one wants to have done after they die. Advanced directives may involve legal aspects such as wills choosing a power of attorney, health information and such things as a living will, whether they wish life support to be used, and personal information such as funeral wishes, the location of letters and notes for family members."

The student nurse was writing as fast as she could, however, she momentarily paused to see Libby smiling at her.

"You remind me of myself when I was your age. I, too, wanted so desperately to know how to help terminal patients and always knew there had to be a better way to help them die with dignity, with more comfort and less pain. That was before hospice, of course! Now you are eager to absorb all that knowledge like a sponge, right now over this short lunch hour!" Libby chuckled.

"This passion you have now in your heart, this desire to be the best you can be as a nurse, is what's important. That drive to be a compassionate and knowledgeable nurse will necessitate your keeping up with classes in order to stay current with ever-evolving medical treatments during the course of your entire career.

"So, darlin,' keep reading, even after you have your RN. The learning never stops."

Nurse Libby glanced at her watch and was startled how much time had passed. She bid Cheryl goodbye as she arose to hurry back to tend to her patients. Both women looked at the food before them on the table. Lunch went untouched that day in favor of an invaluable exchange of information.

At the end of the following year, as Cheryl Edwards proudly walked up to the podium on graduation day, she shook the professor's hand, then kissed her diploma and whispered,

"Thank you my angel, thank you my dear Libby! I know exactly what direction I am going to go from here!"

Ms. Edwards, RN, went on to dedicate her life to being a hospice nurse. The year she embarked on this mission after her graduation from nursing school was the same year that Libby died peacefully in her sleep in hospice Bed 39.

Just as Libby drew her last breath, she opened her eyes to see her husband Clarence. He was on his bicycle built for two with a picnic basket tied to the rack. Libby waved while rushing to give her husband a kiss. They had so much to talk about and catch up on after all these years apart that they were far too busy to bother to eat a meal. Like their first picnic together, the picnic basket was just window dressing and their lunch went untouched that day.

CHAPTER 14

It's Always Hard to Say Good-Bye

I WATCHED LIBBY AND HER husband ride into the Light on their bicycle built for two. They looked so happy. She was a remarkably dedicated nurse that I had watched and admired for more than three decades. Today she left Bed 39 and this hospice for the last time.

I was left to reflect on the truth that only Libby and my beloved Mia made me smile every single time they walked into the 40-bed ward and later into this room. They were the two special nurses for me and probably for literally thousands of other patients over the years. They brought Light to the darkness and minimized the pain and suffering of countless patients.

Mia and Libby not only dramatically improved the lives of patients, but family members as well. They frequently listened calmly to feuding families while strategically quelling their wars so there would be no regrets later.

Of course, it wasn't always family members who were the angry ones. Sometimes, like in the case of Mrs. Bailey, it was the patient. Some were just plain cantankerous, but there also were patients who simply weren't ready to face death yet because there was so much more they wanted to see and do in this life. They clung to denial like it was a life raft! In these cases, if at all possible, Nurse Libby, the other nurses and hospice professionals encouraged the families to be actively involved with helping to make their loved one's last wishes a reality.

Mia chose to leave the hospital shortly after I passed away. She decided her calling was to work with children at the pediatric hospital. Nurse Libby was able to stay on to see the dawn of hospice first hand.

You may wonder why I chose to stay to tell stories of death and dying for those who occupied Bed 39. Surely, most do not want to delve into something so seemingly depressing.

In 1964, I was just a young man with wonderful caring parents and I presumed I had a whole earthly life to live. I hoped I would marry, have many children, and rescue a few cats and dogs along the way as well.

I dreamt about being there to watch my children marry and have children of their own. I figured I would be the fun grandpa who would teach them soccer and other sports, fill them up with soda, sweet yummy treats, give them loud toys and then send them home to their parents. My adult children would shake their heads then tell me how the kids have too much fun and get way too wound up when they were around grandpa! It would be delicious!

Then my grandkids would give grandma and me a kiss good-bye. The hugs would be warm and loving. The grandchildren would look out the back window of their parents' car waving good-bye as they clanged and tooted their noisy toys all the way home.

Makes me smile just thinking about it, however, that was not to be my reality. My soul had different plans. I was to stay on this earth in physical form for just a short twenty-seven years. And I would not recognize the love of my life—Mia AKA Pumpkin—until it was too late to officially, legally marry her because I was at death's door and time had run out.

At first this reality was so incredibly painful for both me and my parents. It was truly torture to witness such grief and I wanted to somehow make it better for all concerned.

For me personally, no cure was possible. But I had hope for others—hope their particular disease could be cured and they could live long, happy lives. I also hoped their death and dying experience would be far better than mine, and that this new modern day hospice would make a quantum difference. I dreamt about advances in medicine and research to enable other young men, women and children to live out long, full lives. Then, after many years when each came to the sunset of their life, they could die with dignity, peace and the comforts of home or at least in a warm, nurturing home-like environment, surrounded by dear family and friends.

Strangely, Bed 39 had been empty for the past day, however another terminal patient would be arriving soon. A sudden glow appeared next to my headboard and I wondered if it was my friend David Tasma. It had been awhile since he visited me and I so missed his stories and friendship.

But it wasn't David, it was something that made me even happier than seeing David, which is saying something! Before my eyes, the most engaging vision transformed in front of me and I could feel my heart beat fast with desire. It was my Mia!

It had never occurred to me that her life would end prematurely. But now, after all these decades, she came back to me, only this time in spirit form. Mia wore an amused expression, like "Surprise, here I am!"

Even though no window was open since hospitals and hospices in this day and age have central air conditioning, her blue floral skirt was billowing softly as if a gentle breeze were blowing. My love placed one hand on the headboard of Bed 39 and one hand was touching her heart over her white sweater. Gone was her hair tightly done up in a bun, instead Mia's hair was loosely draped around her shoulders beautifully framing her sweet, gorgeous face—just like it had on the day we found love at Forest Park.

I was considering my options. Uncontrollable emotions welled up from my soul and I suddenly yearned to walk out of the shadows and constraints of this bed to watch the sunset with Mia so we could revel in our totally unlimited spiritual essences. I became instantly aware that I was ready to complete my journey into the Light with the woman I love.

"Tomas, I've missed you so much and I feel like pulling you right out of Bed 39, so we can embrace once again and walk hand in hand into the Light. That will come my love, however, there has been something I've needed to tell you and what I hoped you may already have known. But if you don't know, get ready to hear something that will make your soul sing and surprise you mightily at the same time. Okay, here goes," Mia teased as she took a deep breath before she made her revelation. I could not remotely imagine what she was about to tell me, but I wanted to hear it as soon as possible!

"The day we found the full expression of our love for the first time in Forest Park was one of the most magnificent days of my life. Being wrapped in your arms, inhaling the fragrant scent of your skin and cloaked in your passion, was something that still sends chills throughout my body—albeit a spirit body now," Mia giggled at the change in state from physical to spirit. "Anyhow, that was a day I will never forget.

"But another equally heartfelt day was to come approximately nine months after your passing. The most heartfelt day for not only myself, but your parents as well, was the day our daughter was born. Yes, Tomas, the birth of our child, our daughter, Annie was the magnificent result of our love. I named her after your mother—I would have named her Tomas, but thought that might cause a few eyebrows to be raised and consign Annie to a life of explanations," Mia laughed.

"Annie was the light of her grandparents' lives and I don't know what I would have done without them all these years! Seamus and his kids continued to work at your parents' deli after you passed away and eventually so did our daughter Annie. She became close with Seamus's youngest son, Mickey.

"Ever since Annie and Mickey were toddlers, they automatically became best friends and that long term friendship blossomed into more when they were working side-by-side at the deli.

"Somehow I always knew they would marry someday and they did. Can you believe they have six children—five boys and only one girl! Three of the boys look like Seamus with their flame red hair and the other two like you, with dark brown hair and green eyes. Their eldest child is twelve and is quite the handful, just like his grandpa Seamus! He was named after his grandpa Bart Kaminski.

"I passed away a couple months ago and I will explain in a minute why I had to wait to come to you. Your father Bart was diagnosed with lung cancer eight months ago. He held on though as long as he could so he could watch his great grandchildren grow. He told them all about you as a child, what you were like and about your ways to get extra tips at the deli with your money-making game face! They loved that story and wanted him to repeat it over and over again!

"Bart's last wish here on earth was he wanted our daughter Annie, her husband and the grandkids to visit Bed 39. It was as close as he could get short of having them meet you in person. Unfortunately, it was after his death when our daughter corralled her husband, the kids and Grandpa Seamus altogether to make a pilgrimage to Bed 39–to their grandpa Tomas in a way. They will be here soon to pay homage to both you and

"Bart did not go to a hospice facility but instead opted for hospice home care which worked out perfectly. He passed away peacefully surrounded by his great grandchild, our daughter, her husband and great grandchildren in the wonderful home Father McCormack had given him and your mother in Dogtown.

"Bart passed away a couple weeks ago and your mother Annie, who had been relatively healthy for her age up until then, died a few days later. I guess it was literally due to a broken heart. They were so close, so intertwined, so inseparable that her soul would have it no other way. They are in the Light waiting for you now, however, they wanted your friend David to explain how you two are connected as family before you meet them on the other side. David should be here soon my love, but for now I will briefly catch you up about my own life after you passed and my death.

"Let's go back to 1964. Once you passed away, I just could not bear seeing Bed 39. Every day I'd come to work the tears would flow when I was visually reminded that you were no longer there for me. At the time, I didn't realize that your soul had become one with the bed.

"So, under the circumstances, I resigned from the hospital and ended up volunteering for decades at the children's hospital. Your mother, father, Seamus, his family and I all remained very close and we saw each other on a weekly basis. I grew to love Annie and Bart like my own parents and I was so grateful that they were such loving, fun grandparents!

"I spent the last three months helping with Sadie, our six-year-old granddaughter. Poor Sadie had congenital heart disease which necessitated a heart transplant. Since Annie and Mickey have five other kids they obviously had to tend to, I tried to be either at their house or wherever I was most needed to help out.

"Little Sadie is the light of my life and I loved reading her books, playing board games, singing songs or sometimes just sitting with her and holding her hand when her parents or Seamus and his ex-wife weren't able to be at the hospital. Now I adore those boys, too, however there was a certain closeness I had with Sadie. She received a heart transplant and we thought she was fine and all was well when suddenly out of nowhere, her new heart started to fail and my little princess was staring at death's door."

Mia stopped to wipe away a few tears.

"Tomas, it was all so very sad! When I thought my little Sadie was going to die, I knelt down at her bedside and prayed,

"Dear Lord, please let Sadie live…please! I've never asked much of anything from you and led my life as a good Christian woman. Lord, I beg you, spare this child and take me instead. I'm 63 years old, lived humbly, donated thousands upon thousands of dollars and thousands of hours of my time to help build this very hospital to save children. Was it all in vain? I ask you Dear Lord, please send me to Tomas…it is my time, not Sadie's.

"I kissed little Sadie and quietly left the room. At that moment, the chaplin entered her room to administer the last rights. Five minutes later I had a sudden cardiac arrest right at the nurses' station. The Lord answered my prayer.
    When my heart stopped, Sadie's heart re-started. I had to stay in afterlife form to be by her side during the healing process. Once I knew she was okay, then I was free to find the love of my life—you!" Mia concluded.

By now, it was me who was crying like a baby and my hand reached out from the confines of Bed 39 to hold Mia's. At that very moment, a loud ruckus erupted in the hallway and I heard children laughing, oops, and someone yelling too! It sounded like my old friend Seamus. Through the doorway walked our daughter, Annie, who didn't look like Mia, but like the blonde woman who used to come to me as a child! Annie had long silky blonde hair, blue eyes and strangely, was wearing a gray business suit. Then to my surprise I discovered David Tasma sitting on the little wooden chair next to my Bed 39. I smiled at my old friend as he began his revelation Mia mentioned would be coming.

"I believe Mia told you I have something I want you to know and that I'd be here to tell you. I believe the time has come for you to know. Tomas, you and I have discovered we have many things in common, but our biggest connection was my sister Dr. Hannah Tasma. I have not mentioned this previously, but the truth is she was your biological mother. Tragically, she died following childbirth and since Father McCormack's best friends were not able to have children, after much soul searching, he gave you to Bart and Annie Kaminiski. Having you was an answer to their prayers and their greatest gift!"

I was breathless with the news and suddenly was certain that the blonde lady in spirit who had visited with me off and on since I was six years old, was my biological mother, Hannah Tasma. The pieces all fell in place and now everything made sense.

Suddenly the sound of short, fast footsteps proceeded the arrival of five rambunctious boys ranging in age four through twelve. The eldest was named after my father, Bart, and he led the pack as they burst through the door. My sixty-five year old friend Seamus brought up the rear but was as loud as the young ones and was still wearing those darn tight jeans!

Mia and I grinned at our grandsons as they all walked in displaying their money-making game faces. Each of them had a little curl above their brow, just like grandpa used to wear! Then there was little Sadie holding her mother Annie's hand. Sadie looked like my Mia, with big brown eyes and long brown hair. At the rag-tag end of the parade a little bundle of energy ran pell-mell into the room. That required old man Seamus to raise his voice,

"Tommie, you can't be running all over the hospital. It's no playground!"

It was funny to see how three of the boys looked like Seamus and the other two like me with their dark brown hair and green eyes.

Seamus hollered again,

"Come on ya hooligans'! We finally found Bed 39! Kids, this bed was located in a big room called a ward and at the time, your grandpa was sick in this very Bed 39. Your grandma Mia was his nurse and they fell in love. Come on kids, gather round before the nurse finds us and kicks us all out of here! I have more to tell ya."

Lil' Bart suddenly piped up with a random question like kids sometimes do,

"Grandpa...I heard our neighbor Old Miss Lilly talking to Mrs. Stanford and she said I was just like Seamus, and she laughed kinda weird like! Grandpa, you're Seamus, so is that good or bad that I'm just like you?"

Seamus's eyes were wide as tennis balls as he recalled the exact same comments having been made about one of his kids decades before! Talk about a repeating cycle!

"Oh my God, save me! Of course it's a good thing, Bart. You're a fine, stand-up kind of guy and I'm very proud of who you are!" Lil' Bart's face lit up with pride from the compliment.

Annie and Mickey each put one hand on Bed 39's headboard and one on their heart. They took a moment of silence to say a prayer to both myself and their mother. Suddenly Tommie yelled,

"Mom, Bart is using his money-making game face to flirt with the nurses! He just ran to their station! I'm using mine for free cookies at the bakery!"

With that, the clan slowly filed out of the room, and Annie blew a kiss toward Bed 39 before she left.

Despite how new this fantastic family was to me, I warmed to them instantly. There was no getting-to-know-you time required! I loved them all on sight! I couldn't help grinning to myself with pride and unbridled delight. I finally had the family I always dreamed of having! And of course, Mia and I will be honored to watch over each of them with great love from heaven above.

A housekeeper entered the room humming a cheerful tune as she proceeded to mop the floor. She seemed to be enjoying the peace and quiet of this seemingly empty room.

Just then a bright white Light appeared in the corner of the room accompanied by a host of spirits. Their faces were indistinct, but I knew they were loved ones, friends, possibly guides and angels as well who were there to usher us into the Light to the other side.

The air in the room responded to the presence of the new arrivals by becoming chilly and almost thick. Often when spirits are present, the energy shifts and human beings frequently experience what they describe as an eerie sensation. It isn't really eerie, just different is all.

Nonetheless, the decided change in the feeling of the room caused the housekeeper to cease mopping. The lights flickered—an often tell-tale sign of spirit presence—then buzzed and soon there was an audible electrical snap! The old woman shrieked as she dropped the mop and fled from the room!

Suddenly a pronounced aroma of flowers filled the room—another common sign of spirit presence which is often a way those in spirit let their presence be known to those on earth. Often a floral scent that the person wore on earth is used to reassure a loved one that they indeed do still exist albeit in spirit form, sometimes it's a smell of smoke. Aromas and manipulation of lights and electricity are two frequently reported types of after death communication. It wasn't surprising both occurred right now since so many spirits were in the room.

I slowly reached my hand out from the bed for the first time in decades. I'd waited all these years to feel Mia's touch and now, finally now...her hand gently held mine. All doubt vanished as I became certain now was the time for me to be with Mia and for us to go into the Light together. My mission had been accomplished and I could go on in peace.

Before Mia and I went into the Light, David Tasma turned to reach for the bed and then looked at us and smiled,

"Tomas, you and Mia must go forth into the Light alone. It's my turn to keep vigil here at Bed 39 now. I will take over and witness the continued evolution of hospice for years to come. Later I will join you when I, too, can walk into the Light with my beloved Cecily."

I walked up to my poetic friend and gave him a warm embrace. David Tasma's life and my life had had such common but unusual similarities including finding great love for the first time in the sunset of our lives literally on our death beds. Not to mention the fact that as my mother's brother, he was my uncle on the earth plane! A tear ran down my face as I thought about how his profound love for Cicely Saunders had impacted not only my own life but eventually millions and millions of lives thanks to his support of Cicely's hospice dreams.

I wanted so much to let him know how much I appreciated all he had done.
"My dear friend, I was inspired to write a tribute for you that I've been wanting to share...your poetic nature awakened my own. Here's a poem I wrote that is dedicated to you, David," I explained.

"It's called, *The Poetry That Is David Tasma*

The gentle soul named David was a poetic, special man
He was forty, dying and all alone yet accepting of God's plan.
He knew the sun was setting and he'd soon be at death's door.
He sadly counted his final hours when his life would be no more.

But then a soul mate entered to usher him with grace,
Into his next existence, a smile was on her face.
The angel's name was Cicely, she shared her hopes and dreams
Of hospice helping people die with comfort it would seem.

This gentle soul named David was poetic in his heart,
Cicely could sense the truth from the very start.
He quickly fell in love with her and with what she saw and told
It touched him to his very core to help her dream unfold.

This gentle soul named David was a poetic, gentle man.
He encouraged Cicely to move forth, to take a greater stand!
Less pain for those experiencing their earthly, mortal death
And dignity and succor for the patient, a family less bereft.

This gentle soul saw Cicely's goal with clarity and vision,
So after death he showed support and gave money for her mission.
T'was quite a glorious ending for his life well-lived on earth
He found true love and enabled hospice to celebrate its birth.

We waved good-bye to our friend, my uncle David, as he became one with Bed 39. We knew we would be united again when he and Cecily entered the Light after completing their missions. Mia and I were thrilled with this newly organized hospice right here in St. Louis, the first of its kind in the state. We smiled as we saw with certainty that a time will come when hospice patients are discharged to return home, to live years longer thanks to advancements in medicine or to leave hospice care because a cure had been found.

I said my final farewell to Bed 39. Tears slowly welled up from deep within and literally cascaded from my eyes. Mia couldn't help but notice and remarked that my teardrops looked like gracefully falling stars slow dancing before they reached the ground. Now who was the poet!

No, I sincerely wasn't sad, just deeply touched. Mia knew with certainty my tears were tears of happiness and indeed they were.

My gratitude knew no bounds for my having been given the privilege of witnessing not death but the triumph of the human spirit, healings at the deepest level, and yes, the very core and foundation of hospice—unconditional love—all from my vantage point of Bed 39.

"It has been a glorious experience," I remarked to Mia even though she knew without question that's how I felt. "And now we're going to move on with each other to another enchanting experience: our romantic slow dancing through eternity together."

Bed 39

Epilogue

BED 39 AND THE HOSPITAL and later the hospice in which it resides in this novel, although fictitious, depict the very real saga of a world-wide movement that has changed the lives and deaths of countless millions for the better. Hospice has indeed become not only the physical place, but the generic term for a service and sometimes a facility that enables terminal patients to live their final days with as much dignity and comfort as possible.

When I researched hospice for this book, I read about an incredible woman who has profoundly inspired me. Cicely Saunders was born in Barnet Hertfordshire, England in 1918 and was raised in a family of great wealth. Over the course of her life, Cicely Saunders had such a strong, caring empathy for the less fortunate that she changed her career focus from politics to nursing.

As so often is the case in life, what appears to be an unfortunate turn of events transmutes into something profoundly beneficial. Such was the case for Cicely Saunders.

Her nursing career was dramatically shortened due to a serious back injury. The physically strenuous nature of nursing finalized her decision to re-enter school to become a medical social worker who specialized in cancer care.

She had a compassionate heart and always felt far more should be done for those who were terminally ill. It was during her work at St. Thomas Hospital in 1948, when she fell in love with a cancer patient named David Tasma, a Polish Jewish Refugee. David was only 40 years of age and knew very few people in London. Cicely Saunders was his social worker and made routine visits to Mr. Tasma. He was an intriguing man with a deep, kind, poetic nature.

Cicely Saunders grew to enjoy visiting her friend to discuss her vision of building a designated facility for the terminally ill. The two discussed Cicely's dream and desire to do more for those in their final days. She felt all terminal patients should be able to die with dignity, benefit from better pain control and to die in the comfort of a home-like facility or at their own home being tended to by hospice.

Cicely Saunders became increasingly determined to develop that plan of action and bring the concept into reality. Her gentle friend would enthusiastically and supportively listen to her ideas and endorse her plans to help those who were terminal. He would frequently say,

"I will be a window into your home."

His deep statement made reference to hospice being an alternative place to care for patients in their final days, a hospice that would be reminiscent of the comforts of a patient's own home.

On February 25, 1948, David Tasma came to the end of his earthly life. He had been a true inspiration and provided the courage to help Cicely Saunders walk forward toward her goal.

It was after his death that Cicely Saunders learned David Tasma willed her 500 pounds toward the establishment of the first hospice. His end-of-life wish was to help her move ahead with her dream to help others who were terminal.

As the years passed, Cicely took the necessary steps toward gaining the credentials that would enable her to have more influence in her quest to build a hospice. Friends encouraged her to go to medical school so she would have a greater voice in caring for those with cancer.

In 1957, Dr. Cicely Saunders graduated from St. Thomas Medical School at the age of thirty-nine. Amazingly, thanks to her wise investment, the first 500 pounds donated by David Tasma eventually became 500,000 pounds!

By 1967, her dream became a reality with the opening of St. Christopher's Hospice in South London. The facility was the first organized hospice in the world!

Cicely Saunders was a nurse, social worker, physician, author, public speaker and knighted by the Queen of England in recognition of her many accomplishments.

Befittingly, on July 14th, 2005, she, too, passed away at St. Christopher's Hospice. Many now walk up to the building and may never notice the large pane of glass at the front of the building or even realize the meaning behind it. The window placed at the entrance in honor of David Tasma was a literal translation of his promise to Cicely Saunders:

"I'll be a window in your home."

The story of Cicely Saunders reconfirms that many have and will continue to associate the word hospice with love. Her love for humanity and deep compassion for others helped build the first organized hospice in the world. For me, it's reassuring that there is a whole trained team to help terminal patients express their last wishes and be heard, and to assist both the patient and their family with end-stage issues including how to cope when one has to say good-bye to those they love.

Today there are now more than 5,800 hospice programs in the United States and over 100 in the U.K. In 2013, according to the National Hospice and Palliative Care Organization an estimated 1.5 to 1.6 million patients received services from hospices in the U.S.

The strides in cancer and other terminal disease research gives us all hope and faith that cures will be found. I am certain it would be Cicely Saunders' greatest joy to see that hospice is no longer needed because all terminal diseases have been cured.

But until that day comes, for now there is hospice. Thank God, thank you Cicely Saunders and David Tasma.

Recommended Reading:

Ice Within The Soul by Shawn Maureen McKelvie
Watch With Me: Inspiration for a life in Hospice Care by Cicely Saunders
Cicely Saunders: Selected Writings 1958-2004 book by Cicely Saunders
Three Stories of Francis by Jerre Cline
Life Without Lisa by Richard Ballo
Faces of Tolerance: Everyone Counts by Ella Nayor
Neon Bible by John Kennedy Toole

Artwork by Tom Bennett

References for: Bed 39

HOSPICE

St. Christopher's Hospice; retrieved from http://www.stchristophers.org.uk/

Hospice & Palliative Nurses Association; www.hpna.org

Cicely Sanders; retrieved from: http://en.wikipedia.org/wiki/Cicely_Saunders ;

http://www.bmj.com//content/suppl/2005/07/18/331.7509.DC1 ;

http://www.myhero.com/go/hero.asp?hero=Cicely_Saunders_06 ;

http://www.hektoeninternational.org/dame-cicely-saunders.html ;

History of Hospice Care | National Hospice and Palliative...

Missouri Hospice and Palliative Care Association www.mohospice.org/subpage.php?page=for consumers

www.nhpco.org/history-hospice-

http://www.thepositiveapproach.info/dame-cicely-saunders-work-for-the-hospice-movement-video/ ;http://www.jacksonvilleu.com/resources/history-of-nursing/cicely-saunders/

http://www.theguardian.com/society/2005/dec/04/health.lifeandhealth

Hospice; retrieved from http://en.wikipedia.org/wiki/Hospice

The National Canine Cancer Foundation - Home www.wearethecure.org

PALLIATIVE MEDICINE
Journal of Palliative Medicine – Stanford; retrieved from
    www.palliativejournal.stanford.edu
Grief.com- Because Love Never Dies- The 5 Stages of Grief; retrieved from
    http://grief.com/the-five-stages-of-grief/

CANCER
American Cancer Society/Lung Cancer- Small Cell; retrieved from
    http://www.cancer.org/cancer/lungcancer-smallcell/
History of cancer chemotherapy; retrieved from
    History of Small-Cell Lung Cancer retrieved from
    http://www.ncbi.nlm.nih.gov/pubmed/21550554
National Cancer Institute – 250 years of advances against cancer; retrieved from
http://www.cancer.gov/aboutnci/overview/250-years-advances
One hundred years of lung cancer. American Journal of Respiratory and Critical Care Medicine; Retrieved from http://www.atsjournals.org/doi/pdf/10.1164/rccm.200504-531OE
American Cancer Society; retrieved from www.cancer.org/fight/timeline
American Association of Retired People (AARP); retrieved from
http://healthtools.aarp.org/learning-center/super/cancer?lcStart=1
Cancer Council Australia; retrieved from:
http://www.cancer.org.au/about-us/history.html
Cancer Research UK; retrieved from   http://www.cancerresearchuk.org/cancer-info/cancerandresearch/progress/a-century-of-progress/
History of Radiation Therapy; retrieved from http://radonc.ucsd.edu/patient-info/Pages/history-radition-therapy.aspx

HIV/AIDS
Timeline of HIV/AIDS; retrieved from
http://en.wikipedia.org/wiki/Timeline_of_HIV/AIDS
AIDS Healthcare Foundation; retrieved from http://www.aidshealth.org/

Timeline of AIDS; retrieved from http://www.aids.gov/hiv-aids-basics/hiv-aids-101/aids-timeline/

Kaiser Family Foundation Global HIV/AIDS Timeline; retrieved from http://kff.org/hivaids/timeline/global-hivaids-timeline/

REFERENCES

C. Everett Koop; retrieved from http://en.wikipedia.org/wiki/C._Everett_Koop

Richard Doll; retrieved from http://en.wikipedia.org/wiki/Richard_Doll

Patient Zero; retrieved from http://en.wikipedia.org/wiki/Patient_zero

Fashion History- Design Trends of the 1940's; retrieved from http://hubpages.com/hub/Fashion-History-Design-Trends-of-the-1040s

News: Christopher Columbus and the Discovery of Tobacco; retrieved from http://www.stogieguys.com/2011/10/10102011-news-columbus-and-cigars.html

Peckham, London; retrieved from http://en.wikipedia.org/wiki/Peckham

Black British; retrieved from http://en.wikipedia.org/wiki/Black_British

Policing Ethnic Minority Communities; retrieved fromhttp://eprints.lse.ac.uk/9576/1/Policing ethnic_minority_communities_(LSERO.pdf

British African- Caribbean People; retrieved from http://en.wikipedia.org/wiki/British_African-Caribbean_people

Young People in Tottenham; retrieved from http://www.huffingtonpost.co.uk/elizabeth-pears/young-people-in-tottenham_b_920390.html

London Burns as Riots Spread to Other Cities; retrieved from http://www.thedailybeast.com/articles/2011/08/08/london-burns-as-riots-spread-to-other-cities-david-cameron-returns-home.html#

London Demographics; retrieved from http://en.wikipedia.org/wiki/Demographics_of_London

Harry Gregg-Official Manchester United Website www.manutd.com/en/players.../Harry Gregg

Ten Facts about Hospice Care You May Not Know | National ... www.nhpco.org/.../ten-facts-about-hospice-care-you-may-not-know

About Us - History/Timeline - Community Hospice of ...
communityhospice.com/...us/hi..

The History of Hospitals and Wards
www.healthcaredesignmagazine.com/article/history-hospitals-and-wards?.

Dogtown.originsofthenameitself
WWW2.Webster.edu/corbetre/dogtown/origin
Dogtown, St.Louis-wikipedia
en-wikipedia.org/wiki/dogtown-st.louis
RootsWeb:Irish-In-StLouis.Somehistoryofdogtown
archiver.rootsweb.ancestry.com 2005-07
Florence Wald - Wikipedia, the free encyclopedia

en.wikipedia.org/wiki/Florence_Wald

Home run king Babe Ruth helped pioneer modern cancer ...
*www.pbs.org/.../august-16-1948-***babe-ruth***-americas-greatest-baseba..*

Rest in Peace Bourbon Armstrong from Dogtown

Shawn Maureen McKelvie Bio:
My love for writing began as early in my life as I can remember. I was always scribbling my version of drama-filled prose on paper. I love words, and I love the stories words can tell. My appreciation and awe for the power and beauty of words woven together to tell a story has been a constant throughout my entire life.

But I also have had another great theme in my life - a deep, burning desire to help people. That dedication led me to earn my Bachelor of Science in Nursing degree from St. Louis University School of Nursing and RN diploma from St. Louis Municipal School of Nursing (AKA-City Hospital). I served as a Registered Nurse for more than 30 years. Over the course of three decades, I trained in an almost century old indigent care hospital, I spent a decade in an emergency room, I had short stints in the ICU, plastic surgery clinic and I even tackled health care marketing for a time.

The past 17 years, though, my heart has been committed to helping my husband Dr. Milton McKelvie with his small animal veterinary practice. My love for Milt as well as animals makes this a deeply satisfying involvement.

Now with this book, *Bed 39*, I am able to combine my love of writing and storytelling with my nursing background and knowledge and even sprinkle in a few passages about animals. Wow, does that combination make my soul sing!

I grew up in the suburbs of St. Louis, Missouri. In the early years North County and later, Creve Coeur – two of those wonderful Americana towns where friendships form in childhood and last a lifetime. Without question it was good for my soul for me to grow up in more simple times when having fun didn't cost a lot of money. I feel a strong desire to share those kinds of rich times and appreciate every chance I have to integrate fond members of yesteryear into the fabric of my various novels.

Now I plan to dedicate my passion, time and energy to giving life to the many fictional stories that are dancing around in my head demanding to be expressed! I have five or six of them lined up on the runway of my mind just like airplanes revving their engines waiting for takeoff.

My most supremely happy times, however, involve spending time with my husband, children, animals and grandkids. It's pure joy being chased by my two toddler grandchildren as they squeal and giggle in an effort to douse me with water from the swimming pool! Of course, I do not recall doing that to *my* grandma, however, I dearly love that they feel free to do so and see me as a bundle of fun! What could be a higher accolade! They make me smile and warm my heart in a way that is truly indescribable.

My husband and I appreciate simple evenings watching our favorite television programs with our furry canine kids. We dedicate a few days each week to working out at the gym and savor sunsets together. When we have spare time, we enjoy seeing the world and have traveled to Europe, New Zealand, Australia and Asia. We are greatly blessed.

And now I have this rich tapestry of my life to draw from as I give birth to fictional tales often based on true life experiences. I am beyond happy and fulfilled as the tales want to flow out of me as if I were the Trevi Fountain in

Rome! Please enjoy both my books, *Bed 39* and the *Ice Within the Soul*. There are many others to come! Thank you for your interest and Happy reading!